KISS
HER
GOODNIGHT

BOOKS BY D.K. HOOD

D.K. HOOD

KISS HER GOODNIGHT

bookouture

Published by Bookouture in 2022

An imprint of Storyfire Ltd.
Carmelite House
50 Victoria Embankment
London EC4Y 0DZ

www.bookouture.com

ISBN: 978-1-80314-336-1
eBook ISBN: 978-1-80314-335-4

To the fans of the Kane and Alton series. I wrote Kiss Her Goodnight especially for you.

PROLOGUE

Trapped in the musty dark stone cell, Deputy Poppy Anderson sat on the mattress and stared at her only form of entertainment. It came in the form of a constant *drip, drip, drip* of water hitting the granite floor, and slithering in a winding rivulet to join the growing puddle surrounding the drain. Despondent, after three months of being confined in hell, she flicked a cockroach from her blanket into the water. It landed on its back, legs flailing and trying to walk on air, as it rushed toward the drain and then spun around and around in the whirlpool before slipping between the metal slots. She lifted her head and stared at the shaft of light coming through the cracks surrounding the door to her prison. It was always the same steady light. There was no way to tell if it was day or night. In fact, time had ceased to exist in her nightmare.

Reality came in the form of terror. Poppy's hands hadn't stopped trembling since the first time she'd pressed her eye to the crack in the door and seen a woman beaten to death. Blood had seeped under her door in a ribbon of horror and the smell of death had lingered for so long she'd gotten used to it. He'd been there, the man she'd first met on a flight to Black Rock Falls,

Montana—the nice man who'd lured her into the woods at the pretense of finding a lost child. He wasn't nice at all. On the flight they'd talked about baseball and how he loved to swing a bat. She swallowed bile. Oh, he liked to swing a bat—but not at a ball.

She'd become a number, and as number twenty-five, she'd been placed on death row. There were others in the jail, but no one said a word. No one dared after he'd made an example out of one who'd called out, cried and demanded to be set free. Poppy had watched her die, one eye fixed in morbid fascination to the slither of light. Her captor had caught her looking at him and smiled with the innocence of a choirboy as he took the life of an innocent woman. She wasn't his first.

Many more followed, and each time, Poppy rolled into a ball, too scared to move or make a sound. Would she be next? There could be no reasoning with this brutal man. The stark reality of being trapped in his storeroom just waiting to die had become her future. Or was he keeping her just to watch him kill? Her thoughts moved from one possibility to another in rapid succession. It was all she could think about because no one would be searching for her. He'd made sure of that by forcing her to email the office with her resignation and intention to head for Colorado. She had wanted to work with Dave Kane and could have convinced Jenna to make her a member of the team, but her one day as deputy at Black Rock Falls had ended in a violent kidnapping. The hope that anyone would come to rescue her had faded long ago and now her imagination centered on him. He was unpredictable and his mood swings chilled her to the bone. Did knowing she watched him kill make it more thrilling for him? Her mind was spinning with the implications, and the next time the screams started, she turned her back to the door and tried to block out the noise. After each murder, she couldn't eat for days, vomiting bile and sitting staring into empty corners. She understood her mental health was suffering but could no longer fight. Her vomiting caught his attention and, as her door opened, fear grasped her by the throat.

"If you make a sound. I'll know. I can see you every second of the day. I watch everything you do. I own each breath you take." The man stared at her, his face passive. "The next time I see or hear you, the others will pay the price of your disobedience."

Days blended into each other, and small sounds gained her attention. The odd cough, the running of a faucet or flushing of a toilet. The scrape of a tray as it was pushed in front of the delivery slot no doubt laden with discarded wrappers just like hers. It had been days without hearing or seeing their captor but none of the others tried to communicate. All followed the rules until they died. When his footsteps came again, without thinking, Poppy went to peer through the crack. The jailer brought supplies in the form of survival rations and pushed them through the slot in the door once a week, but this time he carried an unconscious woman and dumped her into the cell opposite. Like her, the woman wore a skimpy nightie. The cell door clanged shut and the man turned slowly to look along the row of cells. Fear gripped Poppy and she froze on the spot.

"I can see you, looking at me, Twenty-Five." Her captor's mouth curled into a wide grin. "You've been so self-centered all your life, haven't you? How many times have I told you that if you break the rules, everyone suffers?" He opened a cell door and dragged out a bedraggled woman and pushed her hard against the wall. "Lift up your arms."

The woman complied like an automaton, and he secured her to metal loops in the wall. Poppy's stomach lurched. Would he kill her just to prove a point? When he took a horsewhip from a hook on the wall, horrified, Poppy slid to the floor. Over the next terrifying hour, the extent of the prisoners came to light. Apart from her, and the unconscious woman, three others were dragged from the cells. All went without a struggle to receive their punishment for her wrongdoing, but as their screams echoed through the walls, Poppy rocked back and forth, humming, with her hands pressed hard over her ears. *Make it stop.*

The door to her cell opened slowly and a figure blocked the light. She could see the sheen of sweat on his bare shoulders as his rancid stink poured into her space like a thick fog. Terrified, Poppy flattened against the wall, her heart pounding in her ears. Had he come to punish her or kill her?

"See what you did, Twenty-Five? You destroy people's lives without a second thought. Women like you, who flirt and break up people's relationships are all the same. You don't care who suffers because of you, do you? Or what happens to the kids from broken marriages?" He indicated behind him to the woman hanging from her wrists. "She is the same as you. They all are. Did you hear how loud they screamed? Don't worry, I don't intend to kill them just yet, but their time will come."

Refusing to cower to him, Poppy lifted her chin. "You know nothing about me. I'm not like the others. You're mistaken."

"Nah, I can see right through your lies. Can't you see? I'm just putting the world right. It's an experiment in social justice. All of you are nothing more than a bunch of narcissistic para-sites." He narrowed his gaze and took a step toward her. "I'll give you something to think about while I'm away. You can't hide from me. I'm in your dreams, hiding in the shadows." His tongue slid over his bottom lip. "You're close to the top of my list, and I'm gonna so enjoy taking my time with you. Won't that be fun?"

ONE

The summer sun poured through Sheriff Jenna Alton's office window like a beam of hope. She leaned back in her chair, watching the dust motes twirl and spin. As a child, they'd been fairies with gold wings traveling between dimensions on a shaft of sunlight but today they reminded her the office needed cleaning. It was just before eight and she wondered why she'd bothered to arrive so early just to stare at the walls. She'd been doing practically nothing for almost three months and the quietness concerned her. It was like waiting for the other shoe to drop. Something was happening. She could feel it in her bones. Life in Black Rock Falls was very different from her time in Washington, DC, as DEA Agent Avril Parker, but her time as an undercover operative was over. With a new face and name, she'd fought her way to becoming the sheriff of this vast county. She had no idea when she moved to this backwoods town, hidden deep in a forest and surrounded by mountains, that she'd moved to serial killer central.

It was by pure luck the specialized team she'd gathered around her was unique. Her second in command and deputy sheriff, David Kane, had turned out to be an off-the-grid special forces sniper, but another surprise awaited her with the arrival of his handler, Dr. Shane Wolfe, who set up as medical examiner. It had taken three years working with these two men before Jenna discovered they had strong ties to the White House. Now along with her deputies—Jake Rowley, a local Black Rock Falls resident; ex LAPD gold-shield detective Zac Rio; and semiretired Deputy Walters—she'd taken on psychopaths and brought them to justice. She turned in her chair to stare out the window. From here she could see the length of Main and a crowd gathering in the park. She turned to her computer to check the calendar for upcoming events and found nothing. Footsteps came up the stairs and Kane stood framed in the door. At six-five and two hundred and fifty pounds of muscle, Kane was a force to be reckoned with and he just happened to be her fiancé. She frowned at his stone-faced expression. "What's up?"

"I'm not real sure. Maggie got an anonymous call saying we should be down at the park." Kane jerked his thumb over one shoulder. "Want me to go and take a look with Rowley?"

Jenna stood and plucked her hat from the desk. Magnolia "Maggie" Brewster ran the front counter with amazing efficiency, and if she couldn't get a name, nobody could. "I noticed the crowd. We'll go. I'd love to get out of the office. Updating the files is so boring. I'm afraid my mind isn't on work right now. It's set on getting married and being in Florida next weekend." She smiled.

"Mine too, but if it's an argument about picking up dog poop, I'm all over it." He pushed his black Stetson on his head and followed her downstairs. "I've read everything there is to read. I used to look forward to some downtime, but constant inactivity is like watching paint dry."

The next moment, phone ringtones filled the office. Jenna pulled her phone out of her pocket and turned to raise an eyebrow at Kane. "I figure this might be more complicated than dog poop." She answered the call. "Jenna Alton."

"Morning Sheriff this is Susie Hartwig from Aunt Betty's Café. People are coming in and saying there's a body in the kids' playground."

Jenna could hear Kane talking to someone and then Rowley jumped to his feet, phone pressed to his ear. She held up a finger when they both spoke at once. "Okay, Susie, we're on our way. If you can get the names of anyone you spoke to about this, it would be a great help." She disconnected and turned to Rowley. "Was your call about the body?"

"Yeah." Rowley frowned. "In the playground?"

Jenna nodded. "Call Wolfe and bring him up to date, and I'll go and secure the scene with Kane. When you've done that, head down to the park and start collecting names."

"Yes, ma'am." Rowley's phone started up again. "I'm on it." He walked back to his desk.

Jenna thought for a beat. "Rio, grab your camera, but first, I want photographs of the crowd and the crime scene. Use the drone. I don't want anyone slipping away. Check the woods as well. If this is a homicide, killers often mingle with a crowd to watch the fallout of their work." She hurried to the front door.

"Sure." Rio moved past her, heading for the equipment closet.

"Come on, Duke." Kane patted his leg and a bloodhound stood, stretched, gave a doggy yawn, and went to his side, tail wagging. As a tracker dog, Duke was a valued member of the team.

As Jenna climbed into Kane's black truck affectionately known as "the Beast," she turned to him. "I know it's been boring around here lately, but I'd hoped the crime rate would remain low until after our honeymoon. If this is a homicide, we'll have to cancel the wedding."

"Maybe someone just up and died." Kane shrugged as he fastened Duke into the back seat. "It happens." He slid behind the wheel. "Not every incident in town has to be the result of a serial killer." He backed out of the parking space and headed down Main.

People congregated in and around the park like ants around honey. Jenna let out a long sigh. How was it that death drew people? Didn't they understand the memory of seeing a dead body would stay with them forever? She stared down Main. The townsfolk were gathering as if someone were giving out free money. "You know, every time we say we're bored someone gets killed. Perhaps we should drop that word from our vocabulary. Maybe it's cursed or something?"

"Nah." Kane pulled alongside the curb. "Nothing we say makes any difference. They've all been out there doing their thing. We just haven't noticed them yet."

The tension of the crowd was palpable as Jenna stepped out into the morning sunshine. Fear had a smell to it, and it hovered in the air like sweaty socks in a locker room. She waited for Kane to grab Duke, and the crowd parted as they made their way into the park. People pointed in the direction of the children's playground, and the breakfast of hotcakes in Jenna's stomach formed a solid ball. "Oh, please, don't let it be a child."

"It's not." With Kane's height advantage, he could see over the crowd. "It looks like a female or a young guy on the carousel." He glanced around. "Do you want me to disperse the crowd?"

Shaking her head, Jenna plowed through the onlookers. "No, Rio will have our eye in the sky up soon. Whoever did this could be watching. Once he's taken his shots, we can send them on their way."

The onlookers fell silent as Jenna and Kane hurried through the gate to the children's playground. The crowd had remained outside the fence line and all faces turned somberly in their direction. The grass had been freshly mowed the previous day and damp dewy cuttings stuck to her boots as she walked. The playground was half in shade from the forest pressing against one boundary fence, but sun shone on the figure slumped over the carousel. As they moved closer, Jenna stared at the ground, searching for footprints. "One set of footprints in and out." She pointed to the perimeter fence. "They came in through the woods."

"And likely parked on the fire road. It's secluded and they'd be able to move the body through the trees unseen." Kane scanned the area slowly. "If we go in on the right of the carousel, I doubt we'll disturb any evidence."

Moving her gaze over the figure, Jenna followed behind Kane as he picked his way in a wide circle to the carousel. Examining a dead body at a crime scene was so much more than taking a quick glance and leaving the nasty stuff to the medical examiner. The procedure of investigating a homicide ran through her mind in a list. She needed to absorb the scene, but the first responders had a responsibility to record as much information as possible. In her time in Black Rock Falls, Jenna had seen many victims of horrendous crimes, but she reeled back at the shock of seeing this one. It wasn't the blood spatter, because there was none evident, and although the stench of death hovered in the air, the usual stink of bodily fluids was absent. The body appeared to have been washed after death. The face was obscured by a comical plastic mask, the type kids wore when they dressed up as cops. Bile rose up the back of her throat as her gaze slid over the body. The woman's white flesh was barely covered by a skimpy nightie. The skin had turned blue in the extremities and the lower half had a deep rosy hue on one side. All this she'd seen before but not the six-inch metal pins sticking out from the victim's back like a porcupine or the number twenty carved into her flesh.

"Well, this is new." Kane cleared his throat and peered at

the victim. "Are those barbecue skewers? They look much the same as the pack of a hundred I purchased recently."

Pushing on a face mask and snapping on surgical gloves, Jenna held her breath and bent closer. "Yeah, they look the same. That must have taken some time to do and why do it?"

"Torture, maybe?" Kane frowned and suited up. "From the lack of blood. I'd say she was killed somewhere else and dumped here." He glanced up as a tall blond man pushed his way through the crowd barking orders. He resembled a Viking marauder. "Ah good, there's Wolfe."

The medical examiner, Dr. Shane Wolfe, arrived with his assistant and badge-carrying deputy, Colt Webber, and his daughter and ME in training, Emily. Jenna went to his side and gave him a rundown of what they knew. "We figure she was killed off scene and carried here through the woods. The trees block this area from Main and I haven't found the person who first noticed the body. Can you give me anything to go on from what you see here?"

"Hmm. Deep ligature marks on wrists and ankles." Wolfe climbed onto the carousel and examined the body. "The body is emaciated. She was probably kept alive for a time in captivity. We'll get the images and I'll check around for trace evidence." His gaze moved all around. "I'll need to get her to the morgue ASAP. She could have latent prints on her flesh or trace evidence from whoever carried her here. Her feet are clean." He lifted one arm of the corpse and moved one of the legs. "The body is in a state of decomposition and there's no rigor. It came and went already. This would make me believe, unless I prove otherwise, that she died at least thirty-six hours ago. That would be the longest time a body would go through this process. The livor mortis, the dark purple patches on the left side, would indicate she certainly didn't die here."

Above, a humming sound caught Jenna's attention and she noticed the drone moving back and forth like an old typewriter carriage. Rio had become an expert at using the eye in the sky and even sent it to collect takeout from Aunt Betty's Café. Right now, it was recording the scene, taking in the townsfolk and moving off to scour the surrounding area to look for anyone acting suspicious or out of place. Rio had a retentive memory, which was very useful for anyone in law enforcement. He could look at a scene from every angle, take in all the available information, and make a solid judgment call. Jenna could rely on him to carry out his duties to the letter. She turned back to Wolfe. "Okay, we'll talk to the townsfolk and see what we can find and then we'll backtrack from those footprints." She noticed Rowley moving through the crowd. "Ah good, there's Rowley. He's taking people's details, but I need to find out who was first on scene."

"I'll get their attention." Kane walked to the fence line and raised his voice. "Okay, hush everyone. Who was here first?" A few hands raised into the air. "Come here and talk to me."

Glad to be upwind of the body, Jenna stood beside Kane and they spoke to the three people who stepped forward. After speaking to them, they discovered who'd made the frantic 911 call earlier. "Thank you for coming forward, Mr. Lawrence. Tell me how you stumbled on the body."

"I went into Aunt Betty's Café for a to-go coffee, like I do same time each morning, and then headed to the park to give Bingo a walk." He indicated to the golden Labrador standing beside him, mouth open in a doggy smile.

"What time was this?" Kane's pen hovered over his digital notepad.

"At seven forty-five, or as close to it as an angel's breath." Lawrence tipped back his hat. "I didn't see the body at first. I head up the other way most days, but Bingo started fussing and walking around in circles. Then without warning he ran down to the playground and started barking and whining. I figured there must be a bobcat close by, so I went to see what all the fuss was about and then I smelled the body. I took a look and called 911."

Jenna nodded. "Why didn't you give your name?"

"No time." Lawrence indicated to the dog. "Bingo was trying to open the gate to get inside the playground and I had to stop him. I wasn't trying to hide anything. I've watched TV shows and I know about contaminating a crime scene, so I kept everyone away and waited for you."

So do criminals. Jenna smiled. "That's very helpful, thank you."

"Did you see anyone in or near the park?" Kane lifted his gaze to the man. "Anyone in the woods? A vehicle?"

"Nope, only people who came by are those two." Lawrence pointed to the other men who'd stopped to gawk. "Then the entire town showed up." He shrugged.

Jenna nodded. "Okay, give Deputy Kane your details, and if you think of anything at all, call me." She handed him a card and moved to the next man.

After moving through a ton of people, they discovered nothing of interest but at least had a list of names. Jenna turned to Rowley. "Head back to the office and work with Rio putting names to faces. Anyone from out of town, run their names just in case they're felons. If they're locals, check for anyone with priors."

It would take forever to match all the names to the images, but the FBI whiz kid Bobby Kalo would be able to run a match at warp speed. Deciding what to do, she chewed on the inside of her cheek. Calling the FBI for assistance for only one crime wasn't something she'd usually do, but with her wedding planned for Friday, she needed all the help she could get to solve this case. "Call Kalo, and if he's not busy, ask him to run the names for you. He'll be able to get a result faster."

"Okay." Rowley turned toward the twenty or so people

watching Wolfe. "Okay, folks, nothing more to see here. Give the poor woman some respect."

As the mumbles of complaint reached her ears, she turned, hands on hips, and stared at them. "This is someone's daughter, perhaps a mother or a wife. Go about your business and allow us to find out who killed her."

She waited for Kane to finish speaking with Lawrence, and after taking Duke to sniff the body, they walked a parallel path to the disappearing footprints in the dew. Duke was an integral part of the sheriff's team and wore a badge on his collar to prove it. They'd found the bloodhound some time ago at a crime scene. He'd been neglected and left to die. Kane had adopted Duke and nursed him back to health. The dog had issues. He hated the vet and even the mention of a bath sent him running, but he was the best tracker dog in the county. He'd been bred by a Native American out at the reservation and had been recognized at once by their friend Atohi Blackhawk, who'd informed them about the dog's origins and name. A very loyal companion, and an asset to the team, Duke had become a beloved member of the community.

They followed Duke into the woods, but instead of sniffing the ground, he moved from tree to tree. Jenna stared after him. "I've never seen him do that before."

"That's because the killer carried the body in his arms." Kane pulled a strand of hair from one of the tree branches. "I'd say our killer is a man, and he struggled to carry her through the woods. See where the hair is snagged in the trees? If I carried you unconscious in my arms, allowing for head hang, we would find the hair at least eight inches higher for someone my size, so I'd say he's about five-eight. From what Duke is doing, the body was rested against the tree trunks on the way through."

As they emerged from the forest onto the fire road, a terrible feeling of déjà vu hit Jenna. They'd walked the same path hunting down a missing deputy three months previously. She stopped on the fire road and stared at Kane. "See anything familiar to this scenario?"

"Yeah." Kane rubbed his chin. "This is where we lost track of Poppy Anderson, but we checked on her. She's spending a ton of cash in Colorado and she did send us an email saying where she was heading." He twisted at the waist looking back into the woods. "You don't think that's her, do you—the body?"

The idea chilled Jenna to the bone. "I think we need to find out."

TWO

Millions of pine needles crunched underfoot, sending a burst of forest fragrance mixed with damp soil into the air as they dashed back through the woods. Jenna led and took a wider more direct trail and they hit the fence line a little way past the playground. Wolfe had the body on a gurney and was swabbing the carousel. Emily and Webber were crawling over the grass, collecting potential fragments of evidence and placing them in sample containers. Breathless from the run, Jenna hustled to Wolfe's side. "Did you remove the mask?"

"Nope." Wolfe lifted his gaze to her. "I'm not taking the chance of losing evidence. I'll do that in a controlled environment, but from what I can see, it's glued in place. There are drops of glue matting the hair. I'm hoping the killer left a trace of themselves behind. Glue is a very useful medium. When it's wet it attracts all kinds of things." His brow furrowed. "Why the rush?"

Jenna removed her hat and fanned herself with the brim. "It's probably nothing. Do you recall the day Poppy Anderson quit?"

"Yeah, she hightailed it out of town on a truck heading for

Colorado, if I recall. You did a trace on her and she's spending a ton of cash all over." Wolfe's face showed interest. "What makes you think she has anything to do with this case?"

Glancing at the black body bag and then back to Wolfe, Jenna pushed down the horrible feeling Poppy might be the victim. "It's like déjà vu and we know killers like to revisit crime scenes. We tracked Poppy through the same patch of woods when we believed something had happened to her. Would you believe, Duke stopped in the same place as he did before. We know she got into a vehicle on the fire road, or Duke would have picked up on her scent. It just seems a bit spooky, a body of a blonde-haired woman shows up and she arrived here along the same path as Poppy took when she left."

"That was three months ago." Wolfe packed the swabs away and removed his gloves and mask. "The body isn't Poppy, unless she shrunk about five inches. If I recall, she was tall and looked me straight in the eyes. The woman we found is around five-four. You're worrying over nothing. Poppy probably did the disappearing act to gain attention. Kalo has been tracking her movements, and she's where she said she was heading— Colorado Springs." He sighed. "You know how serial killers work. This isn't his first murder, and by this stage, he wouldn't wait three months between kills. Knowing how stubborn you are, you won't trust me and your very capable deputies to handle this case for a few days will you? Do you really want to postpone the wedding?"

The last thing Jenna had on her mind was the wedding. "It will be easy to postpone. It's not as if we hired a wedding planner, is it?" She stared at Kane. "We should be working on the case. We'll postpone the wedding and I'm not doing it for Poppy Anderson. If Kalo is tracking her in Colorado Springs, that's good enough for me."

"See?" Wolfe rolled his eyes to the heavens. "As stubborn as a mule. You've trained your team to the highest level. They're overqualified to handle this case and you'll have Jo and Carter arriving soon to cover for you. You'll have the investigation rolling before you leave. Delegate as usual and let everyone get at it. If we have a problem, we'll call you."

Unconvinced Jenna shook her head. "We'll move the wedding to next month. It will still be summer." She looked at Kane's concerned expression and sighed. "You know I need to be here. I'm sorry, but we'll have to cancel."

"We planned for just this contingency, Jenna." Kane moved to her side. "Rio has worked on plenty of homicides. Let's face it, we have nothing to go on right now and chances are Wolfe won't have gotten too far with the autopsy findings before Monday. We don't have any suspects to hunt down until the grunt work is done and the guys are more than capable of handling that part of the investigation without us. We'll be gone three days max." He stared at her. "Okay, I'd settle for two... or even one night. You can spare one night to be with me, can't you?"

"You're not canceling the wedding, are you?" Emily dragged off her mask. "Jenna you can't. Not at this late date. Everything is planned." She glanced at her watch. "Jo and Ty are on their way now. You can't postpone it. I won't let you."

Special Agents Ty Carter and Jo Wells from Snakeskin Gully had become firm friends and an unofficial part of her team, although she could call them in anytime to take over a case or as consultants. They had arranged to move into the cottage at the ranch to care for the animals over the weekend. Having them around would be an advantage if they decided to go ahead with the wedding. Jenna glanced at Kane, and he shrugged, not giving anything away. "I guess with Jo and Ty to back up Rio and Rowley, it might be possible, but having a wedding and flitting off on a honeymoon in the middle of a murder investigation seems downright irresponsible to me."

"We're not indispensable, Jenna." Kane pushed back the tip

of his Stetson. "Our team is solid. They can manage for a few days. We have to have a life outside of the sheriff's department. You know that, right?"

Swallowing the guilt, Jenna nodded. "Yeah, but I've never walked away from an investigation. Not when it's on my watch. I'm ultimately responsible for the townsfolk's safety."

"We all are, Jenna. You know, Jo and Carter manage to solve a variety of crimes on their own." Wolfe looked at her with raised eyebrows. "Same with Rio, and Rowley is a fine deputy. Most towns of this size have a sheriff and one, and they cope just fine. It's time for you to allow your team to do the grunt work on this case. I'll need time to run tests. There are a ton of things going on here. Finding answers will take days and you can't assist me in the forensics. Even if I work straight through from now until Monday morning, I doubt I'd have enough evidence to present to you to make a case. There are too many questions we need answered."

Jenna could see his rationale but stared at him. "How so?"

"First up, no one has been reported missing." Wolfe held up his hand, fingers spread and turned one down. "Who is she?" He turned down two. "Where was she killed?" He turned down three and continued as he made his points. "Where did the killer purchase the mask? What glue did they use? Has she been sexually assaulted? Cause of death? Has she been in storage, frozen or kept as a sex slave? What damage was inflicted? Was it inflicted post-mortem? Cause of death, drug evidence, trace evidence?" He dropped his hands and sighed. "I could go on and on, Jenna. I figure, you should get married tomorrow morning as planned. Take the weekend and get back on the case on Monday. I might have something for you by then."

Conceding to his argument, Jenna nodded. "Okay, okay, the wedding is on—for now. I might change my mind if anything significant happens later today."

"It won't." Emily grinned at her. "I'll work with Dad over

the weekend and get you some answers and, really, until we identify the body and find out where she's from, there's no trail to follow." She suited up and went to view the body, leaving them alone with Wolfe.

"I'll get Rio to write up a media report and set up a hotline." Jenna's mind was moving ahead at warp speed. "Someone must be missing her."

"She could have been dumped here from anywhere and thousands of people go missing." Wolfe rubbed the back of his neck. "I guess we start local and spread out. One thing you need to consider. The chances of this being their first kill is remote. First kills are messy and rushed. Looking at this victim, this killer is at the top of their game."

Knowing more about murder than she would like, Jenna nodded. "Then the killer will be working inside their comfort zone—they all do. So, they'll be close by."

"Not always." Kane pushed his hands into his front pockets. "Most times, yeah, but some can have a few comfort zones. Some might kill around a favorite vacation destination, for instance. The killing becomes part of the time off work. Then we have people who travel for work, freight drivers, executives. All of these offer a possibility of the expansion of a comfort zone. The thing is, they all have a base to work from in each zone. So, look for anyone who moves around and stays for a time at the same place."

Jenna swallowed hard. "So just about anyone, huh?" She chewed on her bottom lip. "Why now? This couldn't have happened at a worse time."

"Yeah, we've had three months of quiet." Kane shook his head. "It's as if the killer doesn't want us to get married." He moved his gaze to Jenna. "Do you know any psychopaths with a crush on you?"

Snorting, Jenna lifted her chin. "Only one and I killed him. I agree the timing stinks, but whatever date we pick, the chances are something will go wrong." She shrugged. "We have today to get the ball rolling and, like you said, we're only a phone call away if we're needed."

"You do know, it's at least a five-hour trip?" Wolfe narrowed his gaze and lowered his voice. "You need to stick to the plan and leave after the ceremony. We'll be able to get straight back to work." He looked at Kane. "I made a few calls and upgraded your flight. POTUS doesn't want you and Jenna traveling commercial. He wasn't too happy about you leaving the state but has made a consideration for the weekend. There'll be a rental waiting for you at the airport. You have the address of my mom's condo and where to pick up the key. It's nice and safe."

"Going without a weapon will be like being naked." Kane touched the handle of his M-18 pistol. "I can't remember a time I wasn't armed."

"Leave that to me." Wolfe thought for a beat. "I'll have creds for you as a US Marshal by morning. You'll be able to carry a weapon."

"You'll have time to organize that and a badge?" Kane narrowed his gaze. "Seriously?"

"Do you really have to ask, Dave?" Wolfe raised both eyebrows.

"Ah, no. I guess not." Kane chuckled. "Friends in high places, huh?"

Jenna looked at him and shook her head. "I'm sure you'll do just fine if it doesn't arrive in time. We're going to the beach and acting like normal folk for a change. You won't need a gun." She dragged in a sigh. "Come on. Let's get at it. I want to see how Kalo is progressing with the searches."

THREE

Calm flowed through him to such an extent it was as if he were standing still and all around him moved in slow motion. He stared out of the window, mimicking just about everyone else in Aunt Betty's Café as he ate his bowl of chili and washed it down with one of their fine cups of coffee. He dragged his gaze away from the group of people surrounding his gift to Sheriff Alton. Nothing much had been happening in town of late and he liked to see his taxes deployed in a useful endeavor.

Sighing, he leaned over his phone to read a book he'd downloaded about various behavioral traits. One of his friends had called him a psycho and he wondered if this accusation was true, but he doubted it. Surely there was a group of people the same as him? People went missing and showed up dead daily, so it was only reasonable to assume there were more people with the same hobby as him out there. At first, he'd believed his hobby wasn't something he could talk about in general conversation, but the private group he'd discovered on the internet had opened his eyes. There just happened to be hundreds, maybe thousands, of people with hobbies more unusual than his. He glanced at the page. Could he be a sociopath? Nope, he didn't have an antisocial attitude. He mixed well with everyone. Hmm, what about a narcissist? "A person who takes an obsessive interest in himself." No, that wasn't him either. In fact, he'd studied all the psychopaths from Black Rock Falls, and none of them fitted those molds. In fact, it seemed the opposite. Most psychopaths moved through life with ease. They had good jobs, intelligence, and were often admired by their friends... They certainly didn't stick out in a crowd as being crazy. The idiotic generalization that they were antisocial self-loving freaks was just about as stupid as telling a kid that a dirty old man might kidnap them. It seemed to him a psychopath could be anyone and not the foaming-at-the-mouth madman people wanted to believe. He read on and decided maybe psychopath was too harsh a label for him. Maybe *impulsivity* would come close to the mark. After all he did act on impulse, and being smart enough to know and understand his trigger, he'd gained some control.

Reading articles and books written by leading doctors over many years had given him the answers he craved. Now, he understood the affairs his father had enjoyed with a stream of women hadn't been his fault. That sin was his pa's alone. Although he'd suffered the fallout from his angry parents, he'd never forgotten listening to their lies. He'd often pressed one ear to the door as his pa calmed his mom's sobs and promised to be a better husband. His mom had told him that all men were the same and, as soon as he married, he'd be out chasing after "marriage breakers" just like his pa. She warned him about the women who only wanted a man until he left his wife, and then they'd dump him. She'd ranted about the same thing so many times it had become like a mantra running in a constant loop in his head. As a kid he hadn't truly understood her meaning until he'd married a sweet girl straight out of college. At his first job as a married man, a stunning blonde had offered him the world. She'd been irresistible and insisted he leave his wife, but his mother's voice kept on whispering in his mind. Determined not to be like his pa, he'd taken her out for a night of passion. He smiled at the memory. He wasn't like his pa after all, and it had been so satisfying killing her. Yeah, he understood his trigger just fine.

FOUR

It was late in the afternoon when Ty Carter dropped by the office with his Doberman, Zorro, at his heels. Kane smiled at him when he headed for his desk. "All settled in?"

"Yeah, thanks." Carter dropped into the chair opposite and rested one snakeskin cowboy boot on his opposite knee. "You're well organized. I was surprised when Wolfe gave me the keys to Jenna's cruiser. I had planned on getting a rental, so that was very nice of her. Jo is back at the cottage. She wanted to give Jaime a tour of the ranch. Do you mind if we take the horses out for a ride over the weekend?"

Kane hadn't seen much of Jaime, Jo's little girl. "Sure, the paint pony is very gentle, it belongs to Wolfe's youngest, Anna. My stallion is a handful, but Jenna's mare is good."

"Warrior likes me. He snickered when I went by before, so we'll get along just fine. We'll be sticking to the trails around the ranch." Carter plucked a toothpick from his shirt pocket and tossed it into his mouth. "I see that life goes on as normal around here since the engagement. Any second thoughts?"

Wondering what Carter was implying, Kane leaned back in his chair and stared at him. "About marrying, Jenna? No, of course not, and why would anything change around here? She's still sheriff and I'm her deputy. I wouldn't want it any other way."

"And if you have kids?" Carter's gaze remained fixed on his face. "Then what?"

Kane rolled his eyes. "It will be Jenna's choice, but if and when it happens, knowing her as I do, she'll want the baby with her at the office—I figure I will too. We'll build a nursery, hire a nanny...whatever's necessary and maybe Rowley's wife, Sandy, can come work here too and bring along the twins to socialize. It will work out just fine, we don't chase serial killers seven days a week."

"Ah-huh." Carter smiled around his toothpick. "Seems to me you've given it a lot of thought." He sighed. "You know, I've never wanted to settle down, mainly because I had a life that made romance difficult. Seeing you together and Rowley and Sandy, well, I guess a wife and a white picket fence are possible after all."

Surprised the confirmed bachelor was considering marriage, Kane cleared his throat. "Yeah, it can work. Do you have someone in mind?"

"Not yet." Carter chuckled. "I'm planning on seeing how you two go first." He glanced at the images on Kane's screen. "Is that the case from this morning? Kalo mentioned you needed him for research."

Turning around his screen, Kane nodded. "I do, are you interested in lending a hand while we're away?"

"Yeah, but Jo will be working by remote." Carter peered at the images. "With Jaime here, she'll be busy. Give me the rundown."

After Kane explained, he noticed the shadow cross Carter's eyes. "Are you seeing something I'm not?"

"Maybe." Carter zoomed in on the mask. "Glued on?"

Interested, Kane scanned the images again. "Yeah. Have

you seen this before?"

"It was a cold case I studied last year, mainly because we had nothing to do." Carter scrolled through the images. "Women dressed the same with a mask glued over their faces. They had many broken bones. Some had partially healed breaks in their fingers and toes. It kinda proved that the killer had held them for a time. They had one hell of a time trying to identify the bodies and then discovered the ID of only one of them. It was nasty. Six dead women, no missing persons reports, and no clues."

Turning to look at him, Kane picked up a pen. "Where was this? We'll need all the case files."

"Colorado." Carter's gaze narrowed. "Wasn't that where Poppy said she was heading?"

Kane nodded. "Yeah, but the body we found is small. It's not Poppy."

"I'll have Kalo send the files." Carter pulled out his phone and gave Kane a smile. "This visit just got interesting."

Glad to have Carter in town to assist with the case, Kane pushed to his feet. "Jenna will want to know everything you have on the cold case. She's in her office."

"Okay, but rather than repeating myself a dozen times, grab Rowley and Rio as well." Carter stood and shrugged. "Lately, my vacations are becoming more interesting than work."

Kane peered at Duke asleep under his desk. "You coming, Duke?" The bloodhound gave him a bloodshot look from under his lids, sighed, and went back to sleep.

Heading for the stairs to Jenna's office, Kane stopped to gather the other deputies. He knocked on Jenna's door. "Carter recalls a cold case with a similar MO to our murder. Rio and Rowley are on their way."

"A cold case?" Jenna spun toward him in her office chair. "As we don't know how long the victim has been in captivity, Kalo went back five years and found over twenty missing women with the same description." She sighed and leaned back in her chair. "No one has been reported missing in my county. This one is going to be tough."

Unstacking chairs from a pile in the corner, he slid them across the floor to the others and they all sat down to listen to Carter. Kane moved his attention to Jenna. "Wolfe mentioned that the crime scene and kill were too clean. This could be the same person starting up fresh in our county."

"The problem with the missing women is only women people care about are reported." Carter stretched out his long legs. "A killer preying on the homeless, prostitutes, or any number of people living on the edge of society would slip through the net."

"That's true enough." Jenna pushed both hands through her hair and tucked it behind her ears. "And they're easy targets for someone wanting a quick kill. In this scenario, if the killer is keeping them for a time, who would miss them?"

"This is why the case went cold." Carter ran one hand down his Doberman's slick black head and shrugged. "We couldn't identify the victims. One we believe was a prostitute, but only by another recognizing the necklace we found with the body. The lady in question was an addict, so not a reliable witness, and she changed her description of the necklace on two different occasions."

Kane stood and went to pour a cup of coffee from the pot brewing on the counter. "You know, if this is a serial offender, he could be swapping personal items from one body to the next. If he's smart, there's no end to what he might do to hide the victim's identities."

"Yeah." Rio rubbed his chin. "I've seen that happen before. They believe if we can't identify the victims, then the chances of them leading us to them is remote. If this is a planned move, we'd have to assume the current victim is from another county or state."

The phone on Jenna's desk rang and she held up a finger and picked up the receiver. "Sheriff Alton." She listened and nodded. "Okay, that might be significant. Thanks, Shane." She replaced the receiver and stood. She went to the whiteboard, took a pen from the holder, and turned to the team. "Wolfe has started a preliminary examination of our victim and called to inform us that the victim was raped. He didn't find semen or trace evidence of her attacker, but he did find traces of soapy water on her skin. He will run an analysis on the soap and see what he can find. It will take time."

"Ah, you mentioned the similarity to when Poppy Anderson hightailed it out of town?" Rowley leaned forward in his chair with his hands clasped between his knees. "I followed this up with Kalo. He's been keeping an eye out for her as you requested. Seems she is still on the payroll here. A paycheck has been going in her account regular since she left. Another thing, Kalo said she was still using her credit card out at Colorado Springs. She's taking out wads of cash every so often. I figure if she's living somewhere, she's paying cash. She's a cop and would know how to get around a trace if she doesn't want to be found."

Kane exchanged a surprised look with Jenna. "She's on the payroll here? How is that possible?"

"I'd bet my bottom dollar Mayor Petersham is paying her." Jenna shook her head. "You know, I don't recall Maggie saying she'd stopped her pay." She picked up the phone and called down to the front counter. She put the phone on speaker. "Hi, Maggie, did you cancel Poppy Anderson's paycheck?"

"She wasn't in our system." Maggie sounded surprised. *"I can't stop what isn't there. If she's getting a paycheck, it's not from our account."*

"Okay, can you call the mayor's office and find out if he placed her in his system. If so, tell them she resigned. Maybe send them a copy of her email as confirmation."

"You got it." Maggie disconnected.

"From all this information have you got anything, Dave?" Jenna looked hopeful. "Anything at all?"

Clearing his throat, Kane met her gaze. "We have nothing to link the cases yet, no. We'll go through the cold case files and make notes of anything similar between each one and then apply the information to Wolfe's findings. If this is the same person, we'll need to hunt down people who recently settled here or who travel between states regularly. I'd say focusing on the similarities will be the best way forward. I can't offer a profile without information, and we've got zip."

"Okay." Jenna glanced at her watch and then at Rowley and Rio. "As we're chasing our tails right now, it's time to call it a day. I'm off duty and so is Kane from now until we return, so I'm handing this case over to Rio as next senior officer. Rio you have Carter and Jo at your disposal, and Rowley will be an asset. While we're away, I want you to go through the cold case files. Check in with Wolfe and use any information he can offer you. For now, check if any of the victims were sexually assaulted and then make a list of all the similarities. The reason being, this could be a copycat, and right now, we have no proof the cold case murders are even related."

Kane stood and pushed on his Stetson. "I'll drop you and Duke home and then I'm heading back to town."

"Why?" Jenna gathered her things and stared at him. "You going somewhere?"

Smiling, Kane tipped back his hat. "Yeah, Shane, being my best man, insisted on throwing me a bachelor party, and Emily figured you should get an early night. Jo and Jaime are staying over at the ranch to keep you company. I've been banished to the Cattleman's Hotel. I'm not allowed to see you before the wedding."

"Oh, really?" Jenna frowned. "So much for a quiet night at home."

FIVE

FRIDAY

Ty Carter took one last look at the horses in the corral, made sure the water feed was working and headed back to the cottage. Creeping around to make sure he didn't disturb Jo and Jaime, he showered and dressed in record time. He smiled to himself. Man, this town was having a strange effect on him. The previous evening at the Cattleman's Hotel had been amusing to say the least. He'd expected a raucous night of drinking, cards, pool, and women for Kane's bachelor party with Shane Wolfe, Jake Rowley, and Zac Rio, but oh boy, had he'd been wrong. They'd had a good time, but the Black Rock Falls guys liked to keep to themselves. Yeah, women gave them the eye from time to time, and he loved women, but between Shane Wolfe's Viking marauder glare and Kane's blank expression, they backed off. Even his charm had fallen flat and that had never happened before—that was for darn sure. He'd had only two light beers and had driven back to Jenna's ranch as sober as a judge. *I must be losing my edge, or it's getting time for me to settle down.*

He fed Zorro and then filled his cup with freshly brewed coffee and sat at the kitchen table. It was real early and still half-light outside, too early to wake Jo. His phone buzzed in his pocket and he quickly answered the call. "Yeah?"

"We have a problem." Zac Rio sounded serious. "The owner of the landfill, George Brinks, called the 911 line. He found a body at the landfill, right at the front gate against the fence. I'm heading there now." He sucked in a breath. "Protocol is for me to inform the sheriff, but as it's her wedding day, what the hell am I supposed to do?"

Considering the ramifications of not informing Jenna, Carter rubbed his forehead. "As I recall, Jenna put you in charge while she was on her honeymoon. They're away, on vacation—whatever. I figure we handle it and give them the rundown when they get back." He pushed to his feet and, grabbing his hat from a peg by the door, went outside. "I know where the landfill is. I'm on my way." He hurried to the cruiser and opened the door for Zorro before he slid behind the wheel. "Don't tell Rowley—if Sandy notices something is up, she'll tell Jenna for sure—but check out the scene and call Wolfe. We'll have to keep this from Kane too. That man is as stubborn as a mule. He'll want to know all the details and it ain't gonna happen. Not today anyway."

"Copy." Rio disconnected.

It was light by the time he reached the landfill. Rio's cruiser was blocking the road alongside Wolfe's ME's van. A few disgruntled townsfolk lined up along the service road sounding their horns and getting agitated, but he couldn't see anyone on foot. That was a good thing. Bystanders meant interviews and taking statements. It looked as if Rio had gotten there in time to keep people away from the crime scene. Assuming Rio was too busy to disperse the people waiting to use the landfill, Carter drove up the wrong side of the road, pulled on his FBI windbreaker, and walked to the front of the line of vehicles. He gave a twirling motion with his hand, sending everyone back the way they'd come, and once the road was clear, he moved Jenna's cruiser to the entrance to the service road and blocked it by parking horizontally.

He flicked on the flashers and slid from behind the wheel. "Come on, Zorro." He opened the back door and made his way back to the landfill. To one side a gray-haired man was sitting on the side of the road, pale as a ghost, holding his head in his hands. As he moved around Wolfe's van, he caught sight of the body. Another woman, white, bloodless, with blue extremities and wearing a mask. Wolfe was bending over her, and Rio was taking photographs, the ME's usual entourage was missing. He moved closer and covered his nose. "What have we got?"

"It's the same MO as before, right down to the number of skewers along the backbone, but this is number twenty-one. Makes me wonder where the other nineteen bodies are stashed." Wolfe straightened. "Look at all the trash around here. It's pointless collecting samples. They'll be contaminated. Whoever dumped the body here was sure using his brains. A perfect place to hide evidence, and should we find anything, it would be challenged in court. This place is a petri dish of microorganisms." He sighed. "I'll get her bagged and tagged. I'll have to sneak her into the morgue and get her on ice before I'm missed."

Running his gaze over the crime scene, Carter nodded. "If you've got spare gloves and a mask, I'll give you a hand." He took the items Wolfe pulled from a pocket. "This one was left lying faced down by the liver mortis. Is she still in rigor?"

"Nope." Wolfe tossed a body bag on the ground. "I've bagged her hands and feet. If there's any trace evidence, it will be there or maybe in her mouth." He turned to Rio. "Get some close-up shots of the body and under the body when we move it."

"Sure." Rio moved closer with the camera. "I've videoed the scene as well and I'll do the same when you move her. Do you want the scene preserved?"

"Nope." Wolfe headed for his van. "There's nothing we can use. I'll get the gurney."

Carter walked to Rio's side. "Did you get a statement from the old guy?"

"Yeah." Rio kept shooting. "He drove to the gate and saw the body. The road here was deserted. He didn't see anyone hanging around. He went back to his vehicle, drove down the road a ways, and called it in. He was blocking the road when I arrived. No one has contaminated the scene."

Carter walked over to the old man. "Mr. Brinks."

"That's me." Brinks looked up at him. "You know this is the second time someone dumped a body here. It's a shock coming to work and finding a young woman like that." He waved a hand toward the body. "I guess this means I'll have to close the land-fill again?"

"No, the ME will remove the body and then you can open up as usual." Carter tipped back his Stetson. "Don't speak about this to anyone. It's obviously a homicide and anything you say might hinder the investigation."

"Yeah, Deputy Rio already read me the riot act." Brinks ran a finger under his nose. "I won't say a word, although people are going to want to know why they were turned away this morning."

Carter thought for a beat and then smiled. "Tell them we're investigating illegal dumping. That's true and you don't have to elaborate. Why don't you go wait in your truck until we're done here?"

"Thanks, I'll do just that." Brinks stood and ambled off.

Carter scanned the area again and, seeing nothing of interest, went back to the body. Bending to spread out the body bag beside the victim, Carter caught the smell of something familiar. He turned to Rio. "Can you smell that? Like over the stink of the body?"

"You mean trash?" Rio's eyebrows rose over his mask. "Yeah, I smell the trash."

Carter shook his head. "It's... Dammit, I know that smell." He looked up as Wolfe returned with the gurney. "There's a chemical odor here, something I've smelled before. Can you identify it?"

"I have mentholated salve under my nose, so no, I can't smell much at all." Wolfe bent to take hold of the shoulders of the corpse. "Grab her feet and we'll get her bagged."

Complying, Carter lifted the body and stood as Wolfe zipped it up, bending again to lift it onto the gurney. He removed his gloves and the memory slotted into place. He snapped his fingers. "The smell, it's formaldehyde."

"Do you think the killer is preserving the bodies?" Rio shuddered. "That's plain nasty."

Thinking over some of the cases he'd investigated and read about, Carter rubbed his chin. "It's not unusual for a killer to want to relive the kill. Some of them keep a body or go visit a corpse many times before they decompose. If they know how to preserve a body using formaldehyde, it's possible this woman could have been murdered some time ago."

"Maybe, but with the technology we have, we can tell how much the cells have degraded. If a body was frozen or soaked in formaldehyde, the cells still deteriorate." Wolfe pushed the gurney to the van and slid it inside. "I didn't smell traces of formaldehyde on the previous victim, but I'll run a specific test for it ASAP. I inspected tissue samples and took blood. She wasn't drained like this one. Or, let's say, not as much. There was substantial blood loss on the first victim." He sighed. "The most common place to drain blood is from the carotid artery. I'll be sure to check for any other points he might have used. I figure you need to start searching for anyone around town who is buying large quantities of formaldehyde. It's not something most people would use."

"I'll hunt down suppliers." Rio rubbed the back of his neck. "Kalo is still searching for missing women and making a list with photographs. We'll get him to run them through the system. He might hit a match with our victims."

Carter nodded. "I don't like our chances. If these women haven't entered the system as missing, we might never identify them, but if we do, it will give us a start in the right direction." He thought for a beat. "Taxidermists use formaldehyde. There are some working here and in the neighboring counties, and hunt down undertakers. I figure we get a list and check them out as well." He smiled. "Just as well I'm here. If needs be, I can hunt down people across counties and state lines." He clapped Rio on the back. "Let's go. I need to get back to the ranch before I'm missed. We'll meet up at the office as soon as Jenna and Kane have left for the airport."

"Jenna is going to be as mad as hell when we tell her." Rio removed his face mask and crumpled it in his fist.

Carter snorted. "Then say I came in and took over." He tossed a toothpick in his mouth and grinned. "One thing is for darn sure: she can't fire me."

SIX

"Jenna." Jo's voice drifted into Jenna's dream.

The smell of coffee filled Jenna's nostrils and she opened her eyes. Jo was standing beside her bed, with Jaime peeking around her. "Morning." She smiled at Jaime. "Hello, Jaime."

"I'm going to ride a horse after you get married." Jaime grinned at her. "Uncle Ty said you'll be leaving soon."

"Will I?" Jenna sat bolt upright spilling her black cat Pumpkin from the bed. The cat gave a disgruntled meow and jumped back on the bed, curled up in a ball, and went back to sleep. "What time is it? Did I oversleep?"

"No, it's fine." Jo sat on the edge of the bed and stroked the cat's silken coat. "Time will fly by this morning, and I didn't want you to be rushed."

Jenna reached for the coffee. "I'm very organized. I'll be ready. I just hope Dave turns up."

"Why wouldn't he?" Jo grinned at her. "You know that's the top fear on a bride's and bridegroom's lists." She glanced toward the window. "The flowers came about an hour ago and the gazebo looks beautiful. It was such a good idea to build one under the trees. It will be a great place to sit when you have cookouts."

A twinge of worry gripped Jenna. She hated having people unsupervised on her ranch. "Did everyone leave?"

"Yeah." Jo patted her knee. "Carter was there to make sure no one made a mistake. I'll go and start breakfast. You take your time. Are you having anyone over to style your hair?"

Jenna shook her head. "No, Dave doesn't say anything, but I know he likes it around my shoulders. I'll just wash it. I'm all packed and ready to go." She indicated to a small bag near the door. "I'm not taking many clothes. It's casual beachwear there and I'm planning on shopping until I drop."

"Okay, I'll leave you to it." Jo stood and guided Jaime from the room.

A scratching came from under Jenna's bed and Duke wiggled out and shook himself, long ears windmilling around him. He gave an explosive yawn and then stuck his big head on the bed and sighed. Jenna patted his head and then crawled out of bed. "The doggy door is open and Zorro is outside some-where." She looked at Duke's big sad eyes and bent to hug him. "You'll be fine with Carter and Zorro. We'll be back before you know it and Carter said he'll take you down to Aunt Betty's Café for leftovers." She straightened and suddenly wondered why she was talking to a dog but when Duke barked and wagged his long thick tail, she believed he'd understood every word she'd said. After all, he understood Kane just fine.

She showered and brushed her hair until it shone. She pulled on her dressing gown and slippers and went to the kitchen. Carter and Jaime were already at the table, and Jo served breakfast the moment she walked in. She looked at Carter. "I hope you left Dave in good shape last night?"

"Oh, Jenna." Carter gave her a lopsided grin, his green eyes sparkling with mischief. "My lips are sealed."

Jenna ate slowly and sipped her coffee, eyeing him over the

rim of her cup. "So, what are the plans for today? I feel so out of the loop. Dave mentioned something about leaving the Beast at Wolfe's office, so I gather he's coming with him?"

"Yeah, Wolfe's bringing him and I'll do the airport run when you get home, so he can pick up his truck." Carter spread toast with liberal amounts of butter and then topped it with strawberry jelly.

Still worrying about the case, Jenna nodded. "Ah, are you planning on staying after we get back? If you're not busy, I'd value having you both here."

"I guess it depends if you still need us on the case or not. We need a reason to be here apart from a vacation. I personally would move here permanently if I could." Carter shrugged nonchalantly. "Right now, we're just twiddling our thumbs out at Snakeskin Gully. The local counties are handing their own problems just fine. We've asked to be involved anywhere within reach of the chopper but have gotten zip. I figure if it wasn't for the cases in Black Rock Falls, we'd go stir crazy. Life is so slow there we might as well be living in a different dimension. I'd say Snakeskin Gully isn't the end of civilization as we know it, but you can see it from there."

"That's my fault." Jo pulled a face. "When my boss married my ex-husband, she made it very clear my career in the FBI was over. Thankfully, I'm still contacted by law enforcement worldwide for advice, and in the downtime, I'll keep writing my books." She sighed. "Whatever happens here, we'll be flying home on Monday night so Jaime doesn't miss school. She understands I have to work and is very happy with our nanny when I'm away."

"I miss Beau and my friends." Jaime looked up from her plate. "I miss Mommy sometimes too, but we talk twice every day on video calls. Beau can't make video calls, but I spoke to my best friend last night. It was cool."

"I love video calls too." Jenna looked from one to the other as they spoke. Her attention settled back on Jo. "I'm so happy you came and allowed Jaime to be a bridesmaid."

"You've made her a very happy girl and we'll be straight back if you need us here." Jo ruffled her daughter's hair. "We would have brought Beau along, but he gets so afraid of the chopper. We left him with our nanny."

"I have a picture of him in my locket." Jaime beamed at Jenna and unclasped the locket to show her the image of her Boston Terrier. "He's grown since you last saw him."

Jenna smiled at the little girl. "He has indeed. You'll have fun riding this weekend. There are a ton of trails all over my property. You can ride right down to the river and back without crossing any fences."

"Uncle Ty will look after us and I'll take care of Pumpkin and Duke for you." Jaime dug into her cereal. "You just go and have fun getting married."

Jenna chuckled. "I will."

The perimeter alarm sounded, and Carter pushed his last bite of toast into his mouth and headed for the screen beside the front door. "It's the girls." He pressed the intercom. "Come on in."

Emily, and her sisters, Julie and little Anna, soon came through the door with Rowley's wife, Sandy, close behind. Jenna turned in her seat to look at them. "Good morning." She waited for them to sit down and turned to Sandy. Cooper and Vannah, Jenna's godchildren were missing. "Where are the twins?"

"At my mom's house." Sandy gave a nonchalant shrug. "They're teething again and not very happy at the moment. We thought it best to come alone. Jake will be along soon with the food and drinks. Rio's brother and sister have offered to help too, so he'll be bringing Piper and Cade." She patted Jenna on the hand. "Don't you worry about a thing. We have everything arranged. It's just as well you have such a huge house. We'll all fit in the family room just fine."

"Are you nervous?" Emily raised one blonde eyebrow and gave her a look so much like her father, Jenna grinned.

"No, not at all." Jenna sighed. "I'm just happy, but worried about leaving an open case."

"There's nothing to do." Carter leaned against the kitchen counter, coffee cup in one hand. "Right now, it's a waiting game. Oh, and Maggie sends her best and said she'd be opening the office as usual, and Deputy Walters is going to swing by in case there's a problem."

Wondering if Carter was covering something up, she eyed him suspiciously. "I find it hard to believe that Maggie doesn't want to come to my wedding. What aren't you telling me?"

"She's old school, Jenna." Carter sipped his beverage and sighed. "She wants to keep the office open. I told her Walters could hold the fort for a couple of hours, but she said he'll mess up the books if someone comes in to pay a fine."

Shaking her head, Jenna finished her coffee and went to clear the table.

"Oh, no you don't." Jo waved her away. "Head into your room. Em is going to do your makeup."

Horrified Jenna blinked. "I'm sure I can manage. I prefer the natural look."

"That's just what you're getting." Emily put both hands on her hips and glared at her. "It's your wedding day, and we're going to pamper you."

"Here." Sandy pulled a blue garter from her purse. "Something old, borrowed, and blue." She handed it to Jenna. "It was my mom's."

Going misty, Jenna smiled at her. "Thank you."

"You're welcome." Sandy pushed to her feet. "I'll help Jo and hopefully Jake will arrive with the cake."

Feeling as if she'd been thrown into a whirlwind, Jenna blinked. "Cake? What cake? This was supposed to be a quiet informal ceremony and then we head to Florida."

"That was Kane's idea." Carter's mouth curled into a slow grin. "Oh, and he told me to give you this." He pulled a long thin box from his back pocket and handed it to her. "Something new."

With trembling fingers, Jenna opened the box and stared at the exquisite three-colored gold chain. It was so Dave Kane. Not overstated but elegant luxury. She ran her fingers over it and smiled. Since starting her new life in Black Rock Falls, she'd neglected to buy jewelry for herself. The earrings and tracker ring being her only adornment. Now she had an engagement ring and a stunning necklace.

"I don't figure I've seen you speechless before." Carter barked a laugh. "Dave is bringing the wedding rings."

Jenna lifted her gaze to him. "Yeah, that bit I know."

"Okay." Carter rubbed his hands together. "As Dave sent me to make sure everything ran to time, we'd better get a move on. Off you go, Jenna. Leave everything to me." He winked at her. "Don't worry, I'm an FBI agent."

Time moved at warp speed and before Jenna had time to get nervous, the sound of a chopper came from overhead. She turned to Emily. "Oh no, what's happened?"

"Nothing. Dad said he'd fly Dave and Father Derry in on the chopper to save time." Emily grinned at her. "It's just about time, Jenna. Julie will let us know when to head out to the gazebo." She kissed her on the cheek and gave her a hug. "You look beautiful."

Taking a deep breath, Jenna stood and turned to look in the mirror. The necklace sparkled against her tanned skin. The plain white silk dress fit like a glove and fell to her ankles. She'd chosen flat sandals to walk across the grass to the gazebo, and as she turned to go, Julie came into the bedroom carrying a bouquet of white roses and a ring of Montana wildflowers to wear in her hair.

"Complements of the groom." Julie beamed at her.

Overwhelmed, Jenna looked at her four bridesmaids, all dressed in pale blue and smiling. "I guess we better make this happen?"

"Okay, roll the camera." Julie gave a signal to Rio, who was filming the wedding. "Anna and Jaime, off you go, nice and slow now."

It was Jake Rowley who waited for her in the hallway, wearing a new black suit. She smiled at him, remembering the first time they'd met and how he'd instantly become her deputy. When she'd arrived in town she'd been lost and like a fish out of water. Rowley had helped the townsfolk to accept a stranger in their midst. He was a dear friend and had worked beside her from the get-go without a complaint. Now happily married with twins, he offered his arm to escort her. She'd never have believed when she'd arrived in Black Rock Falls, scared for her life and alone, that she'd ever be surrounded by a surrogate family, let alone be marrying the love of her life. As she walked to his side, she wished her mom and dad had lived to see her marry. She pictured them smiling at her. *I'm marrying the man of my dreams, and I know you're happy for me.* She smiled at Rowley. "Thank you, Jake. I'm so glad you're here."

"You're welcome and it's an honor." Rowley blushed to the roots of his hair.

They paused at the door as the little girls went first, Anna giggling, her white-blonde hair glossy in the sunlight and Jaime shushing her loudly. Next Emily and Julie headed to the crowded gazebo. Taking a deep breath to calm her nerves, Jenna walked down the steps and out across the lawn Kane had lovingly tended for the last three months. As she lifted her attention to the gazebo. She made out Kane standing beside his best man, Wolfe, their backs toward her and heads bent together chatting. The next second, as if he'd sensed her coming, Kane turned and smiled at her. Everything inside her melted. Her heart must have stopped beating because she couldn't take a breath. It wasn't a dream. It was really happening. As the bridesmaids took their places, she stepped inside and Kane took her hand. It was as if she'd stepped inside a protective shield. The warmth from his fingers traveled up her arm to envelop her. Intrigued, she lifted her chin to look at the man she'd be spending the rest of her life with, and the sight of him mesmerized her. He was so handsome and smelled so good she hardly heard what Father Derry was saying. Forcing herself to concentrate, she listened and repeated the words to join them forever. After they'd exchanged rings, Jenna thought the ceremony was over, but then Father Derry cleared his throat.

"Is there anything you'd like to say before you kiss your bride, David?" Father Derry's face was filled with joy.

"Jenna." Kane turned to face her. "I can't promise our life together will be easy"—his mouth curled into a smile—"but whatever time we're given, it will never be long enough."

Blinking back tears, Jenna couldn't think of a word to say. She hadn't thought past the ceremony they'd discussed with Father Derry. She swallowed hard and said the first thing that came into her mind. "Um... and I'll try really hard not to burn the toast."

SEVEN

The moment the chopper disappeared over the trees Carter ushered everyone into the family room. "Okay, we have a situation. Sandy and Julie, can you take care of Anna and Jaime? I promised them they could ride the horses and I don't like to break my word."

"Sure. We'll have a great time." Sandy looked at her husband. "Jake, if you leave your truck for me, we'll clean up here, take the girls for a ride, and then drop them at Wolfe's house." She turned to Jo. "If that's okay, Jo?"

"Yeah, that would work." Jo smiled. "You'd like that wouldn't you, Jaime? Anna and Julie live close to the sheriff's office. I'll be five minutes away."

"That sounds like fun." Jaime grinned and gave her mom a hug. "You don't have to worry about me, Mom. I'm not a baby."

"Come on then, girls. Let's get you out of those dresses and back into your jeans." Julie herded them down the hallway. "Then I'll go and grab my things out of the truck and we'll go and see the horses."

When Sandy set off for the kitchen with the leftover cake,

Carter quickly brought Rowley and Jo up to date. "I'll go and change. Do you have spare uniforms at the office?"

"Yeah." Rowley scratched his cheek. "Jenna is going to be like a bear with a sore head when she finds out about this."

"Ty did the right thing." Emily's brow wrinkled into a frown. "Jenna deserves some time away with Dave." She shrugged. "We'll just make sure when she comes back, we have everything under control. I'll head straight to the morgue and meet Dad. We'll need to get started. With two victims to process, it's going to be a ton of work."

Carter pushed back his Stetson. "Okay, let's get at it." He whistled to Zorro and patted his leg for Duke to follow him and then headed for the door. "I'll leave the dogs in the cottage. They enjoy each other's company and we're going to be busy. Jenna insisted that Pumpkin is fine to do her own thing. She has food and water, so I guess I'll leave her be."

"That's a good idea." Jo walked along beside him back to the cottage. "Getting back to the homicides, if it's exactly the same MO in both cases, it makes this interesting." She picked her way over the uneven ground on strapless heels. "I guess we look for symbolism. I'll need to see the crime scene photographs to get a profile up on this guy."

Carter noticed the strained expression on Jo's face. "Sure, but what's up, Jo? I mean apart from the case. There's something troubling you. I can tell."

"It's having Jaime here in the middle of a murder investigation. I shield her from my work, and it's too easy with everyone involved for things to slip out. She's way too young to be exposed to what people are capable of doing to each other." Jo's mouth turned down. "I'd prefer to take Jaime home today if possible. I trust Wolfe's housekeeper, but if I'm worrying about Jaime, I'm not concentrating on the case."

Carter removed his hat as he walked into the cottage and tossed it on a peg. He turned to look at her. "Taking her home isn't a problem, but are you sure you don't want to spend more time with her? You don't have to come into the office at all. We can manage for a time without you. I'm sure Jaime would appreciate a couple more days here on the ranch with you."

"I appreciate the thought, but you need a profiler." Jo smiled at him. "Jaime is very independent and is used to me coming and going. She's not an infant. She is eight now and as smart as a whip. It's not like I'm away every day, but when I am she is in such a great routine she hardly misses me. The video chats help me more than they do her. I miss her when I'm away and she seems to bounce through it like it's just another day." She smiled at him and hung up her jacket. "I owe everything to our nanny. Clara's been there since Jaime's birth and they're very close. She's more like her grandmother."

Carter stopped to look at her. "Okay, I'll go and refuel the chopper and we'll leave as soon as we get the chance. It won't take long if you ask Clara to meet us at the office. You're always worrying about Jaime's welfare, but are you happy, Jo?"

"Yeah, funnily enough I am." Jo shrugged out of her jacket and hung it on one finger. "With school and her dancing lessons, I only get to see her before she heads out to school or in the evenings anyway. Not having a man in my life, I prefer to keep busy." She sighed. "I miss being married. It would be nice to have someone to discuss my day with when I get home. I didn't think it mattered until I watched Jenna and Dave's wedding. I miss that connection." She gave him a rueful smile. "But I have you to watch my back, so it's not all doom and gloom."

"True." Carter headed for his room. "I still can't figure why you chose me as your partner. I'm a lost cause, Jo."

"There's no such thing." Jo followed him down the hall. "Anyway, I like a challenge. We were both broken when we arrived out at Snakeskin Gully and we're honest with each other. I like that we can work together without walking on eggshells all the time. You say it like it is and I like that about you, even if you have a faulty filter at times."

Amused, because Jo rarely talked about her previous life and husband, Carter turned at the door. "You have to admit I've changed." He smiled at her. "Thanks to you and Jenna, I'm almost human again."

"Yeah, but you've always been civil to me, and I appreciate it." Jo kicked off her shoes and bent to pick them up.

Carter regarded her with interest. This was another side to Jo he hadn't seen before. She'd always been ultra-professional with him from the get-go and, as she was his superior, he'd always tread lightly around her. She rarely let her guard down and having her admit her vulnerability surprised him. He smiled at her. "Everyone deserves to have at least one close friend. I've noticed Cage gets all flustered around you. Maybe you should ask him out for a coffee."

"Sheriff Cage Walker is a very nice man, but I'd drive him crazy." Jo giggled. "He's an old soul in a young body and speaks so slowly. Every time we talk, I feel like he's in slow motion and I'm flashing around him." She snorted with amusement. "Now, don't you start matchmaking. I already have Em on my case." She waved him away. "Go and change your clothes. We have people waiting for us to solve this crime." She hurried down the hallway.

Shaking his head, Carter looked after her. She ran circles around him too.

EIGHT

Still bathing in the wedding glow, Jenna hadn't let go of Kane's hand since leaving home. Everything had happened so fast and now, finally alone with her husband, it was taking a long time to unwind. After cutting the wedding cake and posing for Rio to take a million photographs, they'd changed into casual clothes and climbed into the chopper. Excited to be leaving, the last thing on Jenna's mind was murder. Bubbling over with happiness, she'd smiled as they waved goodbye to everyone. Wolfe had taken them directly to the airport and they boarded a private jet to Florida, compliments of POTUS.

Luxurious didn't come close to how to describe the jet. It was like flying in a high-end hotel room. Jenna relaxed in the comfortable leather seat, snuggled under Kane's arm, and just breathed. They'd been in the air for almost two hours when the flight attendant came by to offer them more drinks and a selection of meals. She listened with interest as he spoke to Kane.

"We just heard there's a weather watch for the Florida coast. There is a hurricane out at sea and moving landward. Our orders have changed. We're staying over until Monday in case you need to be evacuated. Here's a number to call if the storm causes a problem. Just make it to hangar eight and we'll take it from there." He handed Kane a card.

"Copy that." Kane's brows knotted into a frown. "Just how bad is this storm?"

"It's a big one, but you know hurricanes. They can change course. It might swing past and you'll be fine. Just check the weather alerts, and if there's a problem, get the hell out of Dodge." He gave them a nod and headed back to the galley.

Staring out at the clear blue sky, Jenna rested her head on Kane's chest. "We'll be fine. Surely nothing will happen in the next couple of days. We'll leave on Sunday if it looks like it's heading inland."

"Yeah." Kane rubbed his chin thoughtfully. "I'll be sure to check for weather alerts on my phone." He smiled at her. "Let's eat and maybe watch a movie to kill some time."

With her mind on sea and sand, Jenna nodded and straightened in her seat. "You choose something." She sighed. "This jet is spectacular. I could get used to this luxury."

"We don't have to work. We could retire and spend the rest of our lives doing whatever we liked." Kane scrolled through the movie choices on the screen. "But after a time, I figure that would get boring. I know it seems crazy wanting to put in the hours solving crimes, but I actually enjoy it."

Considering long and hard about spending a year on a beach in Hawaii and then dismissing it, Jenna had to agree with him. "I love my job too, and grabbing weekends like this together is all the more special because they're hard to come by. I'd hate to lose that appreciation of taking a vacation." She gazed down at the rings on her finger and smiled. "We had to get away for a honeymoon. I think we both need new memories and something to tell the grandkids. Although, I miss Duke and Pumpkin already."

"Me too." Kane lifted one shoulder in a half shrug. "Pumpkin is very independent, and Duke likes Carter and enjoys the company of Zorro. Time will tell if he copes without us being there."

Jenna rolled her eyes. "He'll probably give you the cold shoulder when you get back."

"More like take to having showers with me again." Kane grinned broadly. "For a dog who hates water, he must have been very insecure to do that."

The memory of Kane buried alive sent shivers down Jenna's spine. Without Duke they wouldn't have found him in time. She pushed the memories into the back of her mind. "Let's hope he's never insecure again."

It was late afternoon by the time they touched down in Florida. The heat was stifling and perspiration trickled down Jenna's back as they made their way to the car rental desk. The only vehicle available was a small compact. Jenna shook her head in disbelief. "We reserved a truck. How are you going to fit in there? This is crazy."

"Don't worry. Wolfe said his mom's condo is opposite the beach and everything we need is in walking distance." Kane shook his head and pushed the seat back as far as it would go. He folded himself into the seat. "We just have to get there and back is all." He leaned out the door to remove his hat. "My head is touching the roof and I don't figure the seatbelt will fit."

"I'll snap you in." Jenna opened the door to a wall of blistering heat that rushed out and surrounded her. Sweat stuck her shirt to her back as she lowered herself into the scorching seat. "I wasn't expecting it to be this hot. Crank up the AC to its limit. I'm going to melt in this heat."

"Open the windows. The air will blow out the heat, and when we shut them, the AC will work better." Kane started the engine, entered the address into the GPS, and backed out of the parking space. "I wasn't expecting it to be so hot on the coast." He glanced at her. "We have a private jet at our disposal, maybe we could turn around and head for Hawaii."

Laughing Jenna shook her head. "By the time we get there it will be time to head home. That's got to be, what, nine hours or so from here?"

"Yeah, but it was nice and cool in the plane, and they had food and movies." Kane's eyes twinkled with mischief. "I love traveling on luxury aircraft. Not that I've been on many. I took a few flights with POTUS, but in service, it was usually anything that I could get a ride on. I'd be sitting on the floor most times with trucks and supplies."

As this was her first visit to Florida, Jenna took in the scenery and grinned when the first glimpse of the sparkling ocean came into view. Concern crushed her excitement as she looked into the distance. A band of dark clouds hung over the horizon like a massive tsunami threatening to strike at any moment. "Oh, I don't like the look of that."

"It's a long way away." Kane turned into a beach road. "Most storms look like that at sea. It doesn't necessarily mean it's a hurricane. It might just be a thunderstorm. It's very hot today and they often have evening storms here."

Unease crawled over Jenna. "I hope you're right." She tried to push the worry from her mind. "What else did Wolfe tell you about this place?"

"Like I said, the condo is in a building with a restaurant, coffee shop, and a beachwear store, opposite the beach. He said the food is good, but we can cook ourselves if we want. He also said he left his knucklehead in the garage. It's drained of gas, but his mom left a can of gas in there, if we want to take it for a ride. He's having it shipped to Black Rock Falls when his mom comes down for her vacation in August."

Jenna blinked at him. "What is a knucklehead?"

"A motorcycle, a Harley." Kane chuckled. "It's an old one he restored years ago and rides on his vacations. Since his wife died, he rarely comes here. It has too many memories."

"That's so sad." She pointed. "Look! Palm Drive, turn here. Oh, this looks nice."

As they joined a line of traffic crawling along the beach-front, Jenna's attention moved to the sea. The Google search she'd made of the area showed images of a blue ocean and white crested shore breaks on golden sands. The sea looked angry, reflecting the gray clouds cumulating on the horizon. Huge waves pounded the beach, creating a line of foam, and high winds had lifted the sand, scattering it across the blacktop like gold dust. As they drove past stores, there seemed to be a general unease. People stood at the curb loading up their vehicles and others boarded up storefronts and windows. "Maybe we need to check the weather situation again. The locals are leaving in droves."

"As soon as we get settled. Ah, here's the building." Kane drove into an underground parking lot and punched numbers into a keypad.

The mesh door rolled upward slowly and they drove from brilliant sunshine into a dim space. Jenna tipped up her sunglasses and pointed ahead. "Look we can park in the bays. They're numbered, but if we drive through, there are garages lined up against the far wall."

"They're probably storage areas." Kane parked in a bay. "This is the correct number. We'll leave it here. It's cooler under the building. We'll need to collect the apartment key from a neighbor. Her name is Mrs. Coats." He opened the door, climbed out and stretched. "I sure miss the Beast. If you want to go anywhere, maybe we should use the motorcycle?"

Smiling as she slid out of the sedan, Jenna inhaled the ozone and sighed. "I'm not planning on going anywhere, but I can't wait to get my toes into the sand."

"Maybe later, when it's cooler." Kane's mouth curled into a smile, and he pulled her close and kissed her. "If you recall, this is our honeymoon?"

Jenna giggled. "How could I forget?" She gazed into his eyes. "But the beach later. Maybe a moonlight stroll after dinner?"

"Sure." Kane stepped away and pulled their bags from the back seat. He pushed his hat on his head and his expression change to serious. He dumped the bags onto the hood of the sedan, turned and cupped her cheeks, his thumbs making tiny circles. "You are so darn beautiful, Jenna. Tell me this isn't a dream."

Misty-eyed, Jenna looked into his dark blue gaze and sighed in contentment. "Well, if it is, I don't ever want to wake up."

NINE

BLACK ROCK FALLS

After entering all the images he'd taken at the scene into evidence and emailing a copy of the files to all concerned, Zac Rio stood at the whiteboard in Jenna's office and made notes for others involved in the investigation. All the information he'd gathered remained in his head. Having a retentive memory was good for him, but he sometimes forgot others couldn't read what was in his mind. The procedure for processing a homicide scene and running an investigation was virtually the same for all areas of law enforcement, but being first responder had its obligations. As Jenna had given him the lead, he'd play it by the book. His files were complete, but he transferred his observations of the crime scene to the whiteboard for everyone to see. He included the time he'd arrived and where Mr. Brinks was located. He'd secured the scene and made sure there wasn't a physical threat to his witness. He could plainly see the victim was dead, but he'd checked the body for life signs and then called it in before validating Mr. Brinks' identity and taking a statement. He'd taken images of Brinks' truck, tires, and driver's license for the record.

He'd made a note of the weather and temperature, listed the

other officers on scene, and made a note about Carter smelling formaldehyde. After stepping back and looking at his work, he started another heading for possible uses of formaldehyde and the people who used it regularly. They'd need a checklist to work through during the investigation.

He moved his attention from his list and over to the one Jenna had started on the first victim. Beside her list, he added a heading for victim two and noted the comparison between both victims:

- Caucasian
- Female
- Blonde hair
- Naked apart from a thin negligee
- Mask
- Glue
- Meat skewers inserted along spine
- Ligature marks
- Bruising
- Clean feet
- Number cut into back

As he finished writing, Carter and Jo walked into the office after their round trip to Snakeskin Gully and back. Rowley followed close behind them. Rio waved a hand toward the coffee machines. "There's plenty of coffee if you need it. While you were away, I updated your files. I figure we need to explore the formaldehyde angle as it's all we have right now."

"Not so fast." Jo folded her hands in her lap and stared at him. "Two murders, same MO. Both dumped in town and we have no missing persons fitting their descriptions. This is like waving a red flag at me, Rio."

Interested, Rio dropped into Jenna's office chair and looked at her. "How so?"

"This screams of an organized serial killer." Jo stood and went to the counter to pour a cup of coffee. "There is symbolism here and we need to look more closely at it. The mask and the skewers mean something to this man." She turned and leaned against the counter, cup in hand. "This isn't his first dance, and from the crime scene images, we need to be looking at other murder victims. Carter has seen something like this before, so that's another angle to investigate."

Nodding, Rio cleared his throat. "I agree but we need to find suspects, and if this man is in town and has access to formaldehyde, that will give us a lead to follow. I mean how many people in Black Rock Falls could that be?"

"Maybe more than you think." Rowley looked up from his tablet. "Oh boy, it's used in a ton of things. We figured a mortuary and a taxidermist, but it's used in manufacturing. The recycling plant that takes wood from the landfill and makes it into composite wood products uses formaldehyde-based resins." He scrolled through a page. "And we have a factory on the outskirts of town that makes resins." He sighed. "It's used as a preservative and a disinfectant, so it's just about everywhere."

"I'm sure Wolfe will be able to narrow down what type was used on the body." Carter shook his head. "It wasn't a resin. It smelled like an undertaker's preparation room, or a specimen kept in a jar in a laboratory. That type, strength, or whatever has to be available to a few, not a vast majority. As far as I know, chemicals like that have restricted distribution. We should be able to track down a local supplier once we know what specific one we're tracking. We'll have more leads after the autopsies."

Rio stood and added Jo's observations to the whiteboard. "Okay, so we maybe add schools and colleges to the list? I recall specimens being preserved in formaldehyde or alcohol. It's worth looking into. I mean, even a janitor could have access to a supply."

"So, we work on tracking the formaldehyde until Wolfe has completed the autopsies?" Rowley glanced up from his tablet.

"Something else." Carter tossed a toothpick into his mouth. "The skewers. We'll need to see if they're the same on each victim. We'll need a supplier of these in bulk as well. The killer used a ton of them and, if he purchased them locally, someone would have noticed a guy buying that number of skewers."

"Okay." Rio made more notes. "Anything else?"

"We have zip reports of missing women, here or from the surrounding counties." Jo went back to her seat and placed her cup on the desk. "If these women are out-of-towners or from out of the state, which seems reasonable at this point in time, you won't have jurisdiction to investigate the case. You'll need cooperation from the law enforcement in whatever county or state these women hail from." She spread her hands wide. "This case isn't going to be easy. From what I've seen so far, if this killer is bringing bodies here, he's not just using Black Rock Falls as a dumping ground. He's trying to prove a point. We need to find out what that reason is—and fast. It's obvious he has an ax to grind with someone, and what is more disturbing is that if he has multiple comfort zones and is moving between them, this case could stretch across states."

Considering the ramifications of her statement, Rio dropped into his chair. "Right. Carter mentioned a similar case some time ago. We should pull that up and compare the murders to our victims. Maybe this guy has been in jail and that put a stop to his killing spree for a time. It protected him from being caught if he is moving from state to state." He leaned back, running ideas through his mind. "We'll need to look at offenders released from jail in the last say...year? Also, occupations that would give a killer multiple comfort zones. In my opinion, we're looking for a person who travels around and maybe stays in different places for a short time but knows the location well."

"I agree." Jo sipped her coffee and sighed. "So what occupations are we looking at here?"

Standing and moving to the whiteboard, Rio searched his mind. "Long-distance truck driver, a businessman who moves around within his businesses and has apartments in different counties and states."

"Drillers spend time in different places, especially the offshore rigs." Rowley looked animated. "The oil business employs a ton of people and they move around everywhere."

"Man, this is getting complicated. We're still assuming the victims have been moved, so whoever is doing this is driving, not moving around by air, unless they have their own aircraft or chopper. Around here, there are many cattlemen with their own choppers. It could be anyone from the suggested occupations or just someone on vacation with their own cabin." Carter removed his hat and ruffled his blond hair before replacing the Stetson on his head. "I figure Monday won't come soon enough. Jenna will need all the help she can get, and I'm darn sure we're not going anywhere. She'll need all hands on deck for this homicide."

Allowing the information to settle into place, Rio sat back down. He must take charge and delegate. "Okay, Rowley, you hunt down suppliers of formaldehyde, get a list, call them, and ask them if they'll give us a list of people and places they sell to. That should cut down the grunt work of tracing the chemical."

"I'm on it." Rowley stood and headed out the door.

Dealing with the FBI was surreal, and Rio looked at Carter. "Would you mind hunting down the case files you mentioned so we can compare them?"

"Sure, I'll use Kane's desk." Carter stood and went to the counter to fill a cup with coffee before he slipped from the room.

"What have you got for me to do?" Jo's face brightened. "I can do grunt work."

Rio nodded. "Would you help me hunt down anyone with offenses against women who was released from jail over the last two or three years? Maybe one of them will fit your profile." He leaned forward in his chair with his hands linked on the desk. "When I'm done, I'll head on over to the county records office before they close for the weekend. I'll hunt down the names of out-of-towners who own cabins or weekenders in Black Rock Falls."

"You might need Bobby Kalo to help you with that task." Jo smiled. "He's superfast."

Picking up the phone and calling Kalo's number, Rio nodded. "Good thinking." He frowned. "When I arrived, I had aspirations of being sheriff, and after working here in Serial Killer Central, I don't know how Jenna keeps up the pace."

TEN

"Wind gusts of 85 to 110 miles per hour, north to northeast. If Hurricane Zorba maintains its current heading, it is expected to cross the coast in the next thirty-six to forty-eight hours. Prepare your homes and complete your plans for evacuation. The next update will be in two hours. If evacuation is necessary, follow the advice of the local officials."

Kane sat on the edge of the bed and listened intently to the small radio. He looked up as Jenna came out of the bathroom wrapped in a towel followed by a cloud of honeysuckle fragrance. "It looks like we have twenty-four hours to enjoy Florida before we must leave to be safe. I'm not going to risk our lives hanging around to meet Hurricane Zorba. It looks like the beach walk is off."

"I'm not sure I'd want to hit the beach anyway with a major storm whipping up the ocean. It looks like a horror movie set out there." Jenna stared out the window and let out a long sigh. "I was so looking forward to a swim and the feel of sand between my toes, rather than finding it in my hair and stuck between my teeth. The wind is brutal. In that glimpse of the beach, we had walking from the parking lot, my legs feel as if they've been sandblasted."

"Mine too." Kane stood and wrapped his arms around her, peering at the waves pounding the beach. He frowned as the wind gusts bent the palm trees all in the same direction. "It's getting pretty wild out there. Do you feel like going out to grab a meal before it gets any worse? The restaurant downstairs had a WE'RE OPEN sign painted on the boards covering the windows."

"Maybe later. I think I should call Rio and see how the case is progressing." Jenna picked up her phone.

Kane plucked it from her hand. "Oh, no you don't." He shook his head. "We agreed. No shoptalk. In any case, if you call, they'll think you're checking up on them, and they're more than capable of handling a homicide. This is our alone time together, Jenna. Relax and enjoy it while we can."

"Okay, but it doesn't feel right." Jenna slipped from his arms and looked around the floor. "Where are my things?"

"Here." Kane grabbed Jenna's bag and dropped it onto the bed. "I've been through a hurricane and I'm concerned about the weather. It's getting worse and it doesn't take a genius to see the wind is dangerous. I figure if the storm keeps tracking this way, we should head back to the airport first thing in the morning. We can't risk leaving it to the last moment. If everyone starts to evacuate at once, it will take the entire day to get through the traffic. I've seen people panic and it's not nice." He wrapped his arms around her. "I know you're disappointed, but I'll make it up to you. I'll find a nice safe beach for us to visit the next time we take a break, I promise."

"The weather isn't your fault." Jenna turned and placed her hands on his shoulders. "I just wanted a weekend to remember and have stories to tell our grandkids and now look what's happened. I jinxed our honeymoon."

"No, you didn't." Kane shook his head and smiled at her. "I

figure you wanted a little excitement too, and wishes don't always work out the way you plan them. We had a luxurious flight, and a wonderful afternoon together."

"We sure did." Jenna's mouth curled into a satisfied smile. "Although I didn't know I'd married a US Marshal." She giggled. "You certainly are full of surprises."

"That's a first for me too. Wolfe is a genius." Kane thought for a beat. "I'll drop by the 7-Eleven and make up a survival kit, just in case we have to leave in a hurry. They were open when we came by. They have shutters on the storefront windows. I figure they're used to the weather by now."

"Yeah, we should make that a priority. I feel strange without my sheriff's jacket." Jenna stared out at the darkening sky and shuddered. "My pockets are already full with emergency supplies but it's not enough,"

A clap of thunder rolled across the sky, and under his palms Jenna trembled. He pulled her closer, kissed her, and then leaned back to look at her—his beautiful wife. He still couldn't believe it. A lump formed in his throat and he swallowed it, pushing his wedding to Annie far into the recesses of his mind. He loved Jenna with all his heart, but Annie would always be with him as if watching from afar. He forced his expression to remain calm, although the weather warning had concerned him. As Jenna picked up on his moods, he wanted to keep it light and happy, even with a hurricane threatening to spoil everything.

"You really are hungry." Jenna inclined her head and looked into his eyes as if trying to see his thoughts. "I can hear your stomach growling. I'll get dressed. We'll drop by the 7-Eleven and then find someplace to eat."

"Wolfe recommended the restaurant downstairs. He said it is second to none. We'll have a nice meal and a good bottle of wine. I'll make it an evening to remember."

"That sounds perfect." Jenna yawned and stretched. "If we

can't go to the beach, let's get an early night. I hate storms and all this traveling is wearing me out."

Amused, Kane nodded. "Yeah, I'd like that too."

ELEVEN

"Another day and I'm still alive." Poppy Anderson ran her fingertips over the bumpy stone walls, taking note of the unusual gouges and scrapes. The cold seeped into her from the forever damp walls. The constant sheen of moisture fed a patch of bright green moss. It started in a crack on the floor and tumbled across one corner before climbing up the walls. She had to be imprisoned in a section of caves deep underground. Moving her hands slowly, she examined the rough surface and small fissures. There'd been animal scat on the floor when she'd arrived and a variety of critters—mice, rats, cockroaches, ants, spiders, and maggots—visited daily.

Time seemed to drag by in one endless day, but it had to be summer by now, because the man who'd imprisoned her glistened with sweat when he arrived, as if he'd walked for a time carrying the supplies. She wondered if the caves had once been part of an old mine or used as a prison a long time ago. There had been a TV show about the railroads cutting through the West. In those days towns grew very fast and places like caves were often used to hold prisoners or as storage. Her prison cell was very damp, and some days water ran down the walls to escape into a drain. The plumbing confused her. If this cave was deep underground, her jailer had taken great pains to add a toilet and washbasin. In days gone by, she'd have had a bucket and straw on the floor. Even with the amenities the odor of sweat and sewage clung to the damp stale air.

Keeping her mind active was her only chance of survival. Going stir-crazy meant a slow death. It was as if their jailer used it as an excuse to hurt them. As if listening to her thoughts, a woman pleaded to be set free and pounded on a door close by. Poppy pressed her mouth to the crack in the door and dropped her voice to a whisper. "Calm down. He'll kill you."

She listened in horror as the woman ignored her whispers and screamed, hammering on the door. He'd come now, maybe not straight away, but he'd always walk in real slow. A wave of dread washed over her and she trembled as footsteps, slow and deliberate, echoed through the passages well before he arrived. The smell of him seemed to seep through the door in a miasma of unwashed male. She'd found a tiny crack in the wall to peer through without him seeing her, but panic gripped her. He stood for a time not a hand's width away, looking up and down the rows of cells. As if making his choice, he opened a door and dragged out one of the women. The woman fought back, kicking and biting, but his large hands closed around her throat. As he shook her to the brink of unconsciousness, the conversation was always the same. He inclined his head and stared at her bulging eyes. Bile rushed up the back of Poppy's throat. Surely, he knew his victim could never reply. It was as if asking the questions was a ritual to validate murdering them.

"What is your number?" He lifted them from the floor. "Do you understand the consequences of making a noise?"

The woman's eyes rolled up in her head and he dropped her to the floor. Coughing and gagging, the woman tried to crawl back to her cell, but he was on her in a second.

"You've asked to be punished." He pushed the choking

woman to her knees and grabbed her hair. "Do you figure you can tempt a man to leave his wife now?"

The woman shook her head, gasping for breath.

"I'm going to kill you. Can you make me change my mind?" He bent to stare into his victim's eyes. The woman was clutching at her throat, just trying to breathe. He shook her by the hair. "No? I didn't think so."

Terrified, Poppy shivered. The woman's screams crawled inside her head. She covered her ears and slid down the wall and hummed. The man took forever to kill, as if he savored every painful blow. There was no mercy. Sick to the stomach, Poppy trembled uncontrollably as the only sound coming from outside her cell was the man's heavy breathing and the dragging sound as he removed the body. Fear overwhelmed her and she couldn't move. No sound came from the other cells. Was she finally alone? Would he bring more women to feed his need to kill? Teeth chattering with fear, she crawled to the mattress and curled into a ball. Soon it would be her turn to die unless she could work out a way to escape. She'd laid awake for hours trying to recall the lectures from the crime investigation conferences she'd attended. Reaching deep into her memory, she'd first come up against panic-driven brick walls, but as she relaxed, bits and pieces of information filtered back into her memory. She clearly remembered Special Agent Jo Wells' lecture on the criminal mind. How to interview a psychopath and what not to do if confronted by one. Trying to reason with them never worked because their mental processes didn't recognize their prey as anything of worth. Her jailer showed all the signs of a psychopath. He numbered the women in the cells and this took away any semblance of humanity. She remembered Jo saying that, if captured, the only chance of survival would be to become of some value to them.

It had been a struggle as Poppy tried to keep her sanity and wits. Conversation was banned, but once a week the man would take her from the cell and watch her shower. During this time, she'd make small remarks. Asking how his day had been and thanking him for the shower. Most times he ignored her, treating her less than if he'd just hosed down his front steps. There had to be a way under his guard, she just had to find it. In the meantime, she'd use the time to scan her surroundings. If she got the chance to escape, she'd need to find a way out. During the days in between his visits, she'd think of something else to say to make a chink in his armor. She had to make him realize she wasn't an object for him to brutalize, but an asset. Ideas flooded her mind, foolish maybe, but she would die anyway, so what the heck?

Footsteps came back, and Poppy froze. Fear had her by the throat, but as the key turned in the lock, she scrambled to her feet. The door opened with a metallic creak, and she waited, standing tall and proud. Cowering to this monster would give him power over her. Staring him straight in the eyes, she couldn't miss the blood spatter over his face and bare chest. She swallowed hard, realizing he was naked. What did he want with her? Taking her life in her hands, she pushed down the terror and lifted her chin. She needed to make him understand. "I know why you punish the women. Why do you do everything alone? I can help you."

"Why would you want to help me?" He stared at her with not the slightest hint of expression on his face. "You're just like them. I've seen you in action, remember? You admitted to going to Black Rock Falls to land you a deputy. You must know he lives with the sheriff? It's the worst-kept secret in the county. It's been that way since he arrived in town, and you planned to come between them, didn't you?"

Gathering her nerve, Poppy straightened, not taking her eyes from his face "Forget Dave Kane. I can help because I'm just like you."

TWELVE

FLORIDA, SATURDAY

A strange rushing sound dragged Jenna from a deep sleep. She sat up in pitch black, unsure of her surroundings. She blinked a few times. The readout from the bedside clock was missing and the annoying rattling of the air conditioner had stopped. All the noise came from outside. The promised storm must be wreaking havoc. A howling wind screamed through the night and the shutters on the window rattled like a train going over an old bridge. *Rat-a-tat, rat-a tat, rat-a-tat.* A tingle of worry crept over her. Kane would wake at the slightest sound and she sensed he wasn't beside her. The darkness closed in around her and, concerned, she pushed her hands over the rumpled sheet next to her. The bed was empty and cool. "Dave?"

Nothing.

It was so dark and then a flash of lightning sent spears of light into the room for one blinding second. As thunder followed close behind, Jenna reached for the bedside lamp and flicked the switch.

Nothing.

The storm must have caused a blackout, but where was Kane? He wouldn't leave her alone in a storm. Alarm for his safety gripped Jenna's chest as she eased out of the bed. "Dave, where are you?"

Nothing.

She'd discussed plans with him over dinner to leave in an emergency. The 7-Eleven had everything they needed for their evacuation pack, and Kane had listened to the storm warning updates all evening. The wind had picked up considerably during dinner and the manager of the restaurant was stacking chairs as they ate dessert. It was obvious he wanted to head for the hills before the storm crossed the coastline but before they left he'd offered them a stack of sandwiches to go. As they'd left the restaurant, they ran into a stream of residents filing out of the building. All elderly, they pushed their luggage in an orderly fashion down to the parking lot, and Mrs. Coats, who'd given them the key to the condo, took them to one side and explained the other residents didn't want to take the risk of staying. After checking the weather warning at ten the previous evening, they'd decided it should be safe to leave at daylight. They'd made ready to leave, charged their phones, and laid out clothes for a fast retreat and headed to bed. So, what had changed? Jenna felt her way across the unfamiliar floor searching for the nightstand and her phone. Tripping over her boots, she stumbled headlong into the nightstand, bumped off it and landed in an easy chair. Annoyed for being so skittish, she stood slowly. "Get a grip, Jenna."

The wind howled like a pack of wolves, screaming around the building as if trying every window and door to get inside. The lightning came frequently in blinding crashes, the rolls of thunder a second behind it. In the black interludes, red spots danced across her vision. Spreading her hands wide, Jenna felt all around and eased along the wall to the nightstand. Running her palm over the top until she found her phone, she checked the time. It was almost three in the morning. Using her phone flashlight, she moved around the room. Kane's clothes were no longer hanging over the back of a chair and his boots were gone. She frowned into the darkness. "Where are you, Dave?"

Unease crept over her, but she tried to remain positive. There was no way Kane would leave her alone unless it was an emergency. She tried to call him, but nothing happened and she stared at the screen in disbelief. "Dammit, no bars."

The storm must have knocked out the tower, and of course, she didn't have a satellite sleeve with her. Why should she need one on her honeymoon? The windows shook and shuddered, and things hit the building. Suddenly afraid, she hugged her chest. The hurricane was getting worse. From the reports, they had another twenty-four hours before it was supposed to cross the coast. She chewed on her bottom lip. No doubt, Kane would be trying to get news of the hurricane. Lightning flashed and thunder followed close behind like giant's footsteps shaking the building. It didn't take a genius to know the hurricane was heading their way. Would the building be strong enough to withstand the storm or could they outrun it? Hurrying into the kitchen, she searched the drawers for a flashlight. She found two and a pack of spare batteries and grabbed them. Saving power on her phone might be crucial in an emergency. After visiting the bathroom and collecting her things, she dressed in jeans, boots, and a T-shirt. If the storm increased its ferocity, they'd planned to head for the airport. Standing the flashlight on the nightstand, to illuminate the room, she pushed her things into her backpack and placed it by the front door. She turned to search for Kane's backpack, but it wasn't anywhere to be found. The emergency kit was missing as well. Where was he? Why would he marry her and then disappear in the night?

Terrible loneliness crawled over her, making her heart ache. Her mind was working overtime and fear gnawed at her. Everyone had left the building and she'd never been through a hurricane before. Where could she go? The next second, a gust of wind roaring like a freight train grabbed the shutters on the bedroom window. Transfixed by the surreal sight between each flash of lightening, Jenna stared as they flew open and banged against the outside wall, flapping around like trapped butterflies' wings. Thunder shook the building and the shutters screamed as high winds tore them from the hinges and carried them away into the darkness. The next instant, the glass smashed into a million pieces, spilling like diamonds over the floor. Rain pelted into the room and, borne on a gust of wind, a tree branch flew past her shoulder and speared into the wall. "Dave where are you? We have to get out of here."

Terrified, Jenna picked up the flashlight, grabbed her bag and jacket, and then bolted from the bedroom, slamming the door. Behind her, lamps toppled and smashed as the wind destroyed the room. As she looked frantically around to escape, the wind seemed to taunt her, rattling the shutters in the family room with its deadly fingers. One thing for sure, it wasn't safe near any windows. She ran to the front door, flung it open, and stared into the darkness. Apart from the roar of the wind and the rain beating down, nothing stirred in the dark hallway. Where could she go? Should she stay here and wait for Kane or go look for him? What if he'd gone out in the storm and been hurt? Heart racing, she pulled on her jacket and backpack. After dragging an easy chair across the room and wedging it into position to keep the door open, she moved to the stairs and sat on the top step. Made of concrete with steel handrails, they looked sturdy enough, but was it safer to be in a stairwell in a hurricane or was that an earthquake? Indecision crawled over her. Should she stay or go?

Jenna wrapped her arms around her and peered into the darkness. It seemed like an eternity of doubts and fears assailed her before a light bobbed in the stairwell. "Is that you, Dave?"

"Yeah." Kane's voice echoed up the stairs. "Are you okay?"

Springing to her feet, Jenna headed down to him. "Yeah, but the bedroom is wrecked. The window smashed."

She rounded the top of the next flight and her flashlight moved over him. Her breath hitched in her throat at the sight of a man in a black slicker, a cowboy hat, and rubber boots. "Where did you get the slicker?"

"From the size, I'd say it belongs to Wolfe." Kane stopped beside her dripping water on the steps, removed his hat, and leaned in to kiss her. "Sorry, I didn't mean to worry you. I went to use the bathroom at two and the wind had picked up. The phones were dead, so I went down to the parking lot to listen to the radio in the sedan. It's bad news. We don't have time to get out before it hits. Driving in a hurricane is suicide. I recall Wolfe telling me this building has weathered them before, so we'll be fine, but once it passes the roads will be in bad shape. It will be easier to travel by motorcycle. I went to the garage and pulled out the Harley, gassed it up, and brought it inside. It's in a utility room under the ramp on the first floor. I found helmets and a couple of leather jackets in the garage and stashed them in there too. If it floods, that should be high enough to be safe. There's another slicker in the apartment if we need it in the morning."

Jenna gaped at him. "You pushed a motorcycle up the ramp to the first floor?"

"Yeah, well, it's made for wheelchair access, so it wasn't that difficult." He gave her a lopsided smile. "We'll be riding it down."

"Okay. You're not filling me with confidence, Dave." Walking beside him up the stairs, Jenna stared at the black rubber boots. "Where are your things?"

"Already stashed in the saddlebags. My boots are under the kitchen table." He turned and gave her a long look and shook his head. "You didn't think I'd leave you here, did you?"

Jenna couldn't hide the worry in her expression. "I admit I was kind of scared when the tree branch came through the window and missed stabbing me by an inch. You should have woken me."

"I didn't want to drag you out in a storm for no reason." Kane glanced at his phone. "It's three-thirty. The hurricane will be making landfall anytime soon. We need to hunker down and ride it out. Soon as it's safe, we'll head back to the airport. I'm guessing if the phones are still out, we'll find a payphone there to contact the flight crew. While we're waiting to leave, I'll contact the rental people to go and collect the car, and then see if I can arrange to have the Harley shipped back to Black Rock Falls." He shrugged. "They might even take it on the jet. There'd be enough room in the cargo hold."

Jenna relaxed at Kane's calming influence until the flashlight picked up the tic in his cheek muscle. She'd known him long enough to recognize he was concerned and trying to hide it from her.

"We'll need to grab what we can and get downstairs. I don't know how long it will take to pass over." Kane tossed the easy chair to one side and entered the apartment.

Water spilled from under the bedroom door, soaking the carpet. Avoiding the puddle, Jenna followed him to the kitchen. "Okay, give me the bad news." She dumped her bag on the kitchen table and propped up the flashlight.

"It's bad." Kane leaned against the counter and rubbed his chin. "It's heading our way faster than anyone realized. I had no way of knowing, but over the last hour it increased speed, and the announcer on the radio said destructive wind gusts of over one hundred fifty miles per hour, and it's massive. We're in the direct line. We're in danger, Jenna, and there's no way out. Already roofs and trees are flying around. If this building caves in, our chances of getting out alive is slim to none."

Trying to make light of the situation, Jenna nodded. "Okay. You've survived worse situations, so what do we do to keep safe?"

"We find a small room, with no windows. Eat food if we have it and wait." Kane went to a cupboard in the hall. He handed her a slicker. "You'll need this." He pulled out two aluminum folding chairs. "We'll grab the sandwiches and cookies we purchased and head down to the utility room under the stairs. I figure it's the safest place to hole up." He went to the refrigerator, pulled out the food, and dropped it on the table. "Pass me the bag hanging on the inside of the broom closet door handle. I'll take the water as well. I don't know how long we'll be holed up. I'm hoping the hurricane will break up into a rain depression once it hits land. Rain we can handle but I'm not risking the high winds."

Jenna aimed her flashlight into the broom closet and raised an eyebrow. It was deeper than she'd expected and held hooks with various types of equipment hanging from them. "Does Wolfe's mom climb mountains? There's all kinds of ropes and pullies in here."

"Not that I'm aware." Kane took the bag from her and peered over her shoulder. "It's rescue gear. Probably another of Wolfe's sidelines. Being a military chopper pilot, he'd likely be called on to help out in an emergency." He sighed. "Believe it or not, I know very little about Wolfe's life before Black Rock Falls. I knew about his wife and that he was a field medic. He flew into many dangerous situations to evacuate wounded soldiers, but we don't discuss past lives. He knows nothing about me. At the time, I was Ninety-eight H to him. Just a number in a team."

Jenna noticed the change in Kane's eyes and squeezed his arm. "I doubt you've ever been just a number to him, Dave. From the little you've told me, he got you out of hell, even with his wife dying of cancer. He never let you down, did he? That's a true friend, even if you didn't know each other's names."

"Well, he did call me Dave in the end, and it kinda stuck,

didn't it?" Kane smiled at her. "Let's go." He hoisted the bag over one shoulder and urged her toward the door.

As they hurried down the steps, the building trembled beneath their feet. Jenna gripped tight to Kane's hand. A sound like metal being dragged across the blacktop filled the stairwell. A ripping sound and the tinkle of glass smashing came seconds later and then a massive chunk of metal crashed onto the landing below them. The wind rushed up to meet them in a gush of rain, and debris like fingers pulled at her hair. Horrified, she gaped at Kane speechless.

"Oh, that can't be good." Kane turned and pulled her back up the stairs. "Run."

THIRTEEN

BLACK ROCK FALLS

Medical Examiner Dr. Shane Wolfe listened with interest as Rio brought him up to speed with the cases of the two Jane Does. He'd called them into his office before seven. He'd worked long into the night to get answers and needed a few hours' shuteye. With luck he'd be able to eat breakfast and grab two hours' sleep while he waited for the results of the samples he'd taken from the bodies. "You're saying that even with the FBI scanning the image databases, you still can't identify these women?"

"If they're not in a database, we can't find them, no, but Kalo is extending his search internationally." Rio leaned back against the counter in the morgue examination room and shrugged. "For now, they'll have to be Jane Doe One and Two. Or Twenty and Twenty-One, your choice."

Wolfe shook his head. "I'd never give a killer the satisfaction of naming his victims. It's Jane Doe One and Two."

"That's fine by me. When you have time to take casts of their teeth and DNA samples, we can try again." Carter peered at him over his mask. "With people searching their family trees, we might find a relative, and if the women went to visit a dentist, we might get a hit on the dental records—but that will be like searching for a needle in a haystack, without as much as a state to go by." He crossed his feet at the ankles and took a relaxed pose. "We checked out the masks and skewers but couldn't pin down any particular store. The skewers with hearts on the top are mass produced and can be purchased anywhere in packs from ten to one hundred. The masks are available at general stores, costume stores, and Walmart."

"We're working on a list of people and places that use formaldehyde." Rio rubbed the back of his neck. "Maybe a list of who doesn't use it might be easier."

"Don't worry too much." Carter let out a weary sigh. "Once we've hunted down the names, we'll hand them over to Kalo. He'll cross-match them with local stores and people buying online. His results will give us the best possible candidates for suspects."

"Hey, listen up." Emily came into the room with a whoosh as the door opened and closed behind her. "A hurricane made landfall overnight and wiped out part of the Florida coast." She looked aghast at Wolfe. "I watched the news. They have no communication with anyone yet. I hope Jenna and Dave made it to the airport. It hit right where Grandma has her condo and then turned back around and headed to Bermuda. It's spinning over the Bermuda Triangle."

Wolfe headed for the door, pulling off his gloves and mask. "Give me a minute." He rushed out and headed for his office. He tried calling Kane and then Jenna with no luck. His options were limited. Kane was an asset with a bounty on his head and he had to report him missing. If his fingerprints got into the wrong hands, anything might happen.

Using his keys he located a cellphone, a direct link to his superiors in the military. After giving his code name, he passed on the information and waited. A voice saying a code name he didn't recognize came through the speaker.

"*What do you mean, you've lost contact with Ninety-eight H?*"

Wolfe stiffened. "I'm sorry, sir. I don't recognize your identification. I'm unable to continue this conversation." He disconnected, pulled out the SIM, and tossed it into the microwave.

Dashing a hand through his hair, he paced up and down. Who could he trust? Had his connection to the White House been compromised? He stared at the ground. If Dave and Jenna were in danger, he must go and get them out—if he had a location. He stared at the phone on his desk and snatched it up. The signal from Jenna's tracker alarm inserted into her ring would have sent an alert to his phone. She never took off the ring, so if they were alive, and in danger she'd likely activate it. He took a few deep breaths. He'd ask Kalo to track their phones. They didn't need a connection to find them. He dialed Kalo and explained the situation. "I'm in the middle of an autopsy, but if the signals are stationary, like they might be injured or stuck somewhere, call me." He disconnected and headed back to the examination room.

Wolfe looked at the expectant faces. "I've asked Kalo to track Jenna's and Dave's phones. He'll call as soon as he has anything. We might as well keep busy until we have more information." Forcing his head back to the case of double homicide, he looked at Jo. "So, Jo, any thoughts on this killer?"

"A few but I'd like to see what you find." Jo stood beside the screen peering with interest at the X-rays. "I'll know more if you can describe the process he used to kill them. It says a lot about the type of killer he is and his motive... if he has one."

Wolfe replaced his mask and gloves. He'd already completed a preliminary examination of both bodies. At this point in the autopsy, he'd left the organs intact but had the body cavity open. He'd progress with the autopsy, but from the findings he could use a device to explain the injuries more fully to the observers. "Emily, wheel over the digital anatomy table. I've given you a glimpse of this device before, but by superimposing the images of a victim over the file of a normal body I can demonstrate the nature of the injuries." He activated the machine. "As you can see, it also gives us a 3D image and, by rotating parts of the body, I can display underlying organs. It will give you a concise and visual explanation of cause of death."

"This can't replace a full autopsy." Carter straightened. "It's more like science fiction than fact. How do I know what I'm seeing is the real deal?"

Wolfe glared at him. "Because I'm the real deal. This apparatus was designed for teaching purposes, but in our case, it will demonstrate the damage to the victims in a way you'll understand from the get-go." He turned to Jo. "From the bruising and broken bones, both women were beaten using a blunt instrument. From the bruising, the size and shape of the injuries, I'd say he used a baseball bat."

"And the sexual assault?" Jo cleared her throat. "Can you tell if they were ante- or post-mortem?"

Wolfe moved the slider on the machine to show the depth of the bruising on the arms, legs, and back. "They were both alive when he raped them. He used a condom. I found no semen but found nonoxynol-9, used in the manufacturing, and traces of the powder used to prevent a condom sticking to itself, and luckily enough, lubricant ingredients to identify the specific brand." He raised his eyebrows. "I'm running these for analysis now. A rape kit is the first thing I do when I see the signs on a victim."

"He punished them." Jo let out a long sigh. "For him, rape is the final degradation."

"I disagree." Rio stared at Jo and shook his head. "I'd like to know if that mask was put on before or after they died. I figure he wanted them faceless. He took that away from them too, their identity. They were objects to him, not people."

Wolfe checked through the results coming through on his screen and turned back to them. "I found blood under the mask, some damage to the faces, bruising like from a slap, and a bloody nose. From these findings alone, I'd say he put the mask on postmortem." He cleared his throat. "From the preliminary examination and the damage to the heart and lungs, my first assumption was that the incisions made by the skewers killed them, but on further examination of the bruises on the throat, and from the X-rays and dissection, I concluded the cause of death was asphyxiation caused by strangulation. The lack of hemorrhaging around the skewers would say they were inserted postmortem." He moved the slider on the machine to show the damage to the victim in 3D and looked at Jo. "Can you profile him now?"

"I can." Carter rolled his eyes. "This man sure hates women."

FOURTEEN

FLORIDA

Wind whistled through the cracks in the door, and Jenna buried her face in Kane's chest as they huddled inside the broom closet seated on upturned buckets. Water pooled around their feet and seemed to drip from every crack and cranny. The noise outside had eased some but the creaking and grinding terrified her. Sweat trickled down her back. The humidity inside the claustrophobic closet had made it a very unpleasant night, but in truth, she'd been too terrified to notice it. The thought of dying on her wedding night had dominated her thoughts. Her jaw ached from keeping her mouth shut although she'd wanted to cry out in terror. The hurricane had hit with such force and so fast they'd barely thrown themselves into the broom closet in time. From the ripping and grating sounds, followed by thumps and screaming as the wind tore into the building, they'd been lucky to survive the terrifying onslaught. "Has it gone by yet?"

"I figure the worse is over. The quiet time was the eye going over us and then it started up again. It sounds like the wind is still high but it's moving away." Kane untangled himself from her and grabbed a bottle of water. "Drink your water. We've been sweating for hours. Dehydration is a killer."

Nodding, Jenna lifted a bottle to her lips and drained it. "Now what? We can't sit in here all day."

"We'll go take a look, but the wind gusts are dangerous and things are going to be flying around like missiles. Let's hope the building isn't too damaged." Kane drained his bottle and tossed it into a bucket by their feet. "I'll check our supplies." He opened a bag. "We've four bottles of water and cookies. If the motorcycle made it through, we have the energy bars I purchased from the 7-Eleven stashed in the saddlebags." He stood and stretched. "We'll take the climbing gear. We'll need it to find a way down to the next floor. The stairs were toast before the storm hit, so it won't be pretty now." He tossed the climbing gear over one shoulder, picked up the bag, and then placed one hand on the door handle. "Ready? Stay close."

Heart thumping, Jenna took the long coils of rope from the hook and looped them over one shoulder. "Go, I'm right behind you."

She heard Kane's sharp intake of breath before she blinked into the light and gasped in horror. How had they survived? The apartment was little more than a shell, the kitchen and bathroom the only rooms left standing. The interior walls of the apartment had vanished, leaving a brick skeleton with strips of silver insulation and twisted metal waving in the wind. She stared through the gaping holes to the beachfront and way into the distance, and dismay engulfed her. All along the beachfront was apocalyptic. Roofs ripped off and tossed in all directions, walls half standing. People's belongings, clothes, drapes, toys thrown around or piled up against remaining walls like colorful snowdrifts.

Sand covered the blacktop in a golden hue and water ran through it like newly made rivers. The storm had littered the beachfront with palm trees and debris. An orange sofa, turned upside down and half buried in the sand, sat with foamy waves lapping around it. She gripped Kane's arm as she turned toward the gaping hole where the front door had been. She swallowed hard. They were stuck on the top floor of a wrecked building in no man's land. An uncontrollable tremble went through her. "Sweet Jesus, thank goodness we survived, but how the hell are we going to get down from here?"

"Very slowly." Kane scanned the area and then looked at her. His face had changed into combat mode and that made Jenna feel much better. He held out his hand. "Hold my hand and don't let go. The floor is a concrete slab over a steel frame. Unless the structure is damaged below us, which I doubt because I don't see any cracks, we should be able to get to the stairs. They're the strongest part of the building and we can use the ropes to drop down from there." He moved forward, testing his weight on the floor. "Step by step. Watch your footing. There's debris all over."

Taking his hand, Jenna followed. Under her feet the building seemed to sway, and with each gust of wind, salty rain wet her face. Her boots crunched over broken glass as she followed slowly behind him. They reached the hallway and dismay swallowed her. Most of the walls had vanished and flapping sheets of soaked siding and gaping holes surrounded her. Rubble covered the stairs, making them impassable. As far as the eye could see, personal effects littered the ground. What was left of the hallway looked like a landfill. A photograph album lay open in a pool of water, the images distorted and curling at the edges. Clothes, pots and pans, paper—so much paper was strewn everywhere. Wind whistled through the hallway buffeting them. Apart from the roar of the ocean and the building remnants flapping in the wind, deathly silence surrounded them. No traffic or other signs of life drifted from the streets below. Concern gripped Jenna as she stared through the open walls to the flattened sidewalks. "I don't see anyone moving around out there. What if there are casualties? Should we take the time to search the area?"

"I won't sugarcoat it, Jenna. Right now, we should be worrying about our own survival. If we can get down from here, we'll keep a look out for anyone in trouble on our way back to the airport, but most people would have left before it hit. Locals who live here are overcautious, and search-and-rescue teams will be on their way." Kane straightened. "Right now, we're in danger of this building collapsing and my priority is getting us to safety. Let's hope the airport is still standing, but from what I can see, the main damage is to this strip of the coastline."

Jenna swallowed hard. "What if it's toast or the crew high-tailed it out before it hit?"

"Don't worry. I'll find a way to get you home. There're airports all over Florida." Kane squeezed her hand. "I need you to concentrate on getting down from here first." He leaned over the railing. "There's a ton of damage to the building and wind gusts will be a problem, but this is the only way down. I can see the first-floor ramp and it looks intact. We'll drop down to there and hope the Harley made it through the storm. Or we're walking back to the airport."

Jenna peered into the abyss and shuddered. It was such a long way down. "You want us to climb down there?"

"Yeah." Kane handed her the bag and took the coiled rope from her shoulder. "We have two harnesses and safety gear. I'll lower the bag down as our anchor and we'll follow it. There's enough rope to play out for one trip. He looked deep into her eyes. "You do trust me. Don't you, Jenna?"

It had been a long time since training, and she hadn't repelled down a mountain or anywhere else for a very long time. "You know I do, but I haven't done much mountain climbing."

"You've dropped from a chopper though, haven't you?" Kane gave her a confident smile. "This is much the same, but you'll be on my back."

Swallowing the fear, Jenna gaped back at him. "On your back? What if my hands slip?"

"You won't slip. Oh, don't look so worried. Come here. It will be okay, I promise." Kane pulled her close and kissed her hard. "I love you and I'd never let you fall. All you have to do is relax, keep your eyes open, and I'll do all the work." He stepped back and shrugged into a harness and went about arranging the ropes. One end, he secured to the handrail, the other he tied to the bag of supplies and Jenna's backpack. Dropping them over the railing, he lowered them down to the ramp on the first floor. He handed the second harness to her. "Get this on and climb onto my back. I'll attach you to me. I won't let you fall." He dragged a pair of gloves from his pocket and pulled them on. "It was as if Wolfe had a premonition something would happen. I found gloves in a bag with the harnesses."

Hands trembling, Jenna stepped into the harness and Kane checked the fastenings before turning his back on her. She grabbed his shoulders and jumped onto his back, wrapping her legs tightly around his waist. "Okay, I'm ready."

"Hold on to my straps, not around my neck." Kane hooked up her harness to his. "There, you're attached to me and you won't fall. It's the same as if we were skydiving in tandem." He took hold of the rope and stepped over the railing, balancing on the narrow edge. "Keep your eyes open and don't look down or you'll become disoriented. Lean into me. Hug me tight."

Gripping white-knuckled to the straps of the harness, Jenna's stomach went into freefall. They hung over the drop as he balanced on the very edge of the cement slab. When Kane stepped off and they hung in midair, Jenna's heart raced. She wanted to screw up her eyes and hide but forced them open and pressed against Kane's back. The wind gusts around them sent papers fluttering around them like bats caught in an updraft and then they dropped. As Kane fed the rope out, they fell faster than Jenna would have liked. Heart in her mouth, she held her breath, and in seconds, Kane landed softly on the ground.

"You okay back there?" Kane unclipped her. "Jenna? You can get down now."

Frozen with fear for a second, Jenna unclasped her death grip and slid from his back. "That made my stomach turn over. I wasn't expecting to drop so fast."

"A fast drop means survival." Kane turned and helped her from her harness. "The wind gusts are carrying all kinds of projectiles." He unfastened the harness and tossed it over the railing. "I'll be sure to replace Wolfe's equipment when we get home. I sure hope his mom is insured."

Jenna untied the bags and nodded. "I'm sure she would be."

Scanning their surroundings, she gasped at the destruction. "There's water on the ground floor. I can't tell how deep."

"It's only surface water, look it's lapping at the door. We'll get out okay, but I'll have to clear the broken shutters from the ramp. The utility room is over there." Kane pointed to a door tucked in under the ramp and then headed down the slope. Screeching echoed up the stairwell as he hauled the twisted metal away. "Okay, we're good to go."

Kicking pieces of broken wood and tree branches to one side, Jenna headed for the utility room under the ramp. Sand had piled up outside, preventing her from opening the door. She grabbed a tree branch and dug at the sand as Kane came up behind her. "Almost done."

"Here, let me. You'll get splinters." Kane held out one hand for the branch. "I'm wearing gloves." He made short work of the wet sand and tugged open the door. Water had seeped under the door, but the Harley stood glistening on its stand. "There she is." He smiled at Jenna. "I hope she starts." He ducked inside the room and wheeled the motorcycle onto the landing. "Here goes nothing."

Saying a silent prayer, Jenna collected her backpack and the supplies. The next moment a deafening roar filled the confined space and she heard Kane whoop for joy. She stowed the supplies in the saddlebags and waited for Kane to go back into the utility room to retrieve the helmets and leather jackets. She took the jacket he offered her and slipped into it and then pushed the helmet onto her head and fastened the strap. "I feel like I've gone back in time and we're heading for Route 66."

"You look kinda cute in leather, but I prefer you in a cowboy hat and wearing a gun." Kane flashed her a white smile. "Let's see if we can find a way out through this mess." He straddled the Harley and pushed on his helmet. "You know, I might buy myself a new hat. My Stetson has been buried in mud and now pushed into saddlebags soaking wet. It's going to be wrecked. Although, it does clean up really well and I do like the lived-in look."

Jenna snorted. "We're stuck in the aftermath of one of the worst storms in history and you're worried about your hat." Giggling, she climbed on behind him and slipped her arms around his waist. As usual Kane had found a way of breaking the tension and making her relax with his strange brand of humor. "It's great to see you have your priorities right."

"A man's hat is like... well, like an old friend. At first, it's all new and a bit stiff around you, but after a few years it has a comfortable familiarity." Kane revved the motor and kicked up the stand. "Hang on tight. This is going to be a rough ride." The Harley shot down the ramp and out into the daylight.

FIFTEEN

BLACK ROCK FALLS

Wolfe pointed to the X-rays. "You can see by the fractures in the forearms and fingers on the right hand that this woman made an effort to defend herself on the day she died. However, the bruises all over are in different stages of healing. The ligature marks would indicate the killer restrained her previously and on the day of her death." His phone vibrated in his pocket. It was Bobby Kalo, the FBI IT whiz kid. He glanced at the others. "Just give me a moment. I need to take this. "What have you got for me, Bobby?"

"I've found Kane and Jenna. They're heading toward the airport at Fort Lauderdale. I'm sure they'll contact you soon."

The tension in Wolfe's shoulders relaxed and he smiled broadly. He'd sort out the security problem another time and once Kane and Jenna were safely home. "That's great. Thanks for letting me know." He disconnected, and looked at the others. "Kalo has located Kane and Jenna. They're safe."

"Thank God." Jo pushed both hands through her hair and let out a long sigh. "Where are they?"

Wolfe leaned against the counter. "They're heading for a

Florida airport. That's all I know for now. No doubt we'll hear from them soon."

"Getting back to these ligature marks." Carter peered at the body of Jane Doe One and lifted a blond eyebrow in question. "So, you're saying that the killer has been messing with these women for some time?"

Wolfe turned back to the X-rays. He indicated to the fractures in the phalanges and metacarpals on each hand. "You can see some of these fractures are partially healed. This would indicate beatings over a prolonged time. Bruising goes through various stages of healing and you can see from the colors ranging from red, purple to brown that some of these bruises were inflicted antemortem."

"You're saying this guy enjoys hurting women?" Rio rubbed the back of his neck. "The women are supposedly from out of town. This means we're looking for someone who has a place to keep women locked up without detection. It must be remote or people would hear what he's doing." He scanned the faces around the room. "Any ideas?"

Carter gave him a look of incredulity. "You're the one who lives here. Why are you asking me?"

Suddenly missing Kane and Jenna's professionalism, Wolfe let out a long sigh. "How about we concentrate on the autopsies and try and make some headway in the case." He looked at Rio. "Talk to Rowley. He's a local and might have some idea of where to look. If you recall, we had a killer that used the caves at the base of Bear Peak to hole up in, but there are thousands of them up there. That mountain has tunnels running all over. Add to the fact it's difficult to drag an unwilling woman through the forest, maybe we should be avoiding the obvious and think outside the box."

"Yeah. That's what Jenna would do." Jo walked along the screen array peering at the X-rays and photographs of the deceased. "I figure this guy has a big setup somewhere close to town. He knows the area and the location of the CCTV cameras. He is way too comfortable and has an expanded comfort zone. I think we should look deeper. We're missing something here."

"We'll need to expand our investigation to a wider area." Rio scratched his head. "If these women aren't missing from local areas, he has to be collecting them from other counties. There must be more reports of similar crimes in other states or counties apart from the ones Carter heard about. This isn't this killer's first dance."

Wolfe gave Rio a long look. "He's using formaldehyde to preserve the bodies so he can move them. I can't think of any other reason why he would preserve them. From the tissue samples I've taken, one of these women, Jane Doe Two, was murdered almost a month ago. I'll be able to make a more defi-nite determination over the next few days."

"Unless he likes to visit them post-mortem." Jo grimaced. "It wouldn't be the first time."

"There sure are some freaky people out there." Carter shook his head. "But you can usually recognize them by the stink of rotting flesh on their clothes."

"Yeah." Rio looked disgusted. "I've read about them."

"This brings me to another important question we need to discuss." Jo narrowed her gaze at Wolfe. "Can you determine if the women were raped once or repeatedly during their time of capture?"

"Both had been sexually active prior to their deaths." Wolfe moved to the screen array and ran the file forward to display a set of images. "I did consider this as a possibility and conducted a colposcopy on both victims. As you can see from the images on the screen taken during my examination using a colposcope, the tears on both victims in the region of the labia minora and posterior vagina would indicate rape. I used tolui-dine blue to highlight areas of injury. This is a highly sensitive device that gives us a clear picture of even the most subtle injuries." He indicated to the pictures on the screen. "From the evidence on these images, I made my determination that the damage occurred during the final assaults on the victims, and I agree with Jo the killer used rape as the final degradation."

"He uses rape as a weapon?" Rio let out a long breath and shook his head. "As if killing them wasn't good enough."

"It's often used as a means of control." Jo's brows crinkled into a frown. "He likes to dominate women. Beating them to death is him punishing them. This is what satisfies him. He kills them because he's tired of them. Once they've given up, they're no use to him anymore."

"Okay." Carter scratched his cheek thoughtfully. "So, what we've got here is a guy with access to a secluded property in Black Rock Falls, who moves around, maybe from state to state, or someone who takes frequent trips." He looked around the room. "I figure he must be someone who has returned recently. Or has been in jail. There has to be a reason for the interval between murders. These are possibilities we must consider going forward."

"I took everything you mentioned into consideration at the get-go." Rio frowned at him. "There was only one recent release from county in the last six months. He wasn't a person of interest. We need to look farther afield if we're ever going to make headway in this case."

"Then get your minds around this problem." Wolfe indicated to the images on the screen. "As you can see, the skewers on both victims follow the same pattern along the spine, which would suggest they hold significance to the killer. Have any of you seen anything like this before?"

"Yeah." Carter moved closer to the screen and peered at the pictures. "I've seen a similar use of skewers, but the perpetrator in that case was using them to create a halo around his victims' heads." He glanced at Jo. "Do you recall the Michelangelo Killer? He dressed up his victims like angels?"

"Yeah, I do recall the case." Jo shrugged. "He's locked away in the state pen on death row. There's no way this is the same person." She drummed her fingers on the counter. "The skewers mean something to the killer. Symbolism is a very big part of this killer's MO. Both the skewers and the mask represent something in his past. We'll need to discover why he's using two different symbols to convey his hate for women."

Wolfe took in the worried faces. It seemed very unusual that this team of highly skilled people were stymied. "I figure you are overthinking this, so break it down. You have two symbols. We know the mask likely means he considers the women faceless and nameless. Doing this is relevant to him and significant as it's his MO. The skewers are something else. They represent another aspect of his psyche. Jo, you deal with symbolism all the time. This can't be something you haven't seen before?"

"I haven't seen skewers used in the back of the victim like this before, no. It could be very simple like the halo example or complicated as in a twisted memory from childhood that's only relevant to the killer." Jo lifted her hands up in the air and dropped them at her sides. "I sure wish Kane and Jenna were here to discuss this with us. Kane always has some case or another to refer to and Jenna thinks outside the box and always has a ton of angles to consider. Without any strong evidence or suspects, we're chasing our tails like amateurs."

"You can say that again." Carter raised both eyebrows. "Just how long does it take to fly from Florida? The sooner they get back home the better."

SIXTEEN

Who did Twenty-Five think she was, trying to slip under his defenses and pretending to be just like him? No amount of convincing could make him believe that a person with her destructive nature could possibly understand why the women in the cells needed to be punished. He inhaled the formaldehyde solution in the bathtub and sighed. There was something about the smell that made his heart race with excitement. It was an accomplishment to steal a woman from her home town, keep her prisoner, and then turn her into a warning of what would happen if the others didn't behave. Smiling at his ingenuity, he wished he could share his achievements with others online, but for now this was his secret alone. He'd overcome temptation again and would return to his wife a loving and dutiful husband. *I'm not like my pa.*

He'd made plans for Twenty-Two and they would take time to organize. Using the solution would ensure the decomposition would be kept to a minimum and the body presented at its best. The townsfolk of Black Rock Falls needed to know adultery was a sin and his warnings needed to be heeded or they'd risk the consequences. He wanted women to be afraid and would keep leaving faceless bodies until he'd gotten results. The first two had gotten their attention, but it was obvious they needed more encouragement to comply. It was the same in every town he visited. He shook his head, recalling how Susie at Aunt Betty's Café had hung all over him and made her intentions clear. She knew full well he was a happily married man. Taking her from town would be risky, but if she flirted with him again, she'd be waking up inside one of his cells real soon.

Carefully dropping the body into the bath, he kneeled beside it, taking in the perfection of the bruises so neatly administered along both thighs and back. He ran a finger down one arm, tracing the outline of each bruise. He loved the way the colors had changed and now stood out on the white bloodless flesh. The older bruises had a yellow hue and the ones inflicted moments ago remained red or blue. Dead bodies fascinated him, especially the way the blood collected to the side he left them on, leaving a dark purple mark on the skin, or the way the eyes remained fixed in the same position, just like the fish sitting on ice behind glass in the local store.

After positioning Twenty-Two face down in the tub, he washed her hair and meticulously cleaned each nail. He'd leave her in the solution overnight and turn her in the morning before leaving her for another day and then carry her to the plastic-coated bench for her final adornments. The skewers came fresh from the package, all shiny and bright. He laid them out in a neat line, beside the new hammer and caressed each long sharp spear with the tips of his fingers. The cool aluminum sparkled under the overhead lighting, each little heart-shaped end carrying a memory of the past. It wouldn't be his fingerprints on the silver shafts because he always protected himself with gloves. He'd taken every precaution and his own flesh was devoid of hair apart from his head. He'd draped his naked body with a rubber fisherman's apron that covered him from neck to knee to prevent skin flakes falling on the body.

The mask and glue sat on one side. He prided himself with his ingenuity in disguising each of the homewreckers. They came to him as faceless annoyances and would leave the same. He'd never hunted them down; they came willingly and with an agenda. It was always the same. They would play on his weaknesses by making themselves attractive to him and creating doubts about his own relationship. He understood now this was a ploy they used on any man they decided was an easy target. They were all the same. It was as if he'd been watching the same movie over and over again. In constant fear of becoming just like his pa, it had become his duty to rid the world of the pestilence. No marriage was safe while toxic women continued to walk the earth.

He stood and walked to the cells, wiping his hands on a towel. Number Twenty-Five intrigued him and he wanted to take another look at her. This one was different. She didn't cower away from him like the others, and there was something about her he couldn't fathom. Opening the trapdoor, he peered at her through the bars. She gave him a belligerent stare and lifted her chin as if in defiance. He shook his head. "So, you think you're like me? Well, little lady, there is no one else like me."

"That's where you're wrong." Number Twenty-Five's eyes flashed with annoyance. "I'm more like you than you could possibly imagine. I can prove it. Just give me the chance."

He searched her eyes, the windows to the soul. There was a hint of something there he recognized. They always say it takes one to know one, so maybe he'd misjudged her intentions toward the deputy. If she was like him and had been luring Deputy Kane into the forest to exact her own kind of justice when he spotted her in the park, he'd misjudged her. Maybe he could beat the truth out of her but not today. He flexed muscles still tingling from his workout. He'd always considered the punishments to be part of his routine. Most people exercised to music, but he preferred the screams of the guilty.

SEVENTEEN

Rain splattered Jenna's face as Kane weaved the motorcycle in and out of the mounds of debris littering the streets. She clung on tight with both hands wrapped around his waist, fingers dug into the leather of his jacket. All around the blacktop was strewn with household items, tree branches, and papers. Negotiating through the damaged streets was a nightmare. They didn't find anyone in trouble, but as Kane turned at an intersection, they ran headlong into a gang of youths. Some carried baseball bats, standing guard while their friends looted the stores. Hordes of them as young as ten ran up the middle of the blacktop carrying armfuls of goods and personal possessions stolen from stores and houses.

Terrified for their safety as the crowd flowed toward them yelling and screaming abuse, Jenna raised her voice over the noise. "What are we going to do?"

"Hang on." The motorcycle's engine roared and Kane mounted the sidewalk.

People jumped out of the way as they flew past stores with broken windows, barely missing upturned tables, chairs, and signage that littered the sidewalk. In fear of her life, Jenna hunched down over Kane's back as shots rang out. The next moment Kane made evasive maneuvers, laying the bike almost down on its side as they took a sharp bend and accelerated away at top speed. As Kane braked hard and almost unseated her, she cried out in terror. She'd just regained her hold on him when they shot down an alleyway. Branches from overhanging vegetation whipped her cheeks and tore at her clothes. She closed her eyes tight as they moved through another group of looters who used them for target practice. Sticks and stones bounced off her leather jacket and pinged against her helmet. They were outnumbered twenty to one and had no choice but to keep going. The motorcycle weaved in and out of the streets at full speed. Suddenly a crowd was descending on them from all sides and Kane pulled to a halt, scanning the area. Heart thundering, Jenna stared all around too. There was no escape route. To one side of them an alleyway led to a flight of stone steps and down onto another road below, ahead and behind a mass of people, armed and dangerous running toward them screaming abuse. There was no way out this time. Kane was armed, but against so many, they didn't stand a chance. "Why do they want to hurt us?"

"Mob mentality. Get closer to me." Kane turned his head toward her. "Grab on to my belt. Lock your fingers in real tight. We're going down the stairs."

Pressing hard against Kane, Jenna slipped her fingers around his belt. There was no time to think or even hold her breath as Kane pointed the motorcycle down the alleyway. It tipped dangerously forward as they bumped down the steps. Teeth chattering from the vibration as they careered down the stairs, Jenna held on for dear life. Petrified as the angry mob rushed after them, she kept her head tucked into Kane's back. At last, they reached the bottom and bounced onto the blacktop. With a roar of the powerful engine, Kane accelerated away at full speed, slowing only to weave around household items spilling from damaged houses. The hurricane-ravaged buildings flashed past and they soon left the path of destruction far behind them.

Shaken by the ordeal but confident in Kane's driving, Jenna chewed on her bottom lip until they reached the highway. Seeing the open road ahead of them, she sighed with relief. The rain had stopped at last and the air was cool against her sore cheeks. High above, the search-and-rescue helicopters swept back and forth. Trucks and local authorities streamed past them into the disaster area. The highway was clear and it seemed all the damage had been restricted to the coastline.

By the time they arrived at Fort Lauderdale airport Jenna's back and arms throbbed and no doubt she'd be bruised all over come morning. Hands numb from holding on to Kane so tight, she slid off the motorcycle, shook out the cramps, and grabbed her backpack. As she looked at Kane, she noticed a trickle of blood running down one cheek and staining the front of his T-shirt. "You're hurt. Let me take a look."

"It's just a scratch. Don't worry about it." Kane climbed off the Harley and removed his helmet. "Are you okay? Did they get you with the rocks?" His concerned gaze ran over her face, and he pulled her close, stroking her hair.

Trembling all over, Jenna leaned into him and nodded. "Yeah, but I'm okay, just shaken is all. Those guys sure didn't want any witnesses. Can you imagine what would have happened if they'd pulled you off the Harley and found the US Marshal's badge on you?"

"I wouldn't have let that happen, Jenna." Kane turned away to pull his backpack out of the saddlebags. "I would have used my weapon if necessary to protect you. Just be thankful I didn't have to. I would rather not explain to the authorities why I'm carrying a fake US Marshal's badge."

Confused, Jenna stared at him. "It's not a fake, is it? Surely

Wolfe would have made suitable arrangements with the powers that be?"

"I really don't want to find out." Kane shrugged. "Do you?"

"Nope, can't say that I do." Jenna looked around at the people streaming in and out of the airport. "Okay, what next?"

"We'll leave the motorcycle here and go find a phone that works. I'll call the flight crew and Wolfe to let him know what's happening. They'll know about the hurricane and be worried about us. Hangar eight is on the far side of the airport. It will take some time to submit a flight plan and get the aircraft ready to leave. We'll rest up some and then I'll arrange to transport the motorcycle back home and go speak to the rental people about the sedan. It's insured and they'll arrange to collect it from under the building if it's still drivable."

Jenna took his hand and they hurried into the building. When Kane showed his US Marshal's badge to the desk clerk, she practically threw the phone at him. After contacting the flight crew and making arrangements to take the Harley to Black Rock Falls, Kane called Wolfe to explain their situation. The airport was in good shape and all the stores inside open. Many others had taken refuge inside and people lined up at the diners, but they eventually found a place to get something to eat. They took the Harley down to hangar eight and sat down on the floor to wait for the flight crew to arrive. Jenna pulled the first-aid kit out of her backpack and tended the cut on Kane's face. They waited for a time sitting in stunned silence, just drinking coffee and nibbling at sandwiches, before Jenna turned to Kane and smiled. "Well, that was a weekend I won't forget in a hurry. I know I wanted something to tell the grandchildren, but we barely got out alive."

"I figure this one beats all." Kane gave her a broad smile. "Although, there were some parts of it I enjoyed." He cupped her chin and stared into her eyes. "It wasn't all bad, was it?"

"Fishing for compliments, huh?" Raising one eyebrow

Jenna chuckled. "The short time we had together was wonderful, but a hurricane? I mean, really? How many people have gotten stuck in a hurricane on their honeymoon?"

"I told you to be careful what you wished for." Kane squeezed her hand. "Don't worry, we've gotten the bad luck out of the way and now there's only good memories to come."

EIGHTEEN

It was so good to touch down in Black Rock Falls after such a chaotic trip. Bone weary and eyes filled with grit, Jenna waited on the tarmac as Wolfe's Harley was unloaded from the back of the private jet. A cool breeze brushed her face, bringing with it the delicious smell of pine trees and fresh air. It wrapped around her in a fragrant hug as if the mountains and forests were welcoming them home. She'd called ahead to inform Wolfe they'd be arriving outside the medical examiner's office in a few minutes and to open the gate for them. The moment she climbed on the back of the motorcycle and the wind brushed her face, the feeling of being home engulfed her with peace and contentment. It was a shame she had a murder case to deal with. She wanted to spend more time alone with Kane. It should be their time together and not business as usual, but as the sheriff, homicides were her responsibility.

Wolfe was waiting for them at the gate of the medical examiner's parking lot and waved them through with a broad smile. As Kane parked the motorcycle, Jenna slid from the back and collected their things from the saddlebags. She turned to Wolfe.

"Well, we had a disaster of a honeymoon. What progress have you made with the case?"

"I'm afraid we have another body." Wolfe rubbed his chin. "The team is on it. We have nothing on their identities or where they came from at all. Kalo is running their prints as we speak. There's not much else I can tell you. Rio would be the best person to bring you up to date." Wolfe's attention moved from her and concentrated on the motorcycle. "It's such a long time since I've seen my baby." He looked at Kane and smiled. "How did she handle?"

"Like a dream." Kane slapped him on the back. "You do know this means I'll have to get one now. I enjoyed flying down the highway with the wind in my hair and hearing the roar of a powerful engine."

Astonished, Jenna stared at Kane. "I'll never understand how you take near-death experiences in your stride." She looked at Wolfe. "He's not going to mention we were caught in a hurricane and almost died, and had people shooting or throwing rocks at us on the way back to the airport?"

"That would be a walk in the park for him." Wolfe met her gaze. "The hurricane was only along the beachfront I hear."

Jenna gripped his arm. "It was really bad, and I'm so sorry, Shane, your mom's condo was completely destroyed."

"Don't worry, it's insured." Wolfe turned with a shrug. "Hurricanes happen all the time in Florida." His gaze traveled over her face. "Kane said you weren't injured. You're sheet white, are you okay?"

Jenna rubbed her bruised forearm and nodded. "Yeah, I guess. Just a few bumps and bruises. That's what happens when people throw rocks at you. We came through the hurricane just fine once we'd climbed down from the top story to the first floor to escape the building before it collapsed. The hair-raising ride through Armageddon to get back to the airport was just peachy. I know that you and Kane are used to living on the edge, but right now I figure I need a week to get over it." She turned and walked to the back door of the morgue. "I hope you have fresh coffee brewing. I have a feeling I'm going to need it."

The conversation concerning motorcycles followed her into the morgue. She headed for Wolfe's office and dropped into a chair. "We're in the middle of a homicide investigation and you're both chatting about motorcycles. I think we need to get our priorities right." She turned to Wolfe. "You mentioned a second victim. Is it another female? Are they in the morgue?"

"Yeah, they're both here, and I've completed the autopsies. I believe the team is still at the office." Wolfe went to the coffee machine and dropped in two pods. "To be perfectly honest, we haven't made much headway in the twenty-four hours or so you've been away, but the team has been working nonstop."

"Where did you find the second victim?" Kane sat down beside Jenna and sighed. "Same MO?"

"Yeah, exactly. She was found outside the landfill leaning up against the fence." Wolfe handed them both a cup of coffee. "Mr. Brinks called it in." He leaned against the counter, looking at them. "We've got nothing solid and no suspects. Kalo has checked all the databases for missing women matching their descriptions and fingerprints and these two seem to be ghosts. Another thing, Jane Doe Two was bathed in formaldehyde, which as you know is a preservative. We don't know how long the killer kept her prior to leaving her at the landfill. I'm running tests to determine the rate of deterioration of Jane Doe Two's flesh to give me a more accurate time of death. Both women were raped antemortem and bruises of different maturity on their bodies would indicate they were beaten over a period of time." He looked at Jenna and shrugged. "It's early in the investigation and I need more time to make a determination. Although cause of death of both victims was asphyxiation due to strangulation. I'll get my report to you as soon as possible."

Concerned the killer had escalated so fast, Jenna ran both

hands through her hair and stared at Kane. "I would love to go home and shower and change, but we'll have to go into the office and see if they've made any headway." She finished her coffee and stood and then removed the leather jacket and handed it to Wolf. "Unless you want us to view the bodies now?"

"That can be done tomorrow when you've rested. It isn't a pretty sight, Jenna." Wolfe shook his head. "You know, it might be best if you went home and started fresh in the morning. You've both been through a traumatic experience. You're both exhausted and won't be thinking straight."

"Thanks, but we're good. We had plenty of time to rest on the flight." Kane dragged his jacket out of his backpack and shrugged into it. "You know darn well Jenna won't be able to sleep unless she's gotten to the bottom of this case." He tossed Jenna her jacket. "Let's go. The Beast is out back."

It was no surprise to Jenna when Kane pulled up outside Aunt Betty's Café. She'd listened to his stomach growling for the last twenty minutes or so and expected him to stop somewhere to get something to eat. To her surprise he asked her to wait and dashed inside, coming out with a ton of pies. When she walked into the sheriff's department, she was surprised to see Rowley on the counter. "Hi, Jake. Where's Maggie?"

"As it's after five on Saturday, I sent her home." Rowley smiled at her. "I'm real glad to see you made it home safely. Bad luck about the hurricane." He indicated with his chin toward the hallway. "The team is in the conference room. Not that they've come up with anything yet. This case sure is a tough one."

Jenna nodded. "Thanks, it's good to be home, and with two murders in town, it's just as well we're here." She stared down the hallway and then back to Rowley. "Is Jo here too? Where's Jaime and what's been happening here?"

"They took Jaime back to Snakeskin Gully after victim two showed." Rowley rubbed his chin. "On Friday, after you left, Jo and Carter went out to view the scene, and Sandy and Julie went for a ride with the girls. Jaime told me that she had a great time riding the horses."

Smiling, Jenna's mind filled with images of the little girls dressed in their bridesmaids' dresses. "Oh, that's good. At least her visit wasn't ruined." She turned to Kane. "I guess we'd better get at it."

A low mumble of voices came from the conference room, and Jenna walked in with Kane close behind. In a flash of black and brown Duke flew out from under the desk and hurled himself at Kane. She plucked the bag of takeout from Kane's arms just as the dog circled him in an affectionate yapping doggy dance. She grinned as Kane wrestled the dog into submission by rubbing his ears and telling him that everything was okay.

"Well, won't you look at what the hurricane's blown in." Carter grinned around his toothpick. "And they've brought food too. It's a double bonus. Now be honest, you missed us, didn't you, and couldn't wait to come back."

"Well, let me think—a weekend in Florida with Dave or working a case with you?" Jenna smiled at him. "Sorry, Dave wins." She turned back to the whiteboard. The copious notes made by Rio's neat hand in columns with headings were concise, but it was obvious no conclusions had been drawn about the killer. The column marked PROFILE was empty, which surprised Jenna as Jo was an expert in her field. She smiled as faces turned to her. "Okay, guys, what have you got for me?"

After listening to Rio's update of the cases, she sat down at the table and rubbed her temples. "So, we have no suspects at all?"

"We hunted down the obvious users of formaldehyde." Rio rubbed the back of his neck. "The undertaker and the two taxidermists we know about in town. We interviewed them and they all had rock-hard alibis for the time the bodies were dumped."

Unsatisfied with his reply, Jenna frowned. "I want details—names, places where they work, and their alibis."

"We went to the Black Rock Falls Funeral Home and interviewed Max Weems, the undertaker, and his son." Rio leaned back in his seat and stared at her. "They were at Aunt Betty's around the time of the dumping of the first victim and for the second they were collecting a body from the hospital."

"We checked out their alibis." Rowley consulted his iPad. "They're rock solid."

Agitated Jenna tapped a pen on the desk. "Is that all? What about the taxidermists?"

"Me and Jo handled the interviews of the taxidermists with stores in town: Colin Drury and Austin Berry. Drury has been in Helena for the past week, and Barry lives with three other guys. All of them confirmed he was at home and we spoke to them separately." Carter smiled around his toothpick. "They checked out too." He chuckled. "You see we can work when you're not here, Jenna. In fact, we've been gathering information since you left."

Trying not to roll her eyes at Carter's self-satisfied grin, Jenna pushed the hair from her face. "With all this information gathering, we still don't have a list of suspects. There must be other people who use formaldehyde that we haven't considered yet."

"There are plenty of taxidermists in town who do it for a hobby." Kane sipped coffee. "We've run into a few before. They should be licensed. It's a lead we need to chase down."

"Okay." Rio made a note on the whiteboard. "I'll get on it but that's all we have for now."

"This is a tough one but this is only day three. So far you've all followed procedure. That's all I can ask of you." Jenna turned to Kane. "Any suggestions?"

"Yeah, why do you figure the killer used a fresh victim for Jane Doe One when he had Jane Doe Two in storage?" Kane looked at Jo. "Would you consider this guy is a necrophiliac? What do we need to know to give him that label?"

"No, I don't think so." Jo folded her hands on the table. "Those guys enjoy the smell and like frequent visits to the corpses, usually to indulge their sexual fantasies. I see no evidence of that behavior in this case." She cleared her throat. "I believe he used the formaldehyde for one reason only and that is to preserve the body so he could move it from place to place."

Considering the update from Rio, Jenna scanned the file and met his gaze across the table. "In your report you mentioned a previous case in DC." She turned to Carter and raised one eyebrow. "I assume you've checked this guy out?"

"We never arrested the killer; he remains in the wind." Carter moved a toothpick across his lips and narrowed his gaze. "My question is: why would the killer go to this extreme and then stop for a long time before starting up again? If these victims are numbers twenty and twenty-one, where are the rest of them? I don't recall the killer in DC carving numbers in the flesh of the other victims. It might not be the same perpetrator."

"I researched a similar pattern of behavior but I'm sure Jo knows more about it than I do." Kane reached into a bag for a peach pie. "In the case I read about, the killer was married with children. It seemed he could control his urges, which is unusual as you know."

"Not really." Jo's expression became interested. "There is a type of psychopath who can quite comfortably lead a double life and take breaks between murders, or kill and return to their life without any change in behavior. They have the ability to compartmentalize people, memories of murders or fantasies. They become expert at putting them away and not thinking about them. When the need arises, they can easily access their fantasies or switch between imagination and reality in a blink of an eye."

Fascinated, Jenna poured herself a coffee and leaned back in her chair. "Are they the same in other aspects? Do they lack empathy and not think of the victim once the murder has been committed?"

"In this case, I doubt it." Kane stretched his long legs and sighed. "He must be thinking about them or he wouldn't be preserving them. This brings me to another question. Do you think he could be married and have a family?"

"Married or a loner, both are possibilities. We know many leave double lives." Jo opened her hands. "One thing for sure, this killer is consumed with making people suffer. I believe he becomes sexually aroused at seeing the women struggling. If he is married, he might blame the victim for making him aroused and beats them to death as punishment."

"Oh, he's a sadistic SOB." Carter tossed his toothpick in the trash and reached for one of the pies in the takeout bag. "Wolfe said he'd been beating these women over some time. He used rape as a punishment. I don't think he was getting any gratification out of it. It was just another weapon in his arsenal." He shook his head. "He's as smart as a whip and, just like all the others of late, seems to know his way around forensics. I blame TV shows and the internet for giving too much information on forensic investigations, because it's becoming more and more difficult to find DNA or, let's face it, any evidence at all against these killers."

Determined to get more information on the illusive killer, Jenna turned to Carter. "It would help if you could send the image files and video from the drone to Kalo. He'll be able to run it through the facial-recognition software against driver's license pictures. I want the names of everyone in the vicinity at the time the bodies were discovered. It's not unusual for the killer to be watching. Some of them return to the scene of the crime to see the reaction of their work." She ran a hand through her hair. "If we find anyone out of place, it will give us a starting point. At the moment, we're chasing shadows."

Taking a beat to stare at the whiteboard, Jenna scanned the list of uses of formaldehyde and the various industries where it was commonly found. She turned back to Carter. "Ask Kalo to cross-reference the occupations of the people at the crime scene with anyone working with or involved in any way with formaldehyde. There has to be a link, and if he can hunt down people who showed at the crime scenes and use formaldehyde for any reason whatsoever, we'll have a list of suspects to investigate."

"Good thinking." Rio glanced down at his iPad. "I'll send him all the additional information I discovered today."

"Okay. Is there anything else we need to discuss?" When the room fell silent, Jenna glanced at her watch and, seeing it was after six, turned back to the tired faces around the table. "That's all we can do until we hear from Bobby Kalo and Wolfe sends over the autopsy reports. I figure we'll need a day to catch up on the information in the case files. So unless anything breaks in the meantime, we'll start fresh on Monday."

Chairs scraped as everyone except Carter got to their feet. Jenna ran down the list of files on her tablet to make sure she had all the information on the case and then collected her things, ready to leave. Every inch of her body ached from the bruises, and her muscles had stiffened from traveling. The delicious thought of going home to the ranch and soaking in the hot tub for an hour or so was very tempting. The hot water would be very soothing, and she would have plenty of time to catch up with the case after dinner.

"You look exhausted." Jo moved to Jenna's side and stared at her with a worried expression. "Would you like me to come over to the ranch house and cook dinner tonight?"

"No need. This time I'm gonna insist you join us at Antlers

for dinner and I won't take no for an answer." Carter pushed to his feet. "That peach pie was nice, but I have a feeling Kane would prefer a ten-ounce steak with all the trimmings."

"You can say that again." Kane grinned at Jenna. "I'm starving."

"You don't have to head back to the ranch first. You could take a shower here. I know you have clothes in the locker room." Jo moved to her side. "Come with us. It will be your first meal in Black Rock Falls as a married couple. It will be relaxing and you deserve some time together, seeing as your honeymoon was ruined."

Shaking her head in resignation, Jenna nodded. "Okay, I'm hungry too and a steak sounds like heaven."

NINETEEN

SUNDAY

As usual, Kane woke at five and slipped out of bed, leaving Jenna sleeping. She'd taken the brunt of the street gang's attack and was covered with bruises. The hot tub had helped some, but she needed to rest if she planned to hit the ground running with the case the moment she woke. He dressed in silence and, with Duke close on his heels, headed straight out to the barn to do his chores. Summer in Black Rock Falls was an exquisite mixture of warm sun and fresh clean air. He inhaled deeply as he walked toward the barn, recognizing the scents of the various wildflowers spread out in colorful patches turning the lowlands into an exceptionally beautiful quilt. A grunting noise coming from the barn slowed his stride, but when he peeked inside, he found Carter making short work of the mucking out. A wheelbarrow set to one side was already filled with hay and manure. Never far from his side, Carter's Doberman, Zorro, was sitting like a statue at the back door. He strolled inside. "You're an early riser. Not many people beat me to the chores in the morning."

"Well, as it's still technically your honeymoon," Carter

smiled at him around his toothpick, "I figured it was the neighborly thing to do."

More than happy not to be ankle deep in horse dung, Kane tipped back his hat and smiled. "Well, thank you kindly."

"You're welcome." Carter picked up the wheelbarrow and headed for the manure pile out back of the barn. "Warrior is acting a little skittish this morning, so I'll leave him to you."

Kane opened the stall that contained his black stallion. "He doesn't like critters in his stall. It was probably a mouse." He ran one hand down the sleek black coat. "He seems fine to me."

After giving his horse a thorough grooming, he took him by the halter, led him out into the brilliant sunshine, and over to the corral. The other two horses whinnied in greeting, and he opened the gate to let the horse run free. He watched it frolicking for a few moments before turning back to the barn. "Come on, Duke. We have chores to do."

"I'm just about done here." Carter walked back into the barn, brushing his hands together. "I figure after wrestling with a hurricane yesterday the last thing you'd need to do is work out this morning, so if it's okay with you, Jo will drop by to cook breakfast... unless you'd rather be alone?"

Kane slapped him on the back. "We're good and we'd like that just fine. I know Jenna is anxious to break down the case with Jo. She's been discussing it with me all night."

"Okay." Carter whistled to his dog. "I'll grab a shower and we'll meet you at the house."

After breakfast the team made their way to the family room. Kane scanned the notes Carter had made about similar cases, but he needed more information. "You mentioned the Michelangelo Killer used skewers. What else do we know about him?"

"Bruno Vito, the Michelangelo Killer, murdered sixteen women. All were prostitutes of various races but around the same age." Carter paused for a beat and then cleared his throat.

"He liked them between the ages of twenty-two and twenty-six. The strange thing is that Vito was married to a very attractive wife and has six kids. He worked as a baker and his wife had a job in the school canteen. His wife had no idea he spent his spare time killing people. From what Jo says, he represents a classic case of double-life psychopathy."

"It says here he's on death row in a state pen." Jenna leaned forward in her chair looking interested. "Have you interviewed him, Jo?"

"No, I haven't, but he's on my list. If I can get to him before he's executed. I believe he is at the end of his appeals. So, his time may be limited, although what he has to say would be invaluable for my research on psychopathic behavior. The problem is, if he's been appealing the charges against him, getting him to admit killing people will be difficult. Right now, I have no reason to believe that this current killer is a copycat of the Michelangelo Killer."

"I'm not so sure." Jenna scanned her iPad. "I see many similarities between the two of them. Both of them keep the women captive prior to their deaths. I've made a quick comparison. Both get enjoyment out of inflicting pain. Both used skewers to represent something in their fantasies. If we can't get any hard evidence to hunt down suspects, would you consider interviewing the Michelangelo Killer? It would be interesting to see what information he could give us that might help us with this case."

As Jenna's suggestion made sound sense, Kane nodded in agreement. "Yeah, that would be a good idea. I recall reading a paper from an FBI agent who went to the source to obtain information about a certain type of behavioral pattern. He straight out asked the psychopath for his help with his current case. The prisoner got a kick out of being asked by the FBI. It gave him bragging rights in jail and gave the FBI investigator a valuable insight into the behavior of the killer they wouldn't have gotten otherwise. If our guy is on the same wavelength as the Michelangelo Killer, we might be able to discover what makes him tick."

"That sounds feasible, but in practice it might be a little more difficult." Jo ran a hand through her hair and sighed. "We might be lucky if he's a talker. Some of them enjoy reminiscing about their murders as it gives them a chance to relive the thrill of the kill. Others deny everything and refuse to say a word. As he's had so many appeals, there's a chance he might figure by talking he's admitting guilt."

"He's got nothing to lose." Jenna smiled at Jo. "Your powers of persuasion are incredible. If anyone can get him to talk, you can."

Kane looked from one to the other. He agreed with Jenna. If the killer they were chasing had been influenced by the Michelangelo Killer and was just a copycat, it would mean an entirely different line of inquiry was necessary. If they could get Vito to divulge his innermost feelings, they could use the information to more accurately profile the man responsible for the recent murders. At the moment, they had no hard evidence to point them to a group of possible suspects. "I figure it's worth a try. How long would it take you to arrange an interview?"

"Not long at all, providing the prisoner agrees to the meeting." Jo raised both eyebrows. "We'll have to assume he won't be willing to cooperate for nothing. We'll have to come up with something to make it worth his while."

After reading so many papers on psychopaths, Kane understood that a majority of them enjoyed notoriety. Being the top dog in prison was a big deal to them and they loved to read about themselves or watch any newspaper or TV documentaries on their murders. "The fact that he's on death row will help. I figure he'll want everyone to remember him. You could offer to feature him in your book, and if he wants to be one of the ten most notorious serial killers in history, he might well enjoy telling all."

"Well, it worked with James Stone, didn't it?" Jenna drummed her fingers on the arm of the chair. "Unless we have some hard evidence real soon, we'll need something to give us a clue to the identity of this killer."

Not having the information on the Michelangelo Killer in front of him, Kane looked at Carter. "What's the MO in the Michelangelo case?"

"From what I recall, the Michelangelo Killer's motive was firmly based in a radical religious upbringing. He believed by murdering the prostitutes, dressing them up like angels and adding a halo, he rescued them from their sins." Carter scratched his cheek. "That's all I have on the case, but if you want details, I'll have the files sent to us ASAP."

"Thanks." Jenna turned to Jo. "I know you haven't gotten much information, but have you made any headway at all in profiling the killer in these homicides?"

"I do have a few thoughts on this killer." Jo's expression was serious as she looked at Jenna. "I think it's pretty obvious he has a problem with women for some reason or whatever. We've had so many serial killers who've had manipulative mothers. As you know, often the trigger comes from childhood abuse. Abuse happens in many different ways and it doesn't have to be physical. If a child is exposed to violent behavior from one or both of their parents against each other, they might develop psychosis against both parents. In this case it's obvious the police were involved. The use of the Halloween mask is a significant feature of this man's fantasy."

All the cases that Kane had read about percolated into his mind as he listened to Jo discuss the profile of the killer. He leaned forward in his chair. "I believe the skewers used in the same pattern on each of the victims represent something from his childhood. I've been racking my brain trying to think where people use skewers apart from in cooking. Do you figure the killer's parents argued or fought in front of him, and then, for instance, the wife or husband cooked a special makeup meal using skewers each time, it would impact to this extent on the child?"

"It all comes down to what he associates with his trigger memories. People associate smells or actions with memories good and bad, so it makes sense that they also trigger a psychotic episode in a psychopathic killer." Jo's eyebrows met together in a frown. "You have a very good profiling mind, Dave. I would assume our killer has more than one trigger, or he requires both the mask and the skewers to complete his fantasy. As we have no idea how many women he's murdered, but if our Jane Does are numbers twenty and twenty-one, then he could have had breaks in between, or he simply decided to start on number twenty."

"No way." Carter shook his head. "From the crime scenes, there is no way in hell that these murders are his first dance. In all the cases I've been involved with, the first kills are messy, rushed, and the killer makes mistakes. There would be more evidence at the scene. I'm seeing a well-organized killer here and one with experience. He takes his time and enjoys it. It's going to be hard to catch him."

"Okay, taking that into consideration"—Jo stared at her notes and then looked back at Jenna—"if he hasn't being released from jail recently, we have to assume he doesn't live alone. He'd need people around him to use as alibis. I would say he is a Caucasian male between the ages of thirty-five and forty. He has a job that allows him to move around without constriction over a wide area."

"He can't possibly be married. How could a married man possibly hide a bunch of women from his wife over a sustained period?" Jenna raised both eyebrows in question. "Most women would notice if her husband came home smelling of a woman.

We notice these things and if he is, as you say, someone who is away from home frequently and comes home smelling of perfume or whatever, I would imagine that would be very difficult to hide from his wife."

"I don't think so." Carter looked amused. "We know this guy can hide his DNA and any trace evidence from the bodies, so it's pretty obvious he wouldn't be going home stinking of perfume. He's too smart for that, but I agree he moves around frequently. If he is living with someone or is married, he'd need an excuse to be away from home at regular intervals. I figure he is either a truck driver or in sales, and I would go with the latter because sales representatives are usually well dressed and presented. They'd have a better chance of attracting a woman. They would look safer than a roughneck. If we're talking about prostitutes, they'd be looking for a guy with plenty of spare cash."

"You have a point." Jenna nodded an agreement. "As the victims haven't been reported missing, we have to assume that they're either street people or prostitutes, but they don't look like they've been living on the streets. Their hair and teeth are in good condition and if they lived on the street, they wouldn't have the money to go to the dentist. Wolfe hasn't established if they are drug users, but I would assume they're high-end prostitutes, and if you're theory is correct, then our killer is picking them up in bars or off the streets."

Listening intently to the conversation, Kane nodded. "Then he'd need a vehicle to transport his victims. So, we can strike a truck driver from our list of occupations because, as sure as hell, he wouldn't risk using an eighteen-wheeler to pick up prostitutes."

"Okay, so we're looking for a sales representative or some type of executive who moves throughout the state, maybe in a managerial position with a decent vehicle and who deals in a manufacturing process that involves formaldehyde." Carter leaned back in his chair and stared at the ceiling. "That narrows it down to about one or two thousand people. This state has so many different industries and I have no idea how we can pinpoint this killer to any one of them."

"Really? That's a defeatist attitude coming from you, Carter. We haven't even scraped the surface of the evidence yet. Wolfe will find something. He always does." Jenna shook her head. "We've had tougher cases to solve than this one and we're just getting started. I'm darn sure I'm not giving up just yet."

TWENTY

Horrified, Poppy pressed her hands to her ears to block out the begging and screaming of her jailor's current victim. The conversation she'd had with him ran through her mind in a constant loop of agonizing terror. Using every ounce of courage she possessed, she'd done what she needed to survive and offered to assist him with his next victim. Their conversation had been limited and she hadn't been able to gather much information on why he was killing the women. Terrified, she'd watched him change visibly in between the times he spoke to her and when he murdered. Could he be demonstrating a split personality or was she seeing both sides of a psychopath? Having no professional experience in dealing with someone in a heightened state of aggravation, she'd kept her voice low and never looked away from him when he was speaking to her. From what she'd witnessed, showing fear made things worse. When his terrified victims fought to escape, he changed in a split second. The more they screamed and wriggled to get away, the more he enjoyed it. The intense look in his eyes frightened her and his cruel twisted smile reminded her of a deranged clown. It was as if he'd turned into a different person.

Fear gripped her by the throat as the sound of the baseball bat hitting the floor and rolling away signaled the end of the first phase of the woman's punishment, but the moans of the beaten woman continued as he completed his final degradation. She fought for breath trying to keep calm because the next time he opened the door, she would need to be ready to pass his test. Poppy stiffened her spine, swallowing her fear. To fool him into believing she was just like him she'd need to be ready to deal with whatever gruesome job he intended to give her. She'd seen dead bodies before and attended autopsies. If she could look at what he had done in a clinical way, she might not lose it. Scrubbing both hands down her face, she paced up and down the small cell. *Come on, Poppy, you can do this. Just concentrate.*

Locked away with no chance of escape, she couldn't help anyone, but if she gained his trust, there would be at least a slim chance of getting away and alerting the authorities. She had to face the next few minutes without cringing away. He would be finished soon, and it would be time for her to prove her worth to him. Trembling, she ground her teeth together so hard her jaw ached as the sound of him dragging his victim down the passageway seeped into her brain. She would hear the tortured screams of the women he'd murdered in her dreams forever.

Footsteps, slow and deliberate, came down the passageway toward her cell. Heart thumping, Poppy sucked in deep breaths and stared at the door. It opened slowly and her jailer stood before her splattered with blood. She lifted her chin and looked him square in the eyes. "I'm ready. What do you want me to do?"

"Come with me. I want you to remove your clothes because we don't want any DNA evidence on the body, do we?" He stood to one side to allow her to pass. "Then you'll take a shower and I'll give you something to cover your hair." He tapped her on the arm, leaving long streaks of blood. "Don't make the mistake of trying to escape, Twenty-Five. You mean nothing to me and I would be stupid to trust you. I haven't forgotten that you're a cop. You could be next. Just keep remembering that and we'll get along fine."

TWENTY-ONE

MONDAY

The early morning summer sunlight flashed through the trees as Jenna headed with Kane for the office. She had planned her entire day, rising early to make a list to delegate her deputies to specific investigations. This had been her way of rationalizing her situation. Having her dream honeymoon destroyed by a hurricane had disturbed her more than she had imagined. It was supposed to have been a special time with memories to carry with them into the future, but theirs had been cruelly snatched away. She shook her head in dismay. How many brides had a psychopath running around killing people on their wedding day? It seemed that Jenna's life had become a pendulum swinging back and forth to the rhythm of an endless number of psychopaths' insanity.

It had been difficult dragging herself out of bed this morning and concentrating on the case, rather than staying home to spend time alone with Kane, but as usual, her life had to be placed on hold when duty called. Leaning toward him, she squeezed his arm. "Is it always going to be like this? Short breaks and then weeks of craziness? How does Rowley cope, raising his twins with the threat of another serial killer moving into town? I want us to have a family too, but the worry of a constant stream of psychopaths walking the streets concerns me. What if our child becomes a target? Look at what's happened to Wolfe's daughters. No one is safe here."

"Bad things happen in every town, no one can be one hundred percent sure nothing is going to happen to their kids. I'm afraid that's the world we live in. We'll take precautions like we do now. The ranch is like a fortress and the Beast could take a bomb blast." Kane took his hand from the wheel and squeezed hers. "And then you have me and I'll keep you safe. If or when we have kids, we'll do exactly what we've always done and take it one day at a time. We have a great support team around us, and all of our friends are like family. You do trust them don't you, Jenna?"

Since the trauma of surviving the hurricane, Jenna's thoughts had centered on her time as sheriff. They were married now and that shouldn't make a difference. They'd always been a team but suddenly the thought of losing Kane haunted her thoughts. He'd come close to dying so many times on her watch. How many lives did he have left? One? Twenty? As sheriff if anything happened to him, it would be her fault. He'd take a bullet for her without flinching and that was one heck of a responsibility to carry. She'd been seriously afraid during the storm, believing the happiness she'd yearned for would be snatched away from her in seconds. Trying to hide her concern, she turned to him. "You know, I trust you to look after me and the team will always have our backs, but it seems every-thing is against us."

"Nothing has changed, Jenna. It's been like this since the first day we met. You're the sheriff and I'm your deputy. We'll catch the killers same as always. I figure you're seeing a problem where there isn't one. We've been married for only a few days, and so far, it seems to be going just fine. We haven't tried to kill each other yet anyway." Kane chuckled and wiggled his eyebrows at her. "Please stop worrying, Jenna, and do what you do best and concentrate on catching this killer. Everyone on the team looks to you as their leader, so stop second-guessing yourself. You know instinctively what to do and we trust your judgement." He squeezed her fingers. "Look what happened when we were out of town. Without you to point them in the right direction, they were chasing their tails."

Although Rio's handling of the case had been faultless, Jenna enjoyed the ego stroke and nodded. "Yeah, I guess they did miss us. Maybe you're right and I should get my head back in the game and stop feeling sorry for myself."

They had just turned onto Main when her phone chimed in her pocket. She checked her caller ID, put her phone on speaker, and accepted the call. It was Deputy Jake Rowley. "Hi, Jake. What's up?"

"A call came in on the 911 line, a delivery driver spotted someone leaning against the WELCOME TO BLACK ROCK FALLS sign just outside town to the north. He could see it was a woman and pulled over to ask if she wanted a ride into town. Long story short, it's another body. From what he described, it's the same MO. I have the man's details and he'll be waiting on scene. I'm heading in that direction now, but you will probably beat me there if you've already left home."

A sinking feeling filled Jenna's gut and she glanced at Kane raising both eyebrows. Another murder so soon and they didn't have any clues on the other two yet. She sighed. "Yeah, we're heading down Main now and will be there in five. I'll get Wolfe on scene, and Jo and Carter are right behind us. What's the name of the man who discovered the body?"

"His name is Alan Woods. He is out of Louan and makes a regular delivery to the general store Monday through Friday."

Rowley sucked in a deep breath. *"I wonder what number this one will have carved into her back? I hope this time he's left some evidence behind so we can lock him up for a very long time."*

"So do I, Jake, so do I." Jenna disconnected and then called Wolfe and Carter.

It would never be a normal day's work for Jenna to deal with crime scenes. It took a toll on anyone having to constantly witness such carnage. Every case that she worked on she'd made her responsibility and cared for the victims. They were never faceless corpses and she remembered each and every one of them. Trying to gather her thoughts on how to proceed with yet another crime scene, she stared out of the window. The town was just waking up. As usual, Aunt Betty's Café was open and delicious smells of baking pies wafted into the truck's open window. She smiled when Kane's stomach rumbled, glad of a little piece of normality in a day that promised to be traumatic. She'd cling to anything she could get right now to ease the burden of solving the current homicides. "Mmm, I smell cherry pies. Now those are my favorites too, so when you pick up your order make sure there's enough for all of us."

"I'll see what I can do but I'm not making any promises." Kane flashed her a smile. "Susie mentioned pecan pies, so I ordered them as well. I figured it was going to be a long day, so I've arranged to have a bunch of takeout delivered to the office at ten. I figured we're gonna need a break by then."

"We sure will." Jenna pointed at a white delivery van with a logo on the side that read LOUAN'S FRESH MEAT PIES. "There, can you see the guy spewing into the bushes?"

"Yeah, he's hard to miss." Kane pulled in behind the van. He slid out of the Beast. "I'll grab the forensics kit."

A breeze brushed Jenna's face, bringing with it the stench of rotting flesh and vomit. She walked over to the witness. "Did you see who dumped the body or anyone in the vicinity when you arrived?"

"No, ma'am." The man turned a shade of gray. "I'm gonna spew." He headed for the bushes.

Jenna turned to speak to Jo and Carter. "I'll go and check the victim with Kane, if you don't mind interviewing the witness? He didn't see anything, but we'll need his statement. Wolfe is on his way."

"Sure." Carter looked over her shoulder to the man spewing in the bushes. "I figure I'll give him a few moments to catch his breath." He wrinkled his nose and pulled a mask out of his pocket. "Man, it sure stinks around here."

Jenna nodded. "It sure does. I know the witness used his vehicle to conceal the body, and it saved us worrying about bystanders showing up and contaminating the scene, but can you ask him to move it back aways? Wolfe will need direct access."

"Yeah, no worries." Carter headed for the witness.

Taking the face mask and gloves from Kane, Jenna headed toward the victim. It was exactly the same as the previous two. A battered woman wearing a mask and a flimsy negligee with skewers down her spine and a number carved into her flesh. There was no doubt now they had a very dangerous psychopath in town. From the smell, this woman hadn't been washed in formaldehyde. The distinctive odor didn't linger on the corpse and the position of the body was also different from the other two. The two prior victims had been discovered lying face down, sprawled with arms and legs in disarray, but this one was sitting up, propped against the sign. Her head was facing down, which made her hair fall over her face, concealing the mask. She turned to Kane. "Do you figure that positioning the corpse this way was done to make it look as if she were waiting for someone?"

"No." Kane crouched down to view the body. "In my opinion, placing her on the side of the road so everyone could see her as they drive past is degrading. He has discarded her like trash. This is the final insult for someone he despises."

"He's escalating." Jo walked up beside Jenna and peered at the body. "And he's getting careless. The other two victims were meticulously presented, their hair brushed, and this one is untidy in comparison. It will be interesting to see what Wolfe discovers. Killers always make a mistake sooner or later, and by looking at this poor woman, she was a rush job. Maybe he had to leave town in a hurry."

"Which would confirm he moves around in his occupation. It's Monday morning and it makes sense that if this man is working out of town. He could have dropped her here on the way to work." Kane straightened and pushed back his Stetson as he scanned the dirt alongside Stanton. "I can't see any tire tracks close to the side of the road. So, he stopped some ways away and carried her here. He wouldn't risk doing that in daylight, so we must assume he is an early riser and usually leaves home before dawn."

Listening with interest, Jenna walked beside Kane around the perimeter of the murder scene, searching for footprints or any other evidence a person might leave behind. The rancid smell of death followed them, leaking through her mask as they walked away. Jenna lifted her face to the breeze coming from the mountains, seeking some respite. Finding nothing but a few animal tracks, she turned to look at her own footprints, clearly visible in the soft dirt alongside the highway. "This is a waste of time. The man responsible for doing this obviously parked on the road and carried her along the blacktop."

"Yeah, I figure he stopped just about there. This is a typical oil leak from a stationary vehicle. If it were a continuous leak, we'd see a line of small droplets, not a pool like this. Which would suggest the vehicle was stationary for a time." Kane went to the edge of the highway and squatted down peering at a patch of oil staining the blacktop. "It looks fresh, and I can't see anything floating on the top of it. There's no dust or pine needles from the forest. I figure it's only been here a few hours." He searched in the forensics kit for what he needed. "I'll take a few samples and mark it in case Wolfe wants to take a look."

As a truck came barreling along the highway in their direction, Jenna stepped out onto the blacktop. Her jacket with the fluorescent insignia of SHERIFF written in bright yellow six-inch-high lettering across the front was easily recognizable. She held up her arms, making slowing-down motions to the eighteen-wheeler as it came close to where Kane was working. The truck continued on by in a rush of wind that lifted the hair of the victim, exposing her grotesque mask and moving her negligee as if she were alive. Jenna swallowed hard and kept her attention fixed on the oncoming traffic. Most of the vehicles had slowed at the sight of the Beast and her cruiser parked on the side of the road with their blue and red lights flashing. Drivers hung out of their windows staring in morbid fascination at the victim, each one trying to catch a glimpse of what had happened. Jenna waved them on. "There's nothing to see here, move on."

"I'm done here." Kane stood and came to her side, pushing the swabs he'd taken into clear plastic cylinders and sealing them. He stared into the distance. "Ah, there's Wolfe, and Rowley is right behind him."

After making a particularly careful examination of the area around the oil spill and all along the blacktop on the way back to the body, Jenna greeted Wolfe and his team as they climbed from the ME's van. She was glad to see Wolfe had used his van to conceal the body from the road. Standing to one side, she waited for him to complete his preliminary examination of the corpse. When he straightened, she moved to his side. "What have we got?"

"This one is fresh." Wolfe narrowed his gaze at her over the top of his face mask. "She is in only the first stages of rigor.

I've taken the body temperature and I'll be able to give you a reasonable time of death. There's no indication of formaldehyde on this body but all the signs are there that this is the same killer. Something else is screaming out at me. The other victims had been scrupulously washed but I can clearly see this woman has something under one of her nails. It looks to me as if our killer is getting careless. I'll be able to tell you more when I get her back to the lab." He waved his assistant over. "Webber, bag her hands and feet, and we'll get her into a body bag. "Emily, I want you to search every inch of the ground beneath her to make sure the killer hasn't left any evidence behind."

"Is that something in her ear?" Emily bent close to the victim's face. "Maybe soapsuds or something similar? I didn't notice anything like that on any of the other victims."

"Yeah, that looks interesting." Wolfe bent low over the victim and brushed back her hair. "I'll collect a sample of it before we move her." He reached into his bag and pulled out a kit. "This might be the breakthrough we've been looking for."

Moving closer, Jenna looked at him. "Kane collected samples of a patch of oil just back there on the highway. We didn't find any footprints anywhere near the body and figured he parked on the blacktop and carried her here. It will be another piece of evidence we can use if we get a suspect driving a vehicle with an oil leak."

"Used engine oil is great evidence." Wolfe collected the sample from the woman's ear with care and slid it into a plastic cylinder before straightening and turning to Jenna. "It tells a story. For instance, all oils have different properties, so we'll know the brand. Different vehicles produce different contaminants, which we can pin to a particular engine. It's almost as good as a fingerprint."

Encouraged by the good news, Jenna smiled behind her mask. "How long before you can do the autopsy? This one might give us the information we need to hunt down a few suspects."

"There's no reason I should delay an autopsy, as it's an obvious homicide. I'll conduct a preliminary examination when I get her back to the lab. If you scan her prints and run them with her description through the database, you may hit paydirt. Looking at the condition of the body, this one was kidnapped recently. I'll give you a call when I'm ready to proceed with the autopsy. It will be a few hours yet. There's a ton of evidence to process on the body before I start."

Staring past Wolfe to the witness, Jenna nodded. "That's good. I've some leads to chase down. Do you want to speak to the witness who discovered the body? He didn't see anyone."

"No, not if you've taken his statement. If I need any more information, I'll catch up with him later. I think it's more important to get the body on ice and collect as much evidence as possible. For instance, if you want to know if she has drugs in her system, I'd need to get the tests underway without delay." Wolfe surveyed the crime scene and then turn back to her. "We can handle it from here. If I find anything interesting, I'll call you later this afternoon."

It was like a great weight had lifted from Jenna's shoulders. Having Wolfe to take over the crime scene gave her time to fast-track the investigation. "Thanks, I'll leave you to it. We'll see you later." She walked to her team and waited for them to turn to her. "If you have everything you need from here, we can head back to the office." As everyone headed for their vehicles, she made her way to where Mr. Woods was leaning against his van. "Thanks for your assistance. We'll be in touch if we need any more information. I want you to keep this information to yourself as a respect to the family of this woman. I'll need to discover her identity and inform the next of kin before it's released to the public."

"Yeah, I understand. I need to get these deliveries to the

general store and then I might go home for the rest of the day." Woods turned away and climbed into his van.

Jenna walked up to the Beast and slid inside. She looked at Kane and let out a long sigh. "If this body is fresh, maybe we'll be lucky and find a missing persons' report. She must be somebody's daughter. Someone out there must care."

TWENTY-TWO

By the time she arrived at the office, Jenna's mind was working overtime. She informed Maggie that the team would be working in the communications room and led the way up the stairs with everyone following close behind, including the two dogs. When everyone was settled, she turned to the expectant faces and cleared her throat. "I want everything you've got on the formaldehyde users in town. Have you cross-referenced any of them with recent releases from jail?"

"We have a few possible suspects lined up for you." Rio glanced down at his iPad. "We found two hobby taxidermists in town who are currently registered. One is Joshua Salmon, who works at the meat-processing plant. He lives on Maple. The other is Tom Parsons, a long-haul trucker out on Pine." He sighed. "We haven't had time to interview them yet."

Jenna made notes in her case file and then looked at Rowley. "Did you find anyone recently released from jail who might use formaldehyde?"

"Yeah, Kalo sent us a list of possibles." Rowley scanned his iPad. "Released in the last three months we have Big John Oates, who was convicted on an assault charge after a fight at the Triple Z Roadhouse. He lives at Miners Ridge—that's a very isolated place and forms part of the lowlands. He works at a factory where formaldehyde is used. The next person of interest is Lucas Davies, convicted of arson after setting fire to a neighbor's vehicle. He'd discovered his wife was having an affair with the owner of the vehicle. He's a merchandiser out of Green Tree Lane, Black Rock Falls." He glanced up at Jenna. "Then we have Sam Bright, who was jailed for five years for indecent assault. From the records, that was the third time he was convicted of the same crime. He likes to break into houses and attack sleeping women. He's living out of Long River, Black Rock Falls, and is a road driver."

Considering the information Jenna nodded. "What exactly does a road driver do?"

"Road drivers usually pick up and deliver cargo trailers. They travel to various destinations, usually long distance." Kane leaned back in his chair. "The occupations that travel from one county to another or on long distance routes would fit in perfectly with the profile of the killer. Do you agree, Jo?"

"Yes, I do." Jo nodded and turned to Jenna. "We have Jane Does and, with no positive IDs to link them to our area, we must assume that these women are from another county or state. The killer is moving the bodies somehow without anyone noticing, so we have to assume he's frequently traveling from one place to another and driving a vehicle that is commonplace in town."

Listening with interest, Jenna turned to Rio. "I figure everyone you've mentioned is a possible suspect. Would you add them to the whiteboard so we can all keep track of their names and where they live?" She glanced back down at her notes. "I believe Sam Bright would be on the top of my list. He travels long distances and there's also a record of indecent assault. As the victims were raped, he already has two strikes against him."

"He definitely is a possible." Kane leaned forward in his chair. "Do you want me to hunt him down?"

Jenna smiled at him. "Yeah, that would be a good place to start." She turned to the others. "I suggest we split up this list, hunt down these people's locations, and go and interview as many of them as possible. It's a long list and we need to cut it down." She perused her notes again and then lifted a head and looked at Rowley. "What made you add Lucas Davies in the equation? What does a merchandiser have in common with formaldehyde?"

"His company deals with all types of cleaning products, and formaldehyde is one of them." Rio turned from the whiteboard to look at her. "He travels around and fits the profile."

Thinking back over all the cases that she'd worked on over the last four years or so, Jenna couldn't recall any of the people Rio mentioned. "The names you mentioned that were released from jail recently are all kind of familiar, but I can't recall arresting anyone for those particular crimes. When was this?"

"These were before your time. You'd likely remember the names because they would be on the current list of recent parolees sent to the office each week." Rowley looked up from his screen. "The records before you took over are very sketchy, mainly because their computer system was toast. All I could find was the information from the county jail, which is sent prior to the prisoners' release. We could call Deputy Walters? He might recall the cases. He would've been in the office at the time."

Jenna shook her head. "That would be a waste of time. All the information would still be available from the DA's office and county would have copies. If necessary, we'll contact them and get the files."

"The problem I see with this list of suspects"—Kane drummed his fingers on the arm of the chair and stared at Jenna —"is we know the killer has a fixation or fantasy with policewomen. There must be some tie-in with the masks he's using and none of these people were arrested by a woman. There weren't any women working in law enforcement in this office before you."

"Which would mean that something substantial happened to the killer concerning a female police officer." Jo raised one eyebrow and looked at Jenna. "It could be something simple like a teenager's attraction being rebuffed or the officer humiliated them in some way. She could have been the trigger that started him on his killing spree from the get-go. If they were recently released from jail, perhaps seeing you in town wearing your sheriff's jacket might have triggered a memory. If it is one of the recently released men, it would account for the break in the killing spree, if we assume this is the same person Carter mentioned. They never arrested him, did they? For all we know, this person has been murdering women over the entire country. If this is so, it would give the impression that his killing sprees are spasmodic, but in truth, he could be killing weekly and just dumping the bodies on his travels." Her gaze moved around the table. "You do realize that this doesn't have to be a trucker? It could be anyone who goes fishing or hunting on the weekends or murders on vacation. We shouldn't limit ourselves to people who move around in their profession."

"Don't worry, I won't." Jenna split up the names of potential suspects and handed them out. "Okay, you each have the name of someone to hunt down. When you find their current where-abouts, write it up on the whiteboard and head on out to inter-view them. We'll keep it to our usual teams." She let her gaze linger on Rowley. "This killer is dangerous and I don't want anyone playing the hero and interviewing anyone without backup. Is this clear?" When the heads around the table nodded, she smiled. "Good. Let's get at it."

TWENTY-THREE

It took Kane all of ten minutes to hunt down Sam Bright. He checked out the paperwork that came from the jail and contacted his parole officer, who gave him all the details he needed. His phone buzzed and he smiled as Bright's work schedule popped into his inbox. He glanced over it, noting Bright was in town around the time the bodies showed. He should be at home now as he'd just checked in with his parole officer when he'd called. The guy had mentioned Bright was going home and wasn't due to head out again until Wednesday. Kane turned to Jenna. "I've located Sam Bright and we need to get there now." He stood and grabbed his jacket from the back of the chair.

"I've found Tom Parsons." Jenna let out a long sigh. "He's married. I called the company he works with, and they said he loaded his truck and was due to leave on a long-haul trip late last night or early this morning. He'll be away overnight and they expect him back late tomorrow or Wednesday morning." She stood and took the jacket Kane handed her. "Let's go."

The moment Kane shrugged into his jacket, Duke was by his side. After the shock of someone kidnapping the dog from the back of his truck, Jenna had made sure, apart from the sheriff's department badge hanging from his collar, the same insignia was prominent on all his coats. Everyone in Black Rock Falls understood Duke was a valuable part of the team, but Jenna wanted to be sure the criminals knew as well. Kidnapping or injuring a patrol dog was a serious offense. After rubbing Duke's head, Kane hurried out of the communications room to catch up with Jenna. "As Parsons is away, we should drop by and speak to his wife. It's a golden opportunity to find out exactly where he was and when."

"Yeah. That works for me." Jenna pulled open the glass door.

They headed out into the sunshine and climbed into the Beast. Kane turned to Jenna. "You said Tom Parsons lives on Pine. We go right by his place on the way to Long River. Do you want to drop by and see his wife now?"

"Sure." Jenna smiled at him. "At last, things seem to be moving along in this case. I hope that Wolfe finds something we can use in the autopsy tomorrow. If this killer is getting careless, he might have made his first mistake. The fluid in the last victim's ear sure looked like spittle to me. If it is and he is one of our parolees, then he'll be easy to identify."

Kane backed out his truck and headed down Main. "That sure would make life easier but somehow I don't figure we're that lucky."

"We'll have to get a break sooner or later in the case and I'm banking on Wolfe finding something." Jenna leaned back in her seat. "This is the first time Wolfe has found anything under one of the victim's nails. I hope it's something we can identify, to pinpoint where this lunatic is keeping these women. The areas around town are so diverse it should be easy. I had a good look at the last victim's hands and I'm sure I saw dirt and maybe grass under her nails."

On Pine the houses spread out over their lots and sat back

from the road with long driveways. The road was aptly named as brown and green pine needles covered the treelined blacktop. Kane pulled into the wide dirt driveway and followed it to the house. The ranch-style residence sprawled at odd angles, as if many additions had been added over the years. Some distance away at the end of a gravel track sat a tall wide garage. He assumed Parsons housed his truck there. The yard was wild and unkept, but the house had been freshly painted and it appeared that they had recently replaced the steps to the porch. He pulled his truck in beside a red Colorado and turned to Jenna. "How do you want to play this?"

"I'll take the lead. We'll keep it friendly and informal." Jenna slid out the truck and walked toward the porch. "See what you can get from her body language."

Kane went up the stairs and knocked on the door. A woman he assumed was in her mid-thirties with a two-year-old boy on her hip opened the door. The odor of wet diapers rushed out to meet them. "Mrs. Parsons? I'm Deputy Dave Kane and this is Sheriff Alton. Could we have a few minutes of your time?"

Mrs. Parsons leaned against the doorframe and frowned at them. "Is there a problem? Has something happened to my husband?" She ran a hand self-consciously through her untidy hair and smoothed her wrinkled floral dress.

"No, no, nothing's happened to your husband." Jenna stepped up to the front door. "We're just looking for information. As your husband is a trucker, we figured he might have been in the area of Stanton early this morning or on Main yesterday morning. We're hunting down witnesses for illegal dumping." She pulled out her notebook and pen and looked at the woman expectantly. "Does he often go to the local landfill?"

"I have no idea where he goes. I don't recall what time he left; it was dark outside. That's the life of a trucker's wife. We're used to being alone." Mrs. Parsons waved a hand behind her. "I have too much to do with the children to worry about where he is twenty-four hours a day. Yeah, he goes to the landfill, but everyone goes to the landfill. There is often a lot of packing material left in his truck when he comes home. So, he does often drop it there. The other days maybe he was there at those times. I wouldn't know. You'd have to ask him when he gets back. I'm usually asleep when he leaves in the morning, so I can't tell you when he left."

Jenna made a few notes and then looked back at the woman. "When he's away, does he stay away for one night or a few nights at a time?"

"He owns his truck, so it depends where the job takes him." Mrs. Parsons eyes flashed with annoyance. "One thing for darn sure, he never dumps his litter on the side of the road. So, if you're looking to pin this on him, you've got the wrong man."

"I'm not trying to blame anyone, Mrs. Parsons." Jenna folded her notebook and put it in her pocket. "I'm more interested in finding anyone who was passing through the area and might have seen a vehicle parked on the side of the road around the time of the dumping."

A baby cried inside the house and Mrs. Parsons looked around and then back to them. "I have to go. My youngest is teething. Tom is due back tomorrow, but I wouldn't be surprised if he stays out longer as we're not getting any sleep lately. If you want to catch up with him, I would suggest that you drop by again tomorrow afternoon or maybe leave it until Wednesday. He's not due out again until Friday morning."

Kane pushed his hands into the front pocket of his jeans and leaned casually against the porch railing. "What type of goods does your husband carry?"

"Anything that doesn't need refrigeration and he don't carry animals." Mrs. Parsons looked over her shoulder toward the wailing baby. "I can't leave her crying. Give me a minute." She hurried away down the hallway.

"What do you think?" Jenna had lowered her voice to a whisper. "Should I ask her about formaldehyde?"

Kane scanned the area, his attention fixing on the garage. "Maybe we won't need to. Keep her busy."

Bolting through the long grass, Kane ran into the garage. The smell of oil hit him in a wave of humidity. The building was massive, big enough to accommodate an eighteen-wheeler. Patches of oil stained the cracked cement floor and Kane bent down to inspect them. He ran his fingers through the oil. It was dry and had been there for some time. Straightening, he walked to the back of the garage and peered into the incinerator, finding only ashes. He moved on to a shed and peered in the window. A bench held a variety of tools and heads of various animals adorned the walls in rows. Out back in a lean-to, he discovered five plastic gallon bottles labeled formaldehyde and lifted each one to judge their contents. He pulled out his phone and took photographs of everything he'd found and then headed back to Jenna. As luck would have it, Mrs. Parsons hadn't returned to the front door. Just as he climbed the steps, he could hear her footsteps coming down the hallway. He gave Jenna a slight nod.

As the woman came to the front door again, Kane smiled at her. "I hear your husband is quite the artist. I believe he has some fine taxidermy. Does he work in the house or does he have a place somewhere else? I guess it would be too stinky to do around kids."

"He keeps all that garbage in the shed." Mrs. Parsons grimaced. "I'm not a fan of taxidermy. All those dead eyes following me like I'm to blame for killing them, I won't have them in the house."

"I'm not a fan either." Jenna smiled. "I prefer my animals alive and free. It's an unusual hobby. I imagine you have to order all the formaldehyde that's delivered here? Does Tom use it to clean the inside of his truck after consignments as well?"

"No, I don't order anything for Tom. He handles everything

to do with the business, all the books, the ordering, and the contracts. I have enough to do bringing up his kids and running the house." She pushed a strand of long greasy hair behind one ear and stared at him. "Is that all? I need to get back to my children or the next thing you know we'll have Child Protective Services knocking on my door."

"I'm sorry we took up so much of your time." Jenna smiled at her. "Children are a ton of work. You've been very helpful and we appreciate it." She backed away from the door and then turned to look at the woman. "If we need more information, we'll be sure to drop by when Tom is home."

As they headed down the long dark winding driveway, Kane turned to Jenna. "There are three empty bottles of formaldehyde at the back of the garage, and two full ones." He handed her his phone. "The oil on the floor of the garage is old. It's unlikely that Parsons' truck made the oil patches we found on Stanton near the body. It seems he's using formaldehyde for his hobby. I did see a ton of taxidermy on the walls in a shed. There are tools and a bench. He's the real deal. Although, formaldehyde is used as a disinfectant as well, but I don't think he carries anything that would require that amount of cleaning. Most truckers would hose out the back of their trucks."

"Unless he's a clean freak." Jenna flicked a glance at him and shrugged. "Although by looking at the yard and the smell coming from the house, I would hardly think so." She chewed on her bottom lip; something she always seemed to do when she was working out a problem. "Formaldehyde and oil spills kind of make me suspicious, but then he does have a rock-solid alibi as he's married. I honestly believe that most wives would protect their husbands. Maybe not after discovering that they've murdered three or four women. But in the initial investigation I would assume they would. Then again, she could be telling the truth and she's so involved looking after her children that she doesn't really know what he's doing."

Kane turned onto Stanton and headed for Long River. He shrugged. "It would be a perfect setup for a psychopath, wouldn't it? Just think about it, Jenna. A guy who can be away from home at any time, and his wife wouldn't become suspicious. If he's aware of the more common psychopathic profile, he would know that the majority of them are single Caucasian males." He stared at the blacktop winding through Stanton Forest and sighed. "If it is him, it will be very difficult to get a conviction. We would need absolute proof. Circumstantial evidence wouldn't cut it with his wife as his alibi."

"We'll keep him on the list. I'm more interested in what Bright has to say for himself." Jenna scrolled through her iPad. "This guy is at the top of my list at the moment. I think you should take the lead in the interview. It's obvious to me he has a problem with women. Or he has no respect for them. Men who rape don't respond well to a woman questioning them. You're intimidating and might have a better chance of getting information out of him. If he's on parole, there's no way he'll want to go back to jail. So, lean on him a bit and see what happens. I see from the GPS that there's a lot of land around his property. I might leave you to it and make an excuse to take Duke for a walk. It will give me the opportunity to take a look around."

Kane frowned. "Be careful. You know as well as I do that we don't have permission to search the premises and without a search warrant anything we find wouldn't be admissible in court." He blew out a long breath. "If we can establish probable cause, we can get a search warrant and go back later."

"I do know what to do, Dave." Jenna laughed. "Is there something about this case? Is it spooking you more than usual?"

Kane looked at her and smiled. "You mean you don't think I should worry about sending my wife into the potential clutches of a raping psychopath? We know Bright is suspicious, but what we don't know is if he's working alone. He could be living with an accomplice. You always need to be on your guard. Especially when you're alone."

"You shouldn't worry." Jenna squeezed his arm. "I wouldn't think twice about defending myself if necessary. Once upon a time, I held the opinion that people could change but since we've been dealing with psychopaths, I understand it's an out-of-control mental problem and there's no cure."

"That's good to know." Kane turned onto Long River and the voice on the GPS instructed him to turn into the first driveway on his left.

Bright lived in a log cabin-style ranch house in the middle of a cleared well-maintained grassy yard. Scattered wildflowers spilled across the lawn, adding a pleasant fragrance to the air. Kane parked the Beast out front. A late-model silver GMC truck was parked in a lean-to attached to one side of the house. A few other sheds and a dilapidated old barn lay toward the back. He climbed out of the truck and opened the back door to let Duke jump to the ground. The bloodhound stretched and looked up at him, wagging his tail, waiting to receive his next command. The one thing that Duke liked was to be involved in a case. Being an experienced tracker dog, his contribution to the team was invaluable. Kane reached into the back of the Beast for his forensics kit and pulled out an evidence bag. He handed it to Jenna. "There is a rag in here carrying the smell of formaldehyde. Give me a few minutes to get Bright occupied and then show it to Duke and see if he can hunt down any on the premises."

"Good thinking." Jenna held the bag behind her back and waited by the truck as Kane went up the steps.

The front door was opened by a man in his mid-thirties wearing a T-shirt and jeans. Neat and tidy with the fashionable stubble men wore on their chins of late, his eyes widened when his eyes traveled to the badge on Kane's belt. Kane straightened to his full height. "Sam Bright?"

"Look, Deputy, I know I was fifteen minutes late for my parole interview, but there's no need for you to come knocking on my door."

Noticing the prison tattoos on Bright's forearm and not liking the way he stuck out his chin in defiance, Kane pulled on his combat face and fixed his gaze on Bright. "This has nothing to do with checking in with your parole officer."

"Okay." Bright stiffened as he looked past him to Jenna. "Is that the sheriff?"

Kane nodded. "Yeah, do you mind if she lets the dog stretch its legs while we're talking?"

"Nope, there's not much it can hurt around here." Bright stood to one side. "Do you want to come in?"

On full alert, Kane smiled at him, but he'd never risk turning his back on a potential psychopath. "Sure. Lead the way."

He followed him inside a surprisingly neat family room. Bright sat down in an easy chair beside the fireplace and looked at him expectantly. His demeanor had changed significantly, from defiant to pliable. It seemed Bright knew how to work the system and pull the wool over people's eyes. The difference between the man on the steps and now was remarkable. Kane remained standing and slowly pulled out a notebook and pen from his pocket. He took his time perusing a blank page to give Jenna as much time as possible to search the outbuildings. "I've spoken to your parole officer this morning and he's given me details of the trips you made in the last week or so. Being a road driver, I assume that you deliver various vehicles to their new owners?"

"Yeah, that's right. I drop one off and bring another back here. Sometimes they're new vehicles. Other times I go to pick up used vehicles." Bright's face filled with concern. "You're not suggesting that I've been carrying illegal substances between states, are you? It was hard to miss the FBI agents moving around town the last few days."

Very astute and proves he was in town. Kane shook his head. "Nope, the two FBI agents are not with the DEA."

He paused a beat as another change came over Bright's disposition. Now he was having a problem sitting still. One knee bounced up and down in obvious agitation. Kane made a note in his notebook to give him time to bring himself under control. When he lifted his gaze, Bright's effort was noticeable. A sheen of sweat had formed on his brow and the stink of fear was filling the room. He had something to hide. "How often do you pick up hitchhikers? Is it all the time or just occasionally when you get the urge to rape someone?"

"I didn't rape her." Bright looked at him incredulously. "Do you think I would risk my parole and go back to jail? That woman was willing. I can't believe she reported me because she didn't even ask me my name."

Standing feet apart and shoulders straight, Kane leveled his combat gaze on Bright. "You haven't answered my question. How often do you pick up hitchhikers?"

"Okay, I admit it." Bright pushed trembling hands through his hair. "They come up to me at the truck stops and beg me to take them to the next town. I don't like to refuse them. Don't you figure I'm doing the right thing? Leaving them out on the side of the road is dangerous. Some of them are just kids."

Kane's mind was moving in all directions. This guy was a minefield of possible criminal activity. Just how many of these young women had he raped? He drove a different truck every time he went out. Even if the victim gave a detailed statement. The chances of them having his correct name or the type of truck that he was driving would be minimal. He stared at him. "Do you ever bring any of these hitchhikers home with you?"

"Yeah some." Bright gripped the arms of the sofa, his fingers white with the pressure. "I was just being neighborly. I give them a place to sleep and a meal before they leave. There's no law in doing that, is there?"

Kane shook his head. "Nope. Do you live alone?"

"Yeah." Bright shrugged. "I like my privacy."

Kane kept his attention fixed on the man. "Do you have a cellar or any other storage areas on the property?"

"You can see for yourself there are sheds and cabins all over my property." Bright jumped to his feet and his mouth twisted into a sneer. "If you want to search them, you'll need a warrant. I sure as heck don't trust you." He lifted his chin and glared at Kane. "I figure I've said enough already. You'll twist everything I say and I want you to leave now."

Kane nodded and slowly closed his notebook and pushed it into his pocket. "Not a problem. Thanks for your time. I'm sure we'll be dropping by to see you again real soon." He made a show of testing the slide of his weapon in and out of the holster and then, neck prickling in warning, headed for the door.

TWENTY-FOUR

The outbuildings on Sam Bright's land sat beneath the shade of the trees like a patch of mushrooms. Joined together by dark narrow alleyways, Jenna assumed they'd been used for some type of cottage industry a time ago. Moss covered the walls of the wooden buildings and weeds tangled the long grass. The window frames still clung to a little white paint but most had peeled, leaving a confetti of paint flakes over the walkway. She peered into grime-covered windows but dust that had built up over a long time obscured any view of the interior. Locked doors prevented any chance of entry. As she moved across a small clearing to the next clutch of buildings, the smell of acrid smoke filled Jenna's nostrils. Motioning for Duke to come to her side, she peered around the end of the shed. The information on Sam Bright was that he lived alone. So, who was out back burning garbage? On full alert, Jenna placed a hand on her weapon ready to draw. Unease crept over her as she moved forward. Kane had mentioned the possibility of an accomplice and it seemed he was correct. Moving along the wall of one of a pair of small log cabins, Jenna made out the shadowed figure of a man tossing things into a flaming fire pit.

Beside her, Duke whined and then moved past her and sat down. She stared at him, recognizing this as a sign he'd smelled formaldehyde. The man burning the garbage was an unknown quantity and she had no backup. Indicating to Duke to follow her, she edged her way back down the alleyway and made her way silently to the perimeter of the other buildings. She pulled out her phone and sent a message to Kane. He must have finished the interview with Bright, as seconds later, he came running across the long grass toward her. When he reached her side, she turned to him and dropped her voice to a whisper. "There's a guy burning something out back of the two cabins on the other side of the old sheds, and Duke reacted to finding formaldehyde."

"We should split up and go in on either side of those cabins." Kane peered down the alleyway. "We'll have the drop on him."

Stomach churning, Jenna nodded. The idea of confronting a possible psychopath in the act of destroying evidence concerned her. Particularly one who hated women. She ran the image of the man through her mind again and looked at Kane. "I didn't see a weapon, but it was only a brief glance as he moved between the buildings. I'll call out and identify myself. If there is a problem, he won't see you coming in from the other side."

"Wait a minute. We don't know what we're walking into here." Kane pulled out wireless earbuds from his pocket and pushed them into his ears. "Use your phone's earbuds. I'll call you and we'll keep in contact."

Jenna nodded and reached for her phone. She waited for Kane's call, gave him a nod, and then headed through the alleyway. He followed behind her silently, and when they reached the perimeter of the outbuildings, he headed in the opposite direction, moving around one of the cabins and disappearing from view with Duke close behind him. Heart thundering in her chest, Jenna kept her back to the wall and eased through the shadows to the end of the building. From her position she could easily make out a man throwing handfuls of clothes into the fire. The smell of burning wool and man-made fabrics rushed toward her, searing her nostrils in a blanket of choking smoke. In the fire pit, fragments of clothes flared up in dancing flames and others smoldered, glowing red as their blackened remnants curled, falling to ashes and dancing away in the wind. "I have eyes on the suspect. He doesn't appear to be carrying any weapons. Can you see anything hidden on him from your angle?"

"Nope. He's not even carrying a knife sheath. I figure you're good to go." Kane cleared his throat. *"Maybe make a noise to get his attention so you don't creep up on him. If he's destroying evidence, he'll be a little jumpy, and we can't see what's in that bag by his feet."*

Sliding her weapon from its holster Jenna took a deep breath and moved forward into the open. "I'm going in."

Keeping her gun alongside her body and pointed to the ground, she moved toward the man and raised her voice. "Sheriff's Department. Keep your hands where I can see them and turn around and face me."

The man jerked as if he'd been stung by a bee and spun around to face her, fists clenched at his sides. He glared at her, his mouth turned down. "What gives you the right to creep up on a man and then draw down on him? This is private property and I have my rights."

"I have you covered." Kane's voice came through her earpiece.

It went against her training to holster her weapon, but knowing Kane had the man in his sights, she straightened her spine and walked confidently toward him. "You're not Sam Bright, who happens to be the owner of this property, so what are you doing here?"

"I'm his cousin Derek and I don't need your permission to

burn garbage in our backyard." He knuckled his fists at his waist and stuck out his chin. "The question is: what are you doing here, sticking your nose where it's not wanted?"

Catching a glimpse of Kane in her periphery with his weapon aimed at the man, Jenna took a few steps closer and peered into the fire pit. "What is it you're burning there?"

"Old clothes." Derek shrugged and went to pull another handful out of the bag. "They stink and I wanted to get them out of the house. They belonged to our grandma. When she passed, she left the house to Sam and me. I've been cleaning out the rooms and getting rid of the junk."

A shiver of apprehension slipped down Jenna's back as her gaze slid over the bag on the ground and the handful of jeans T-shirts and sweaters in his hand. "Don't throw anything else on the fire. I can't speak to you with the smoke in my eyes." She lifted her chin to observe him more closely. "How old was your grandma?"

"In her nineties, I guess. Not that that's any business of yours, Sheriff." Derek dropped the bundle of clothes on top of the open bag and stared her down. "Are we done here? I've got a ton of work to do today."

Jenna waved Kane toward her and turned her attention back to Derek. "No, we're not done here yet. I see there are a variety of different styles and sizes of clothes in that backpack. All of them appear to be exceptionally modern and high end. These are not what we usually see ninety-year-olds wearing in Black Rock Falls. I'd expect to see those labels on women in some of the big cities, maybe LA or New York, but not here in town. We buy more practical clothing because the weather is so changeable." She poked the bag with her toe. "The sizes are dramatically different, and it makes me wonder why you didn't donate these to Goodwill, rather than burn them. I'm sure many people would be able to make use of them."

"More to the point, where did you really get them from?"

Kane walked into the open holstering his weapon. "Think seriously before you answer, because what you say now will reflect on what happens next."

"What the heck are you talking about?" Derek spun around to stare at Kane. "Like I said, I took them out of my grandma's cellar. She had boxes piled up to the ceiling. Maybe these belonged to her when she was younger? Who knows, and who cares? I sure as hell don't. I just want to get rid of the junk."

"Just how much of this have you burned already?" Kane stared at the bag and then slowly back to Derek.

"I've been burning stuff all week, but I just started on this pile today. Why does it matter to you?" Derek pushed a hand through his hair. His eyes flashed with agitation.

"Oh, it matters." Jenna motioned him toward the house. "We need to speak to you and Sam together. Leave this for now." She turned to Kane. "Escort him back to the house. I'm taking Mr. Bright and his cousin in for questioning."

"Questioning?" Derek stared at her in disbelief. "Are you arresting us? On what charges?"

Jenna pulled the phone out of her pocket. "I'm not arresting you. I'm taking you in for questioning and I'll be holding you pending further investigations after obtaining a search warrant for this property. I have reason to believe that you're destroying evidence from a crime."

As Kane escorted him back to the house, Jenna took photographs of the fire pit and the bag of clothes. First, she called old Deputy Walters to come by and pick up the prisoners in his cruiser. Rowley and Rio would be heading out to the lowlands to hunt down Joshua Salmon at the meat processing plant and Big John Oats at the adhesives factory.

Her next call was to Carter. She ran through the evidence with him and forwarded the images. "I'm bringing them in. They can cool their heels while you get started on a search warrant. I know this sounds sketchy, but this is the only solid lead we've discovered. I figure we need to run with it."

"Three naked victims and you find a guy destroying a bag of women's clothes. That sure sounds like probable cause to me. I'm on it." Carter disconnected.

Letting out a sigh of relief, Jenna headed back to the house. She might be grasping at straws with this lead, but at this point in the investigation, she would take any snippet of information and run with it. Sometimes the smallest clue gave the best reward.

TWENTY-FIVE

The smell of blood clung to every pore of Poppy's body. It seeped into her soul and stuck there like a fly trapped in a spider's web. The long night of bone-jarring terror with a psychopath during a killing frenzy would haunt her forever. She stood at the small aluminum sink and scrubbed her nails. Hands red, raw, and swollen, she persisted rubbing the soap over her skin and using the small nail brush her jailer had given her as a small consideration for her help. Disgust shivered through her. She sobbed in desperation and scoured the brush over tender flesh, but nothing would remove the blood from under her nails. She met the eyes of her reflection in the mirror above the sink, hardly recognizing the image staring back at her. Dark circles rimmed haunted eyes and blood still spattered her face. Horrified by her appearance, she lathered her face with soap. The promised shower her jailer had offered her had never eventuated and she'd sat all night stinking of blood, terrified of what would happen next. This morning he'd arrived and ushered her down a long dark passageway and ordered her into a different cell away from the others. Inside and set high on one wall, a cobweb encrusted light bulb secured within a metal net offered a small amount of illumination. The cell was similar to the others: Walls hewn from solid rock. No windows. No escape.

Claustrophobia had gripped her in a wave of panic, but she'd smothered it and tried to act casual, as if she enjoyed living in a dark damp dungeon. Although this cell wasn't as bad as the one she'd left; in fact, it had a few luxuries. Against one wall stood a military-style cot with a pillow and a few rough blankets to cover the canvas bottom. Soap and towels sat on the bed beside an old pink cotton seersucker summer dress that appeared to be out of the 1950s. Too afraid to move, Poppy had waited for instructions, sagging against the wall and shivering from a long night naked and in shock. He'd said nothing, pulled the door shut, and turned the key. After his footsteps had died away, he'd not returned. She knew his routine by now. When he left after a kill he was usually gone for a couple of days or as long as a week, but traumatized, she'd waited, too scared to move. Her hands stiff with dried blood, she'd picked at the crusty crimson streaks cracking with each bend of her knuckles. After an hour or so had passed she'd gained enough courage to go and wash away the stink. It had been impossible to remove all the blood from her skin using only her hands, cold water, and a small piece of fragrant soap usually found at some of the better motels. She'd washed many times and, moving toward the light, examined every inch of her body that she could see, searching for any smears she'd missed.

As she dried her cold body with freezing fingers, her stomach clenched with hunger, and although sick to the stomach, the first rule of survival was to eat when possible. It was usual for her jailer to leave survival packages in a box in the corner of the room. These were the same as soldiers used during their tour of duty in isolated areas. He usually left enough for a week or so, and when she showered out in the hallway, he would collect the garbage and replenish the food.

After pulling the dress over her head, and wrapping one of

the rough blankets around her, Poppy peered into the box of supplies and blinked in surprise. On top of the usual packages sat a Thermos and a bag of takeout with the name AUNT BETTY'S CAFÉ printed on the paper sack. At least, it seemed she hadn't left Black Rock Falls. Uncertainty gripped her as she opened the Thermos and sniffed the hot fresh coffee. The bag contained jelly donuts with a liberal coating of powdered sugar. Her jailer had no empathy, no compassion. Why would he be giving her treats? What else did he expect her to do? Or was he luring her into a false sense of security?

TWENTY-SIX

It was good to be away from the office on a summer's day, and Rowley buzzed down his window and inhaled the fresh breeze coming from the lowlands. The scent of summer wouldn't last long. Ahead, the landscape had become a sea of wheat-colored grasses, whipped into waves by the wind. Occasionally a dust devil would escape the vast openness and dance across the blacktop as if playing chicken with the traffic. As soon as he and Rio drove into the parking lot of the meat-processing plant, the air would be filled with the smell of livestock and hot blood. He turned to Rio, who was riding shotgun. "The phone signal is pretty sketchy in this area. If you need to make a call, I suggest you use your satellite sleeve."

"Okay." Rio snapped the sleeve over his phone and looked at him. "I've read a case file about the owner of this processing plant going crazy and stuffing people into a shredding machine and turning them into fertilizer. He nearly got you too, didn't he?"

The horror of that particular case slid into Rowley's mind like a nightmare he'd rather forget. He headed for the parking lot and pulled into a space opposite the main entrance. "Yeah, I came close to being fertilizer, but Jenna threw herself onto the conveyor belt and pulled me off just in time."

"I sure hope the new guy in charge is cooperative." Rio checked his iPad and smiled at him. "It was closed for a time. Where did people go to get their kills processed?"

Thinking for a beat, Rowley shrugged. "I'm not a hunter, so I'm not sure. I guess most hunters are capable of processing their own kills. Although, I do recall the processing plants at Louan running a pickup service during the hunting season. They have a refrigerated storage building, which is really good for the tourists. They can donate their meat to the local charities. It's frozen and stored in an easy place for them to go pick it up." He climbed out from behind the wheel and headed toward the office.

The office was spread out into different departments. As luck would have it, signs on each wall pointed to the various departments within the complex, and Rowley found the manager's office on the ground floor. The strong smell of disinfectant wafted toward them as they turned the corner and sidestepped a cleaner mopping the tiled floors. They edged their way around the wet patches and went into the manager's office. A woman in her thirties wearing a cream blouse and gray skirt looked up at them from her desk, and her eyes widened. Rowley smiled to put her at ease. "Ma'am, we're looking for Joshua Salmon. Could you check the roster and see if he's working today?"

"I'm not sure I'm allowed to give out that information." She indicated toward the office door behind her. "You'll have to speak to Mr. Wiley about staff issues. Wait a moment, I'll go and tell him you're here."

The woman stood with a scrape of her chair, and after knocking on the door marked MANAGER set out in black letters on a copper plate, she went inside. Through the frosted glass panel, Rowley could make out the woman's outline and a figure seated behind a desk. A few moments later, the secretary came out and waved them inside. He glanced over the rotund man behind the desk. A round face with a pencil mustache and small beady eyes looked up at him. From his expression, he didn't like speaking to law enforcement. Rowley cleared his throat. "I'm sorry to trouble you, Mr. Wiley, but we need to speak to Joshua Salmon. I'm afraid it can't wait until he finishes his shift."

"I've asked my secretary to have him come here. It might take a few minutes. He works on the kill floor. We're processing cattle at the moment and have very stringent health rules. Employees aren't allowed to move from one area to the other without taking the necessary precautions." Wiley leaned back in his chair and his eyebrows rose. "He's not in any trouble, is he?" His expression was indignant. "We don't encourage troublemakers to work here, although I have to admit the odd one does slip through the net."

"We're not at liberty to discuss why we're here." Rio took a notebook from his pocket. "Is there a spare office where we can talk to him in private?"

"Yes. We have an interview room right next door." Wiley stood and led the way through the office and down the hallway. He flung open a door to a small room containing a desk and a few chairs. "If you'd like to wait here, I'll send him along when he arrives."

Rowley turned to Wiley. "Thank you for your cooperation. When we're through, we'll see ourselves out."

He leaned against the wall beside Rio and waited. Twenty minutes or so later, Joshua Salmon arrived wearing white coveralls and rubber boots. He waited at the door, staring at them blankly. Rowley waved him to a seat. "Thank you for coming. We'd like to ask you a few questions about your hobby."

"My hobby? I have a current license, so what's the problem?" Salmon pushed his hands into the pockets of his coveralls but didn't sit down. He just stared at them with an incredulous look on his face.

"Where do you get the animals that you use?" Rio dropped into a chair and looked up at him. "Sit down. You're making my neck ache."

"Roadkill mostly. Some are from neighbors. They bring their pets to me because they can't stand the idea of burying them." Salmon reluctantly sat down. "I specialize in birds but all of them I find I report to the wardens before I use them. I don't kill anything for my hobby."

Rowley nodded. "Did you have any reason to stop in town early on Thursday morning?"

"Yeah, I had an early shift, so I would have gone through town before six." Salmon scratched his cheek and narrowed his gaze at them. "Ah... I know what this is about. It's all over town about finding the body on the carousel in the park opposite Aunt Betty's Café? I didn't stop—not even for coffee. I just drove straight through and came here. You can check my entry in the book at the front door. We all have to sign in and out of this place. It's date and time stamped."

"So cast your mind back to Friday morning. Did you work on Friday?" Rio leaned forward in his chair and stared at him. "Or did you happen to drop by the landfill?"

"As it happens, I did drop by the landfill on Friday morning, but I was turned around by an FBI agent and sent on my way. I dropped my garbage by there the following day." Salmon shrugged. "There must have been twenty or so vehicles lined up on the landfill approach road. Before you ask, I don't remember anybody in particular."

As he was cooperating, Rowley pushed a little harder. The times he had given them put him at the scenes of two crimes. "So, you leave for work in the early hours most days? On Monday you would have driven past the WELCOME TO BLACK ROCK FALLS sign?"

"Yeah, I would have driven past there just after five on Monday morning." Salmon's eyes shifted from one to the other and he moved around restlessly in his chair. "So did about one hundred people on their way through town. What's the big deal?"

Taking his time, Rowley scribbled the time in his notebook and then lifted his attention back to Salmon. "Did you happen to notice a woman standing by the side of the road?"

"Can't say that I did." Salmon rolled his eyes to the ceiling as if seeking divine intervention. "I'm not in the habit of picking up hitchhikers. They're nothing but trouble."

"Would you mind coming outside and showing us your vehicle." Rio stood and motioned him toward the door. "We're not planning on searching your vehicle, but we would like you to move it a few feet out of the parking space if you don't mind?"

"Sure. I have nothing to hide." Salmon stood and ambled toward the door.

Rowley walked beside Salmon, meeting him stride for stride. The suspect was in the right place at the right time on three consecutive occasions and used formaldehyde. This made him a person of interest. If they found a patch of fresh oil under his vehicle, it would be a slam dunk. When Salmon backed the truck out of the parking space, Rowley bent to examine the ground and found nothing. Without an oil slick beneath the vehicle, they only had circumstantial evidence against him and not enough to take him in for further questioning. He waved at Salmon to drive his truck back into the parking space and then bent to peer in through the driver's side window. "Thank you for your cooperation. That's all we need for today, but don't leave town. We might have questions for you later."

He followed Rio back to his truck and climbed behind the wheel. "I thought we had a suspect, but without the oil slick we have nothing."

"Maybe we'll have better luck with Big John Oates. The plant where he works is only a few minutes' drive away." Rio was scanning his iPad. "The business manufactures different types of adhesives used in making furniture. Formaldehyde is a component of just about all of them, so I would imagine it wouldn't be too difficult to steal some from his workplace. Although, this guy was recently released from jail, so he'd be stupid to risk a parole violation. If he knows anything or has seen someone stealing formaldehyde, he might inform on them. Trust me, most of them will talk rather than doing the rest of their sentence."

Big John Oates was well named and big was an understatement. Standing around six-five and weighing in at around four hundred pounds, he would be a force to be reckoned with. It didn't surprise Rowley that he had taken down seven men in a fight at the Triple Z Roadhouse and caused a ton of damage. Once they'd located him, he agreed to go to the parking lot and speak to them. Rowley ran through the same set of questions he'd given Salmon and the only positive response was that he'd driven past the BLACK ROCK FALLS sign on his way to work. He took the same route Monday to Friday and recalled seeing the Sheriff's Department cruisers on the side of the road on his way to work the previous Monday. They checked his vehicle for oil leaks and found none. Rowley had only one more question for him. "Do you ever pick up hitchhikers?"

"Sometimes but never women." Oates let out a long sigh. "With all the killings happening around town of late, I don't want anyone pointing the finger at me. I did my time for a stupid mistake and I'm not going back inside again."

Finding Oats to be honest and straightforward, Rowley gave him a nod. "Thank you for your time. If there's any problem with your boss for speaking to us, just get him to give me a call." He handed him his card. As they headed back to his truck, he turned to Rio. "He looks clean to me. What do you think?"

"It's not him." Rio tipped up the rim of his Stetson and sighed. "He's way too noticeable to get away with dumping bodies around town. It's reasonably busy from the early hours and someone of his size wouldn't go unnoticed. I say we take him off the list."

Rowley laughed and slid behind the wheel. "I figure we'll run it past Jenna first."

"Yeah, good idea." Rio grinned at him. "I do believe being left in charge for a couple of days has gone to my head." He chuckled. "It was sure nice while it lasted."

TWENTY-SEVEN

Waiting for a judge to consider the probable cause evidence to issue a search warrant was like watching paint dry. Jenna spent the time updating her files. When Susie Hardwick arrived with the takeout that Kane had ordered they sat around the conference room eating and discussing the case. She listened with interest to Rowley and Rio's report on the two suspects they'd interviewed. She agreed that Big John Oates was unlikely to be the killer and they removed him from the list. The Salmon interview interested her and the idea of checking out Millers' Garage in town to discover if Salmon had taken his vehicle in for service crossed her mind. Salmon's cooperation went against him. Previous experience told her that most psychopaths were often pliable during questioning and few of them acted aggressively. Many asked questions often to gain information about the progression of a case. Having two experienced profilers on her team was a great advantage when solving crimes, and she played to her strengths. Jo being an icon in the field of behavioral analysis would usually be her go-to person if she was on the case, but as she was cooling her heels at the courthouse waiting for the search warrant, she turned to Kane. "What's your opinion of Salmon?"

"He was in the right place at the right time. He lives alone and doesn't have an alibi for any of the mentioned times the bodies were dumped. He works on the kill floor at the meat-processing plant, so would be used to cleaning up blood and excrement. What happened to our victims would take a strong stomach, that's for darn sure." Kane sipped his coffee and eyed her over the rim. "He could've easily dumped the last victim's body on the way to work and still signed in on time. We're only surmising that the oil leak belongs to the killer. I believe we should keep him on the list and follow up."

The phone buzzed and Jenna reached for it. It was Wolfe. "I was just thinking about you. Do you have anything for us?"

"Yeah, we have some interesting developments in the most recent Jane Doe case. I'll be conducting an autopsy at two. I found DNA in her ear, and I'm running it through the DNA sequencer now. We should have some results over the next couple of hours. I was also able to lift latent fingerprints from the body, and I'm running them through the database, I figure this is the break we've been waiting for. I'll see you at two."

Wanting to punch the air, Jenna smiled at the expectant faces around the table. "Good news! Wolfe might have discovered some evidence. He's running tests now. The autopsy is at two."

"You can't split yourself into two, Jenna." Carter moved the toothpick across his lips and shrugged. "I know Jo will want to attend the autopsy, so I'll go with Rio and Rowley to toss Bright's house."

More than happy to allow Carter to take the lead on the search, Jenna nodded. "Sure, thanks. My first priority is the autopsy. Although, it will be interesting to see what you find at the Bright cousins' house. I hope the judge gets a move on with the search warrant. I can't keep the Bright cousins here for much longer without reading them their rights."

"They're happy enough. Maggie fed them and it's not as if they're in the cells, although the interview rooms are uncomfortable. We had no choice. We had to keep them apart in case they concocted a story." Kane drummed his fingers on the table. "They could be telling the truth. If the old lady did have a collection of clothes in her cellar, she might have been a hoarder. They see a value in useless garbage and take it home. She could have been picking the clothes up from anywhere. Having formaldehyde on the premises and burning rubbish isn't conclusive evidence these men are killers."

"When the search warrant arrives, we'll go over the place with a fine-tooth comb. I'm counting on finding something we can use." Carter met Jenna's gaze. "Seems to me the evidence is stacking up against them. Don't allow them to slip through your grasp." He looked at Kane and shrugged. "We'll agree to disagree. Call it gut instinct. From what you told me, I figure those guys are more than in the ballpark for the murders."

"I'm not discounting them yet." Kane lifted one shoulder. "I just want more evidence. I had one hostile and one cooperative. It didn't feel right to me. Killers like this one are smart and try to outwit cops. Derek Bright was darn right hostile."

"There's still one more person we haven't interviewed." Rio glanced up from his iPad and looked at Jenna. "Lucas Davies. As far as I could ascertain, he is out of town until tomorrow but he was in contact with this office from Thursday through to today, so we shouldn't discount him as a suspect."

Jenna's stared at the whiteboard and sighed. "Okay give me a rundown of his information again, please."

"Lucas Davies was convicted of arson after setting fire to a neighbor's vehicle. He'd discovered his wife was having an affair with the owner of the vehicle. He's a merchandiser out of Green Tree Lane, Black Rock Falls." Rio met Jenna's eyes with a frown. "He fled to Blackwater and was taken down by one of the female deputies. From the deputy's statement of the arrest, it seems that Davies has a problem with women law enforcement officers. Witnesses' statements say he was violent and abusive."

Not planning on leaving any stone unturned, Jenna made notes in her daybook. "Okay, as soon as he shows in town, I want you and Rowley to interview him before he's off on another job." She looked from one deputy to the other. "Keep me updated on his status. I don't want him slipping through the net either. Right now, I'll consider as many suspects as you can throw at me. Sooner or later, we'll have enough evidence to charge one of them."

The door opened and Jo walked in waving a handful of papers.

"I have the search warrant." Jo was grinning widely. "We got the whole nine yards. The house, outbuildings, and even their vehicles."

Thrilled, Jenna stood and high-fived her. "Great!" She turned to Carter. "Grab extra forensics kits from the storeroom and you're good to go."

"I'm on it." Carter stood and waved Rowley and Rio toward the door. "Let's go."

TWENTY-EIGHT

A few scattered puffy white clouds drifted across the endless blue sky as Kane headed the Beast toward the medical examiner's office. Townsfolk ambled through town enjoying a beautiful summer's afternoon oblivious to the fact a killer lurked among them. How long would it take for the murderer to exhaust his stash of captives? Would he risk snatching someone from town to appease his lust for killing or would he be arriving soon with a new woman from parts unknown? With no reports of recent missing persons fitting the descriptions of the current victims, he had no idea which direction Jenna should take the investigation. He glanced at her. "I called Bobby Kalo and asked him to widen the area for the missing persons reports, and although he did come up with a couple of women fitting the descriptions of the victims, all of them went missing over five years ago. I find it hard to believe that our killer has kept these women prisoner for that period of time."

"Really?" Jenna looked at him and raised one eyebrow. "Do you recall the kids who were taken and kept as sex slaves until they were too old to be of interest to their captors?" She shook her head. "Anything is possible. Having a stock of women to murder when the need arises wouldn't surprise me at all. The way psychopaths' minds work, and the fact they are so darn smart, it seems to me this would be very convenient." She looked at him, her face animated. "Think about it. After five years these women have ceased to be a priority and end up in the cold case files. A psychopath who likes to display his victims, like this one, could select a victim from a different state for instance, and the chances of discovering their identity would be near impossible. More so if the woman was a prostitute or a vagrant. It would almost be a perfect crime."

Kane pulled his truck into a parking spot outside the medical examiner's office and turned to her. "Yeah, and after that time, the chances of any witnesses of an abduction coming forward would be long gone."

"If he is doing this, he is very much in control." Jo leaned forward in her seat. "Many would escalate into a frenzy and kill them all. From what I've seen so far, this man's hatred of women is deep set. Which would make me believe his psychosis started a long time ago and he has some control over it. We all agree that this man has killed before and often but now his life-style precludes him from procuring women on a regular basis. Maybe this wasn't his MO in the beginning but now he gains pleasure from keeping them prisoner and making them suffer." She gathered her things from the seat beside her. "Unfortunately, most of our suspects meet that profile. More than one of them move around and could easily have places set up anywhere in Black Rock Falls to keep their victims. The options here are endless. You have the forest, caves, cabins in the mountains, mineshafts, and any number of isolated areas. The thing is that living in a town like this it's not unusual for people to buy large amounts of food or supplies. They can buy just about anything here and not call attention to themselves. It's a psychopath's paradise."

They headed inside the ME's office, and Kane flashed his

ID card over the scanner and they made their way down the white tiled hallway to the morgue. They found the examination room with the red light blinking outside and quickly changed into scrubs, masks, and gloves for the autopsy. The door opened with a whoosh as they entered the cool room. Even with mentholated salve spread beneath his nose, the smell of decomposing flesh seared Kane's nostrils.

"Right on time." Wolfe removed the sheet from the body on the gurney. "We'll get started because this case is complicated and it will take time to explain the subtle differences between this case and the others."

"You mentioned finding DNA." Jenna moved closer to the body. "Have any results come back yet?"

"Not yet but this victim was a minefield of DNA and latent fingerprints. It was almost as if someone deliberately left evidence." Wolfe peered at them over the top of his mask. "You'll recall Emily noticing the fluid in the victim's ear? Of course, my first thought was cranial fluid leaking from the ear due to head trauma. On examination under the microscope, I determined the fluid was spittle. I immediately set up a sample for the DNA sequencer and just before you arrived, I sent them to Kalo, who is currently running the results through the DNA databases."

Leaning against the counter, Kane nodded. "I guess the chances of the victim getting their own spittle in their ear would be impossible?"

"That's the first thing I checked." Wolfe went to the screen array and pulled up some files. "The latent fingerprints don't belong to her either." He indicated to the images on the screen. "Latent fingerprints are those left by body oils and I use a light filter to get a clearer image. From what I collected I can only imagine these were left deliberately because I found a smear of sweat across the cheek of this victim. DNA analysis of the sample was consistent with the spittle in the victim's ear."

"Are you running the prints as well?" Jenna stared at the images on the screen. "I don't see any marks on the victim's neck. This one is different from the others. Have you determined a cause of death?"

"The prints, yeah, Kalo has all the information"—Wolfe let out a long sigh—"and, no, I haven't determined the cause of death at this time. We'll see what the autopsy shows us." He moved back to the gurney, selected a scalpel from the instrument tray, and motioned to his assistant Colt Webber that he was ready to start.

Kane followed along with the autopsy, which was textbook until Wolfe examined the heart. He removed it, set it on a pair of scales, and then proceeded to dissect it. The victim had injuries not consistent with the others. The images they'd taken at the crime scene hadn't indicated that one of the skewers had been pushed into the victim's heart. Although, the killer had placed the others along the spine exactly in the same position as the previous victims. "Is sharp forced trauma what killed her?"

"Yeah. Death would have been instantaneous." Wolfe looked up from his work. "She took a beating. The same as the others, using a baseball bat or similar, and the consistency is that the abuse happened over time. The injuries vary. Some are recent and others as old as six months, maybe more. The bruising, again, is in stages of healing, which would prove that this woman has been held for at least six months."

"I don't see any head trauma on the X-rays." Jenna walked up and down peering at the screens. "For some reason he didn't want to damage this one's face, and by not strangling her, it seems to me he was in a hurry. What do you think, Jo?"

"Stabbing someone in the heart is pretty up close and personal." Jo's eyebrows rose above her mask. "Was she raped as well?"

"Yeah." Wolfe pulled the sheet down to the victim's knees. "Her inner thighs are bruised so I would assume she fought back. Also, there are bruises to the forearms, knuckles, and wrists. In my opinion, this one was a problem for him. He was unable to dominate her into submission and went for the quick kill." He turned to Jenna. "Many people believe death by strangulation is fast and clinical, but it isn't."

"Go on." Jenna lifted her chin as if readying herself for the reply.

"The victim's face swells and becomes blue, the eyes bulge, and blood vessels burst. Mucus pours from their mouth and nose. Their tongue protrudes and their lips swell." Wolfe raised one eyebrow. "I know many killers are addicted to this type of face-to face suffering and it disgusts me."

"Why do you consider stabbing someone is a quick kill?" Jenna stared at the victim on the gurney. "He's always preferred strangling them before, so why would he change?"

"Maybe he was running out of time? That's for you to decide. I just give you the facts." Wolfe shrugged. "The intensity of the grip required to kill someone by asphyxiation takes at least four minutes of continuous pressure. This takes considerable strength and that's the reason many people who kill by strangulation use a cord or similar to twist around the neck to sustain the pressure. Holding someone and exerting enough pressure with their thumbs is difficult because no one is going to sit still and just allow someone to strangle them. Even though it only takes a very short time, ten seconds or so to achieve unconsciousness, the moment the pressure is released blood flows to the brain and the victim regains consciousness."

Kane cleared his throat. "I figure a man capable of strangling would have the strength to break a person's neck. Doing so from behind in one fast movement is not up front and personal. It's fast and silent. He enjoys his killing."

"From the evidence in front of me, I conclude this victim died of sharp force trauma to the heart, causing massive damage to the left atrium and left ventricle." Wolfe looked at Jenna.

"Time of death is approximately six to twelve hours before the discovery of the body."

Nodding, Kane wanted to know if the body had been washed in formaldehyde. "Is there—"

"Just a minute." Wolfe stripped off his gloves and headed for the door. "I have a call coming in and it might be the results I'm waiting for." He turned to look at Webber. "Close her up. I'm done here."

Kane noticed a flashing red light on the screen array and turned to the others. "That will be Kalo. I'm getting out of these scrubs and going to see what he's found." He followed Wolfe out of the door.

"Wait for us." Jenna hurried out of the door behind him.

By the time they piled into Wolfe's office, he was sitting at his desk staring at the screen. Kane leaned against the wall and waited. Wolfe had his phone on speaker.

"Are you absolutely sure?" Wolfe stared at the screen. "Send me the comparison files." He leaned back in his chair, rubbing his chin thoughtfully as he perused the files.

"I'm sure." Kalo's voice came through the speaker. "It's the same Poppy Anderson I've been tracking since she hightailed it from Black Rock Falls. Her DNA profile and prints are on file. It's her. I'm one hundred percent certain. DNA don't lie."

TWENTY-NINE

Dumbfounded, Jenna stared at Wolfe. "What? This can't be happening. You're telling me that Poppy Anderson is capable of murder? That woman is more interested in what color lipstick she's wearing than killing people."

"It would account for the different MO in this case. I figure stabbing a person in the heart would be easier than trying to strangle them to death." Wolfe turned to the coffee machine and started feeding pods into the receptacle. "She's involved or her DNA wouldn't be on the body. Just how much do you know about this woman? It makes me wonder why she was hanging around the conferences and trying to obtain information about forensics when the county she lives in rarely sees more than a traffic violation."

"I see her more as a homewrecker than a psychopath." Jo dropped into a chair with a sigh. "She obviously likes to be the center of attention, and this could be the manifestation of borderline personality disorder or even narcissistic tendencies. It would take an overwhelming fit of jealousy to commit murder, and as none of our victims have been reported missing, I would dismiss them as being somebody's spouse or girlfriend.

It would be very unusual for a husband not to report his wife missing unless he was involved in her disappearance, and then there's the family as well. No, in all honesty, I can't see Poppy being the killer."

"Maybe, she's sending us a message?" Kane stretched his long legs and looked at Wolfe. "She'd likely assume that we'd search for her when she went missing, even though she sent us a cover story. She would know Jenna wouldn't take the email she sent us as gospel." He took a cup of coffee that Wolfe handed him. "I figure we need to take a closer look at the latent prints on the body. Is there any way we can see all of them at once? I'm wondering if there's a pattern. She would know that the prints would be picked up, and I know for darn sure if I was captured and had the opportunity to leave a message only a medical examiner could see, I would use the same method." He sipped his coffee. "Now we know Poppy is involved, it seems to me the smear of perspiration on the victim's cheek was deliberate. I figure she used her own sweat to leave a message. We just need to find it."

"I'll pull up the images of the body and take a closer look." The phone on Wolfe's desk rang and everyone's attention moved to him. "Shane Wolfe." He flicked the phone onto speaker. "That's good. Did you determine the species and origin?"

"Yeah, we sure did." The voice on the other end sounded excited. *"It's a native local species of moss and goes by the name of luminous moss—Schistostega pennata. It's found in caves. The soil sample is indicative of human habitation. We found traces of urea consistent with human excrement from a septic tank or similar. I'll email you the full report."*

"Thanks for prioritizing this for me. I owe you one." Wolfe disconnected and looked at Jenna. "This information confirms the location of the victims. The killer is keeping them in one of the thousands of caves in Black Rock Falls."

Consumed by the idea of finding a message on the body of the last victim, Jenna nodded, but right now, nothing else mattered. This was the breakthrough they'd been waiting for. Why was everyone wasting time discussing possible locations? She wanted to push Wolfe out of the door and into the laboratory to hurry him along. Without more information on the location, the chances of finding anyone in the caves riddling Black Rock Falls would be like finding a needle in a haystack. "That's valuable information but our priority right now is if Poppy left a message on the victim. Do you mind leaving the discussion on where the victims were being held for now and go see the images you took of the latent prints?"

"Sure." Wolfe picked up his coffee cup and headed for the door and then paused to look at her. "It will take time. I'll take a quick look now, but if I don't find anything, I'll keep looking. Sometimes I need to try different light filters to get anything."

With her mind reeling at the implications of this information, Jenna turned to Kane. "You know Poppy. Do you consider her capable of stabbing someone to death? Would she do something like that to save her own life?"

"I don't know Poppy well enough to give you an answer to that, Jenna." Kane walked beside her toward the laboratory at the end of the hallway. "She could be with the killer as an accomplice but what if she's been kidnapped by a psychopath? Who knows what a person might do to save her own life? Everybody's different and she hasn't the training that we have. I honestly don't think Poppy would ever put her life on the line for anyone but herself."

"So not really cop material?" Jo fell into step beside Jenna. "Which makes me wonder why you didn't stand up to Mayor Petersham and allow her to join your department in the first place."

Jenna snorted. "Trust me, I had no choice in the matter. Unfortunately, that woman can twist people around her little finger. It was by Mayor Petersham's request that she join our team for a trial period. He controls our budget and it was a personal request, so what else could I do? She only lasted one day, after all, and sent in her resignation after being rebuffed by Dave. She'd gotten it into her head that he'd invited her to work with him."

"I wasn't that hard on her." Kane shrugged. "I would have been willing to train her but not if her intention was to come between me and Jenna."

"You know it was, Dave. She tried to push her way into our group at the convention." Jo let out a long sigh. "She didn't stop at Dave. She had Wolfe and Carter in her sights as well. Carter could see straight through her, but then it takes a player to recognize a player." She grinned at Jenna. "Wolfe just totally ignored her as if she were part of the furniture or something." She giggled. "I've seen Dave give people the death stare, but Wolfe takes it to a whole new level."

They followed Wolfe into the laboratory. Moments later the screen array lit up, displaying the latent prints on the victim's body. Jenna's stomach gave a twist of apprehension as she examined each image closely looking for a pattern. As Wolfe presented the areas where he'd discovered latent prints, he rotated the images and enlarged them, but no message showed.

Disheartened, Jenna sighed. "Is this everything?"

"Nope, I have images of every part of the body taken at the scene and when we brought her into the lab." Wolfe projected more images onto the screens. "I found evidence of sweat smeared on her cheek and across the skin of her belly." He indicated to the areas of interest. "Obviously there were prints there as well, but I found the majority on the forearms of the victim and concentrated on using them for identification."

Intrigued, Jenna stared at the screen array with renewed interest. "There must be something here. Is there anything we can do to enhance the images of the sweat to get a better look? It seems to me if I was going to leave a message, it would be easier for me to write it in sweat."

"Yeah." Wolfe smiled at her. "I have a few more tricks up my sleeve we can use. Like I said, it will take time. I'll need to review all the primary images of the body. I'll call you if I find anything."

Disappointed, Jenna led the way to the door. She turned toward Kane as they headed for the Beast. "At least we know the women are being held underground in a damp cave." She rubbed her temples in desperation. "I can only hope we get to squeeze information out of one of our suspects, because right now, I could have people scouring the entire county and just maybe, in about three years or so, we might find the darn cave."

THIRTY

"This doesn't add up." Rio stacked the cartons in the back of his truck. "Everything we've found dates to the time Sam Bright was doing time. He can't be kidnapping women from a jail cell. If he'd taken them before he was arrested, they'd have died while he was doing his time."

"Unless his cousin cared for them?" Rowley pushed more boxes into the truck. "They seem pretty close, and Derek looks like a follower to me. I figure Sam told him to go and burn the evidence because he already mentioned to Kane he'd noticed the FBI in town. Maybe he believes we're getting too close for comfort."

"I found these picture albums." Carter laid them on the hood of his cruiser. "It seems to me Mrs. Bright wasn't a fancy dresser and she remained virtually the same size throughout her life. The album is filled with photographs of her, from a wedding day right up to pictures with her grandsons. She was a small woman, probably around five-three. I don't figure she'd have any use for the clothes. None of them would have fit her or been her style. She didn't have any daughters or female kinfolk." He looked up at the two deputies. "These were stored here by somebody else, unless her husband was a trendy cross-dresser."

"Anything's possible." Rowley shrugged. "I'm sure the Bright cousins would know the answer to that question."

Rio locked up the house and then climbed into his truck. "I'm sure Jenna will be interested in what we found but it's not enough evidence to charge anyone. I'm not sure it's even enough evidence to question these guys. We have no proof whatsoever that they even belong to them. I can't find any prints on any of them, apart from the boxes the cousins previously opened. Whoever stored them in the cellar was wearing gloves. This in itself seems to link with the current murders. The killer is extra careful not to leave any evidence behind. Although that plastic bag filled with women's underwear we found in the old nightstand at the back of the cellar might be his downfall."

"I sure hope so." Rowley climbed into the passenger seat. "It will be interesting to know what the autopsy showed. Let's hope it's a breakthrough and we see the end of this killing spree."

"I'll meet you back at the office." Carter pushed the photograph albums into an evidence bag and placed them in the back of the cruiser.

When they arrived at the office, they found Jenna in the conference room with Kane and Jo. Rio waited for Jenna to finish her call with Kalo. She was intent on locating underground prison cells or similar in the Black Rock Falls area. She had a map of the county spread out on the desk and everyone's attention was fixed on Jenna's strained expression.

"Go way back. We might be looking at historical sites." Jenna rubbed her temples. "Any industrial areas that might have been converted into cells at one time. I recall there was an old railroad track that went through part of the mountain and some of it was converted into places for the railway workers to live. We need all the information you can find on anything built underground in the last fifty years or even longer." She leaned back in her chair and sighed. "Thanks, Bobby." She looked up at Rio and nodded at Rowley. "We've had a breakthrough. Poppy Anderson's DNA is all over the last victim." She brought them up to date.

"I can't believe she's involved." Rowley removed his hat and moved it around in his hands. "A victim maybe. She did go missing sudden like. Poppy doesn't seem the type to brutally murder women—and all the victims suffered sexual abuse."

"I'm not making any assumptions on her capabilities to murder. She could be an accomplice. I do know she doesn't like other women. All of them are rivals to her. For all we know, this could be a trap aimed right at me and Jo." Jenna pushed a strand of hair behind one ear and shrugged. "If she's innocent and trying to send us a message, we'll need to search any locations undergrounded suitable for possible jail cells—or that have been used in the past. Kalo will have a list of sites for us soon. For now, we'll keep moving the investigation forward with the list of suspects. What have you got for me?"

Rio gave them a rundown of what they'd discovered at the house. "I figure unless Derek is involved and was keeping the victims alive while his cousin was in jail, these guys are telling the truth."

"That's one possible scenario." Jenna turned to Kane. "What do you think? Are they guilty?"

"No, not a hope." Kane scrolled through the files on his laptop. "Sam Bright was arrested and then given bail until his case went to court. A psychopath would never have risked leaving witnesses alive. He'd been arrested for indecent assault, not murder, and would have believed that part of his life was still private. Psychopaths don't trust anyone but themselves, so there's no way he would have risked leaving his cousin in charge of his captives."

"I agree." Jo nodded. "Just being arrested would've triggered him into a frenzy of murder. He would have killed them all and if they were secured underground, he would have left them there to rot because he knew that no one would have found them."

"Have you made a list of everything you removed from the house?" Jenna leaned back in her chair and looked at Rowley.

"Yeah. I took photographs and we dusted for prints." Rowley nodded. "It's already in the file."

Rio scrolled through the notes on his iPad and the printer in the corner of the room sprang into action. "I'll print copies of the list of evidence we removed. I've sent the image files to your email address already."

"Okay thanks." Jenna smiled at them. "I'll take it from here. When you've taken everything into the evidence room and written it up, you can both take a break."

"Do I get a break too?" Carter tossed a toothpick into his mouth and grinned at her.

"No." Jenna lifted her chin and stared at him. "I want the details on the photograph albums and the bag of underwear you found." She tapped her bottom lip and looked at Jo. "How attached would a killer be to his trophies? Would he react when we tell him we have confiscated them all?"

"Yeah, he'll react." Jo thought for a beat. "It may be subtle or crazy—there's no telling."

"Okay." Jenna nodded. "I'll talk to them." She turned her attention back to Carter. "Leave the underwear with me. I'll go and show them and see if we get a reaction." She looked at Rio and Rowley. "Just enter the entire boxes into evidence. Number them and, if necessary, we'll get Wolfe to go through them and make an inventory if they're relevant to the case."

Rio nodded. "Sure." He turned to Rowley. "Let's get at it." They headed for the door.

THIRTY-ONE

After allowing the new evidence to percolate through her mind, Jenna turned to Kane. "I'm trying to decide which of the Bright cousins we should interview first. Who do you think?"

"Derek seems to be the more volatile of the pair and is subordinate to his cousin. He might be the weak link, so I suggest we see what he has to say first."

"I agree." Jo collected the coffee cups from the desk and put them in the sink. "If we go into the interview as if we know they're guilty, he might roll over on Sam."

"I'm not so sure." Kane stood and collected a statement pad from a pile on the desk. "If Sam is dominant over him, he might be too intimidated by him to risk it. He'd be thinking ahead of time. If they ended up in the same jail, Sam would be gunning for him."

Jenna gathered her things from the desk, pushed the evidence bag of underwear into a brown paper sack, and stood. "Okay, let's get this over with." She led the way through the office and down to the interview rooms.

After swiping her card at the door, Jenna moved inside. The stink of unwashed male crawled up her nostrils as she stared at

Derek Bright. He sat on the floor with his back to the wall his head in his hands and looked up at her with a belligerent expression on his face. "Mr. Bright we'd like to ask you a few questions. Would you mind joining us at the table?"

"I've been sitting here for hours." Derek climbed slowly to his feet and took a seat at the table.

She read him his rights and sat down opposite with Kane and Jo on either side. "Do you agree to answer a few questions?"

"Let's get on with it. I have things to do." Derek leaned on the table and picked at his fingernails. "What do you want to know?"

Jenna switched on the recording device, introduced all parties, and then leaned forward in her chair and looked at Derek. "As you are aware, we executed a search warrant on your premises this afternoon. We have confiscated boxes of clothing and a bag of underwear from the cellar. We have reason to believe that these objects may be related to three murder victims found in Black Rock Falls over the last few days. Is there anything you'd like to say about the clothes you were burning when we dropped by this afternoon?"

"They're just old clothes." Derek gave an irritated shrug. "Are you saying my grandma was a murderer? We buried her over three months ago, so how do you figure the bodies are showing up now?"

"We don't think that your grandma is a murderer." Kane rolled his eyes. "I guess you had a big job cleaning out the house after she passed?"

"Not so much the house. She kept that clean enough, but the cellar was filled with useless junk." Derek linked his hands behind his neck and leaned back in the chair. "I gave a box of trinkets to Goodwill. The other stuff had a strange smell about it, so we decided to burn it."

Needing more information about the trinkets, Jenna leaned forward. "What kind of trinkets?"

"Aw, you know, the things women wear but aren't worth much." Derek dropped his arms and shrugged. "Bracelets, beads, and earrings but nothing precious. I dropped them by this morning."

Jenna exchanged a meaningful glance with Kane, and he stood and left the room. She didn't need to tell him to hightail it down to Goodwill and ask them for the box of trinkets that Derek had given them. She turned her attention back to Derek. "What do you use formaldehyde for at home?"

"Formald... what?" Derek snorted and glared at her. "What are you talking about? I don't know what that is."

"Our tracker dog picked up the scent of formaldehyde at your house this morning. In fact, it was close to where you were burning the clothes. It's a chemical used for preservation and disinfecting."

"Sam said something leaked all over them, maybe that was what he was talking about. I don't know. He wasn't specific." Derek eyed her curiously. "You'll have to ask him."

"Do you think Sam stored these things at his grandma's while he was in jail?" Jo flicked him a glance. "Do you think some of these items could have come from the women he raped? Some men keep trophies."

"Nah, not Sam. He didn't rape anyone; he was set up." He shook his head. "I know he removed all my grandma's clothes from her bedroom and took them to Goodwill. He didn't want to keep anything of hers and told me to burn everything in the cellar. Wouldn't he want to keep them if they were his trophies?"

This man was acting very calm and cooperative. Wanting to see a reaction, Jenna picked up the brown paper sack from the floor beside the chair and spilled the evidence bag onto the desk. Watching Derek's face closely she pointed to the skimpy women's underwear visible through the plastic. "What do you know about these?"

"Absolutely nothing." Derek gave the evidence bag a casual glance and stared back at her. "I've never seen them before in my life."

"So, it's okay if we burn these?" Jo pulled the plastic bag toward her.

"That's fine by me." Derek shrugged and leaned back in the chair. "Are we done yet?"

"Soon. Do you know Poppy Anderson?" Jo lifted her gaze to him, pen raised above her notebook.

"Never heard of her." Derek shook his head. "Can I leave now?"

With absolutely no reaction from him whatsoever, Jenna had nowhere else to go with the questioning and pushed to her feet. "Yeah, we're done here." She switched off the recording device and collected her things. "I'll send someone down to take you back to your ranch. Thank you for your cooperation."

Outside in the hallway Jenna turned to Jo. "I didn't get anything from that did you?"

"Not a thing. He has no attachment to those items of cloth-ing." Jo let out a long sigh. "There's no charges to answer. Like he said, there's no law against burning rubbish in a fire pit on your own property."

Jenna leaned against the wall, hugging the statement books to her chest. "We'll likely get the same story from Sam Bright, although I will be interested to know why he told Kane that he was living alone."

"One thing that puzzles me is where the clothes came from." Jo scratched her head with a pen. "If they don't belong to her grandsons, who else in the family should we be looking at?"

"I guess we'll have to ask Sam Bright." Jenna pushed off the wall and headed to the next interview room. She flashed her card and walked inside.

Sam Bright was sitting at the table with his head resting on his arms. Wasting no time, Jenna read him his rights and turned on the recorder. "You know the deal, Sam. We have a few questions about the clothes Derek was burning. You can either answer them and get out of here fast or we can call your lawyer."

"I've already answered Deputy Kane's questions at the house earlier." Sam gave them both an appraising stare. "What else do you need to know?"

Brushing off the skin-crawling feeling of disgust his penetratingly slow up-and-down gaze gave her, Jenna dropped her things onto the table and sat down. "You informed my deputy that you lived alone. I spoke to your cousin Derek and he told me he was living with you. Why did you lie about that?"

"Because it's none of your business who I live with, and Derek owns half of the property." Sam leaned back in his chair casually. "The rules of my parole say I'm not allowed to mix with criminals and my cousin doesn't have as much as a parking violation." He gave Jenna a slow smile. "What else can I help you with, Sheriff?"

The back of Jenna's neck prickled and she could imagine the horror of waking up and finding this man's smiling face looking down at her. She'd read his case file and wondered how a man who broke into women's houses to rape them had been given parole. "Do you own the women's clothes that were in your grandmother's house?" She tossed the plastic bag of underwear on the desk in front of him. "As we informed you earlier, we conducted a legal search of your ranch today and discovered this underwear in a nightstand at the back of the cellar. Are these garments part of your collection of trophies?" She eyeballed him. "I do know just how much men like you like to keep trophies of your crimes. You like to relive every minute, don't you?"

"I never raped anyone." Sam leaned forward on the desk, an ugly expression cut his face into hard lines. "Those women invited me to their beds. It was a sex game, is all. I did time for something I didn't do." He jabbed a finger toward the evidence bag. "If you took that underwear from the house, then they belonged to my grandma. If you think I'd find them sexy, you're wrong. They disgust me."

"So, you wouldn't mind if we burned them?" Jo grabbed up the bag and shoved it into the brown paper sack.

"Go right ahead." Sam smiled at her. "And if you removed all the other boxes from the cellar, I should thank you. It saves us the work of cleaning it out."

Trying another tact, Jenna paused the interview to write notes. She needed time to allow him to cool down before she questioned him from a different angle. She raised her head and looked at him. He appeared supremely confident—maybe too confident. "We find it hard to believe that the clothes belonged to your grandmother. None of them would have fit her and, from the photographs of her we found, they don't appear to be the type of fashion she would wear. If they don't belong to you, is there anyone else in the family who could have stored them in your grandma's cellar?"

"Nope." Sam let out a long sigh. "This is why we inherited the house. There's no one else alive in the family."

Although Sam Bright made Jenna's skin crawl, like his cousin she had no solid evidence against him. She couldn't prove that he'd stored the clothes at his grandma's house. She hoped that Kane got to the Goodwill store before they sold the trinkets. There might be a small chance that someone would recognize them from previous crimes. Her gut told her Grandma Bright had known the killer. She looked at Sam. "Did your grandma ever have people staying with her?"

"Yeah, she used to rent out rooms during the hunting season." Sam stretched. "She had a notice in the general store window. It was how she supplemented her pension."

With this information, Jenna could feel the end game slipping out of her grasp. Anyone could have left the clothing there.

Perhaps a variety of visitors over many years. She nodded. "Do you recall if she kept records or the names of people who stayed with her?"

"Nope and I never found anything in her papers. Her taxes are paid and the lawyer handled the estate. Like everything else in the house, what we didn't want we took to the landfill." Sam shrugged. "It's not like we were close. Sometimes we'd visit her just to see if she had enough food, but she usually waved us away. She preferred to be living on her own."

"Do you know Poppy Anderson?" Jo stared at him.

"Nope." Sam shrugged. "I've never met her."

Jenna glanced at Jo to see if she had any more questions. Jo gave a slight shake of her head and Jenna switched off the recording device and collected her things. "That's all for today. Thank you for your cooperation. One of my deputies will be along to give you a ride back to your ranch."

Disappointed, Jenna led the way out of the interview room, and they headed along the hallway with Jo keeping step beside her. "That was a waste of time, they gave us nothing we could use and we have no idea if one of Mrs. Bright's visitors paid her to store the clothes there."

"Well, if we've stumbled over a stash of trophies, one thing is for sure, they don't belong to the Bright cousins." Jo touched Jenna's arm. "This is the problem with psychopaths. They can hide in plain sight and don't follow any particular type of person. If we walked past someone on the sidewalk, they could be a killer and we'd never know."

"I still have Lucas Davies to interview. He'll be back in town in the morning." Jenna glanced at her. "I know it might seem like a lost cause at the moment but I'm not giving up yet."

"If you can get someone to cover that for you, I've been offered an opportunity to interview the Michelangelo Killer in the morning, if you're interested in coming?" Jo's expression became animated. "I can't guarantee that he'll give us any information to help with this case, but he might. I figure it's worth trying. The prison warden informed me that he was keen to be included in my book."

Wondering how she could go and talk to a convicted psychopathic murderer, with a killer roaming around town, Jenna stopped walking and turned to her. "How could he assist us with solving this case?"

"He'd be interested because the current spate of murders are very close to his MO." Jo pushed the hair from her eyes and sighed. "I agree it's a long shot but I'm sure any insight into the mind of the killer we're dealing with would be an advantage. I'm banking on the fact that the Michelangelo Killer will be looking at a copycat as hero worship. Maybe if we give him details of the murders, he might be able to predict our killer's next move. We wouldn't have long to question him—no longer than half an hour." She raised both eyebrows in question and looked at Jenna. "You have deputies available to investigate any further leads that come in, and I figure it will be time well spent."

Thinking, Jenna tugged on her bottom lip and then nodded. "We're chasing smoke at the moment. I guess taking a few hours to gain an inside perspective of the case would be to our advantage. If Carter can fly us there, it would save time."

"Yes, that's a given, but it will be an early start." Jo indicated with her chin toward the men sitting in the conference room. "Do you need to run it past Kane before you decide? I'll need time for Carter to submit a flight plan."

Jenna shook her head. "No, of course not. I'm in, but Kane will be coming along too. If we're going to be alone inside a room with Bruno Vito, I want someone on the outside watching our backs. Vito has nothing to lose and might enjoy one last killing spree. I know prison guards can be bought and I'm not taking the chance."

THIRTY-TWO

Swirling mist from the river spilled across the blacktop and filled the sidewalk as Susie Hartwig stepped into the alleyway outside Aunt Betty's Café. After locking the door behind her, she slipped her purse over one shoulder, the weight of her Glock a comfort against her hip. Raised in Black Rock Falls, she'd never needed to carry a weapon for personal protection. As little as five years ago, most folks never locked their doors and children could run wild without fear—but not now. She'd spoken her concerns to Sheriff Alton and the next moment she'd been on the practice range with Deputy Kane. Each time she walked home late at night, his words of advice ran like an earwig through her mind—just like now.

"If someone comes at you or grabs you with the intent to do you harm, don't hesitate. Empty the clip."

Bone weary from working a twelve-hour shift, she made her way out into the darkness with one hand resting on her purse. She took the same way home every night and stepped out with confidence. Since moving to a neat house on Maple, it was easier to walk the few hundred yards than drive her truck, and she enjoyed the solitude of a moonlit stroll after a long shift in a noisy diner. The alleyway behind the diner cut through from Main to Maple and had a streetlight, courtesy of Mayor Peter-sham. The orange-yellow glow appeared to hover over the swirling mist, making the dumpsters look like ships floating on a golden ocean. Always cautious, Susie made sure to listen for any sounds and peer around corners before moving forward. She'd lived in Black Rock Falls long enough not to be naïve about her personal safety. People died in this town and she took extra precautions every time she worked the late shift.

Her mind was on the following morning. She didn't have to show for work until noon and she'd made plans to visit the beauty parlor. Sighing with relief as she reached the end of the alleyway, she made a left into Maple. The houses here were some of the first built during the establishment of the town. They spread out with luxurious-size yards, most of them set back from the road. The gardens displayed an abundance of flowers and their scent hung in the air with a potpourri of perfumes. The moon sat in a cloudless sky—a witch's moon—but not enough to brighten the night. Luckily, streetlights spaced out along the sidewalk offered patches of muted light. Usually, they gave her enough illumination to walk home in confidence, but not tonight. Ahead in the darkness something moved, and she slowed her step. It was unusual to see anyone parked on the side of the road, and the town car seemed out of place. Most people in these parts owned trucks, apart from some of the older ladies who preferred to drive a compact around town.

Wary, she moved closer. Night had turned everything into shades of gray and blended edges, making it difficult to see anything clearly between the streetlights. The mist swirled around a vehicle with the hood raised and somebody leaned over the engine with a flashlight. She heaved a sigh of relief. It wasn't a serial killer lurking in the dark, just some poor soul having car trouble, and by the condition of the vehicle, they probably didn't have the spare cash to join the auto club. As she moved closer the light went out and she could hear muffled curses coming from under the hood. The man was obviously in trouble and in Black Rock Falls stopping to offer assistance was the neighborly thing to do. Stepping a little closer but keeping a good distance from him, she raised her voice. "Do you need help? Can I call someone for you?"

"Nah, I don't want to drag someone out at this time of night. It's a simple repair—just a loose wire. I almost had it when my phone died. If you have a flashlight, I could fix it in a few seconds." He turned and looked at her, but she couldn't make out his expression under the shadow of his hat. "It was impossible trying to juggle my phone and replace the wire at the same time. Do you think you could hold your phone flashlight over the engine for me so I can repair it? It won't take more than a minute or so."

The decision to help him came naturally. Making people happy was part of her job and the success of Aunt Betty's Café since she'd taken over proved her proficiency. Even so her heart pounded in her chest as the voice in her head sent out a warning. She drew a deep breath and opened her purse. Her hand brushed the pistol as she pulled out her phone, turned on the flashlight, and moved closer to peer under the hood.

"Oh, dammit." The man straightened and shook his head. "I've dropped the nut. I'll never find it." He looked at her and his mouth turned down. "I have spares in my toolbox in the trunk. Could you bring the light?" He walked to the back of the sedan and popped the trunk.

Reluctantly, Susie followed. Her flashlight picked out a man in his late thirties, average in height and wearing coveralls. He was cursing under his breath and getting agitated. She aimed her light to the open toolbox. "Maybe I should call someone before my battery is dead too."

"It's just I can't see so well without my glasses. Can you

grab one for me?" He shrugged and pointed at the toolbox. "In there, a nut about a quarter inch wide."

Moving the light over the toolbox, Susie made out a section with oily nuts and bolts. She bent over and sorted through them. She lifted one between thumb and finger and turned to him. "Is this the one you need?"

Pain shot through the side of her head, and she bit her tongue. Her knees buckled and she dropped her phone, the light filling the trunk. Terrified but surprisingly alert, the advice Deputy Kane had given her rushed into her mind in crystal clarity and she pushed one hand into her purse. Her fingers closed around the handle of her weapon but fell away impotent as agony seared a red-hot path through her temple from a second blow. She tasted blood and the reek of oil and gas filled her nostrils. The world tipped sideways and curled in at the edges as she tipped forward. Her purse was torn from her arm, the light from her phone vanished, and she tumbled headlong into the trunk. Red spots danced before her eyes and with her head exploding with incredible torture, she sank into merciful darkness.

THIRTY-THREE

TUESDAY

Enjoying the crisp fresh morning, Kane checked the water feeder and tossed a couple of salt blocks to the feed he'd added to the manger inside the fence line. They'd extended the perimeter of the security fence to include the back paddock and a part of the woods bordering the edge of the ranch. The paddock was rich and lush with grass, and with no worries of bears or other predators breaking through the security fencing, they could leave the horses to run free during the summer. Kane derived a great deal of pleasure from grooming them and a day didn't go by when he didn't tend to them. Gathering the grooming equipment from the fence post, he headed back to the barn. Carter was completing a preflight check of the chopper, which he'd parked in the front yard so they could have a quick getaway this morning. He gave him a wave. "Are we good to go at seven?"

"Yeah." Carter adjusted his Stetson and ambled over toward him. "I figure we should forget the workout this morning. Time is getting away from us." He grinned at Kane. "I think that's the first time I've ever seen you show up this late to do your chores." He chuckled. "Are you still in honeymoon mode?"

Kane returned his smile. "I plan to be in the same mode right up to and beyond our fiftieth wedding anniversary, so you better get used to it." He allowed a small hum of contentment to slip past his lips. "It sure is good being married to Jenna. I figure I'm still in the disbelieving phase. I never thought it would happen but I'm sure glad it did." He bent down to rub Duke's ears and then straightened. Carter obviously had something else to say to him.

"It can be tough on a woman, living with guys like us." Carter peered into the distance and sighed. "We need someone who understands that were not exactly normal. It's not easy finding someone, especially if you make the mistake of dating someone in the military. Most times they have their own ghosts to put to rest and you sure don't need two people carrying that burden into a marriage."

Not intending on discussing the past with Carter, Kane nodded in agreement. What was in his and Jenna's past was need-to-know, and Carter didn't need to know, that was for darn sure. He cleared his throat. "I'm going to take a shower and start breakfast. See you in about twenty minutes?"

"Yeah, sure." Carter gave him a wave and headed to the cottage.

The moment he walked into the house he found Jenna in full sheriff mode. He could hear her on the phone issuing orders to Rowley. While they were at the state pen interviewing the Michelangelo Killer, Rio and Rowley would be hunting down Lucas Davies.

"Before you do that"—Jenna pushed a strand of hair behind her ear and acknowledged him with a smile—"itemize and photograph the box of trinkets that Kane rescued from Goodwill, send the images to Kalo, and ask him to get them out to all precincts. We might hit gold if anyone recognizes them. Then take them over to Wolfe." She disconnected.

It had been Kane's lucky day. When he arrived at the Goodwill store, the box that Derek Bright had dropped by stood untouched on the front counter. Not wanting to make a fuss about the trinkets being possibly part of a murder investigation, he'd offered a generous donation for the entire box. After much raising of eyebrows, the two elderly women behind the counter had nodded in agreement. He'd left the store with "come by again soon" following him out the door.

He sat down to remove his boots and looked at Jenna. "Any updates on possible places the killer is holding his victims?"

"Not yet." Jenna's brow furrowed. "Kalo called. He's sending the list of possible cave sites but isn't optimistic. Historical sites are signposted and frequently visited by hikers. I doubt anyone would risk keeping women there. It's summer and anyone could wander in, so it's doubtful our killer is using them. I called Atohi Blackhawk. He knows the area and couldn't think of anywhere suitable for actual jail cells. He's going to speak to his elders. If he gets any information, he'll call me this afternoon."

Kane stood and nodded. "I'm still confused about Poppy's hand in this, and if she's helping the killer, why wouldn't they be making sure she doesn't leave any DNA? The scenes have been so clean it's out of character."

"I figure we'll find her holed up with the killer. I'm hoping Kalo gives us a place to start a search." Jenna looked up at him. "We can't run around blindly all over the county. They could be anywhere. You know as well as I do a psychopath who has a hatred for women could flip on her at any time. I just hope we find them before she becomes the next victim."

Kane smiled at her. "I know you will. Carter says wheels up at seven." He headed for the shower.

Over breakfast Kane listened with interest as Jenna discussed Jo's list of interview questions for Bruno Vito, the Michelangelo Killer. He sipped his coffee and turned to Jo. "You mentioned this man was married and his wife had no idea that he'd been killing multiple women over a long period." He placed his empty cup on the table. "I'm not familiar with double-life psychopathy. Is there anything we should know before heading into this situation?"

"You won't be in contact with him at all." Jenna squeezed his arm. "He has agreed to speak to Jo and me. I figure he believes he can intimidate us because we're women. He might clam up if you and Carter are in the room."

Kane shook his head. "I figure he'll be in his passive mode, the one he used with his wife, which makes me wonder whether he'll actually discuss his murders with you. Whereas talking to Carter and me, he'd have the chance to boast about his kills." He stood and collected the plates from the table and rinsed them in the sink before stacking the dishwasher.

"Double-life psychopathy isn't the same as personality disorder syndrome." Jo met his gaze. "It's a person who can compartmentalize their lives into two sections that don't cross at any time. They can access the side of their personality they need to deal with the current situation. They switch easily without any problem whatsoever. In fact, I would even suggest that after a kill—should the need arise—Vito would be able to portray the loving husband even though he had blood on his hands."

Kane leaned back on the counter and nodded. "Would it be a form of disassociation or just associated behavior? That seems to be more prevalent in psychopaths."

"Disassociating? Yes, as in managing to forget that he'd just brutally murdered a person and then go home and act normally with his kids. However, many people compartmentalize in their daily lives to cope with unpleasant situations or memories. I'm not saying hiding emotions is a healthy thing to do but it's widespread and quite normal. I'm sure in your time in the military it was necessary for you to compartmentalize bad memories to remain focused on your missions, the same as Carter." She smiled at him. "It might have been necessary at the time, but you don't live a double life because of it, do you?"

Kane caught Jenna's wide-eyed expression suddenly dropping to her coffee cup and shook his head. "Nope, I'm just a deputy in a small town in Montana. My days of working for Uncle Sam are over."

"Time to go if you want to make it back here before noon." Carter stood, scraping back his chair and picking up his hat from the seat next to him. He looked at Zorro. "Stay here with Duke. It's playtime." The Doberman shook himself and gave a happy bark before nudging Duke toward the doggie door.

"Well, won't you look at that." Jenna chuckled. "That dog does understand everything you say."

"Well, he's always been a little uptight." Carter rubbed his chin and looked at the dogs crawling through the hatch. "He needed to be trained to a level where he didn't get blown up searching for explosives, but when we moved to Snakeskin Gully, I introduced a few more commands so he could unwind during our downtime." He pushed his hat on his head and headed for the door. "Wheels up in five."

THIRTY-FOUR

The prison had its own particular bad smell, and it took all of Jenna's concentration not to cover her nose with her hand. Summer had made it worse, and the stink of perspiration mixed with some foul odors seeping from the kitchen would make vomit smell good. She walked through the prison following behind Kane with Jo beside her and Carter watching their backs. The corridor divided the exercise yards and was the only way to get to the interview rooms. Being paraded in front of the inmates, all intent on spitting or hurling abuse at them, unsettled her. Although her shirt clung to her back from the humidity, just knowing that a few bars separated her from a mob intent on getting even sent shivers down her spine. She'd visited the jail before and this time used earplugs before entering the first dim corridors and moving through security. The last thing she needed was to hear threats from inmates and she hummed a tune to block out the noise. She required a clear head to conduct the interview with Bruno Vito and, ignoring the men pushed against the bars, kept her gaze on Kane's back until they reached the interview room. In the anteroom outside, Kane and Carter could observe through a two-way mirror and hear everything being said inside as long as Jenna activated the intercom. The prison's video equipment would be disabled, but Jo would be recording the session. She glanced at her. Jo appeared to be remarkably calm, as if she interviewed psychopaths on a daily basis.

"I'm not sure what mood the prisoner will be in, we'll just have to play it by ear." Jo, a picture of calm professionalism, smiled at her encouragingly.

Nerves clenched Jenna's stomach, and she took a few steadying breaths as the prisoner entered the room and two guards restrained him using chains attached to the table and floor. She scanned her iPad for the questions they'd decided to ask Vito. With Jo as her wingman, the interview would go as planned. She turned to Kane. "Okay, I'm ready."

"You'd better get your game face on. You're sheet white." Kane rubbed her arms and stared into her eyes. "You've done this before, and this guy is no threat to you. He's agreed to remain in chains. Provided you keep in your seat, he won't be able to reach you."

"Trust me"—Carter looked at her with raised eyebrows—"if he as much as twitches in the wrong direction, we're in there."

Pasting a small smile on her face, Jenna followed Jo into the interview room. Before they sat down, she waited for Jo to introduce her to Bruno Vito. The prisoner staring up at her appeared to be anything but a deranged serial killer. He looked to be around fifty, with dark hair graying at the temples, but what surprised her was his eyes. Big brown soft eyes held an expression of compassion. His smile was welcoming, and knowing this killer's MO chilled her to the bone.

"Sheriff Alton. I've heard so much about you." Vito shook his head slowly. "My, my, how did a little thing like you take down so many serial killers?"

Understanding the charm a psychopath used to influence people, Jenna took the chair opposite him and Jo sat beside her.

"I'm sure we could chat about me all day, but we only have a half an hour to speak to you, and you're so much more interesting than me."

"Not for me, but I'm willing to play your game." He opened his hands as wide as the chains would allow. "Maybe next time you come visit me you can tell me some of the details of your cases."

Taking the opening, Jenna smiled at him. "Funny you should ask, I do have a case that might be of interest to you. We believe he is targeting high-risk victims." She scanned her iPad for images and finding a suitable crime scene photo of one of the victims turned it around to show him. "I believe this man is copying your style, but we can't figure out his motive."

A slow smile crossed Vito's lips as he stared at the image. In an instant his eyes changed to a predator's. Trying to act nonchalant, Jenna leaned back in her chair. She'd seen that look so many times before. "Do you have an opinion on this killer?"

"Are all his victims skinny like this one? Can you show me some more?" Vito dragged his eyes away from the image and looked at her. "I can't give you an opinion on one picture."

"Yeah, you can." Jo cleared her throat. "They are all exactly the same, apart from the last one. The cause of death in the first two was strangulation. In the third, sharp force trauma to the heart."

"The first two, he had plenty of time to create the image or fantasy of his desire, but the third one was rushed." Vito sighed. "I'm guessing you know that already, so why are you really here?"

Jenna exchanged a glance with Jo. It would be better for Jo to question him. She had ways of getting information out of psychopaths and would feed him just enough data to make him believe he was taking control of the interview.

"We're here to talk about you." Jo's gaze hadn't left his face. "What made you kill prostitutes? What did the skewers symbolize? I need information if I'm to add you to my book as one of the most notorious serial killers in the last decade."

"My wife was a social worker who had to deal with prostitutes on a regular basis. She wanted to help them, but mixing with them and bringing germs home to my kids annoyed me." Vito stared at his hands. "She had a notion that those women were forced into spreading their legs, but I can tell you no force was ever involved. Offer them a few bucks and they'd do anything for you. If I waved a twenty at them, they'd climb into my truck, no questions asked." He sighed. "So, I decided to help them find God in the fastest possible way, but before they met their maker, they had to suffer the consequences of their actions." He lifted his head and smiled at them. "Once they were in the car, I'd knock them out and drive them to the place I'd chosen. I'd gag them and use zip ties to restrain them, and then I'd bring them around to enjoy the show. I'd explain to them why they had to die." He shrugged. "It took some time hammering skewers into their heads. After a time, I discovered how to keep them alive until the last one, and by that time, they had repented their sins." He flicked his gaze from one to the other as if gauging their reaction and a smug expression crossed his face. "That's not too graphic for you is it, Sheriff?"

A chill ran down Jenna's spine. He talked so casually, as if discussing doing his laundry rather than taking lives. She swallowed bile and kept her gaze steady. "Not at all. I've seen much worse. Your kills were clean in comparison." She shrugged. "I know you selected prostitutes, but you didn't seem to mind what race they were as long as they were between the ages of approximately twenty-two and twenty-six. How did you decide which ones to kill?"

"I didn't choose them. They decided their own fate by offering me sex and climbing into my vehicle." He snorted with obvious delight. "I didn't have to twist their arm or anything. They made the decision, not me."

"Many of the women you killed were never formally identified. Was that part of your plan as well?" Jo looked up from
taking notes. "Out of the sixteen women you killed, only five
people came forward to claim their bodies."

"It was more than sixteen. I stopped counting at twenty-
five, Agent Wells. You have to understand that these women are
pests." Vito linked his fingers together on the table. "When an
exterminator goes into a house and kills the rats, do you see
notices stapled to trees about missing pet rats? No, you don't
because nobody cares. Prostitutes are the same. They swarm
over the streets spreading disease. I offered them salvation and I
was doing the world a favor by taking them off the streets."

Like Kane had said, psychopaths all convinced themselves
they had a valid reason for murder. Jenna smothered a shudder
of revulsion. Vito's lack of empathy was disturbing, and yet from
the information they had on the case, he was a family man. She
had to ask the question. "Did you ever hurt your wife or kids?"

"Why would I? They didn't prostitute themselves." He
snorted. "I did it to protect them from vermin."

"How did your wife react when she found you'd been
killing prostitutes and then going home to her bed?" Jo was
making copious notes. "Does she or the children visit you in
jail?"

"I don't know how she felt." Vito's hands closed into fists. "I
haven't seen her since the day they arrested me. My kids would
be grown by now and, no, they don't drop by to chat."

"Does it make you angry, as you did this to protect her?" Jo
looked up at him a blank expression on her face.

"I would have liked the opportunity to explain to her, but
she obviously didn't want my side of the story." He shrugged.
"I'm not violent in here and others like me talk to each other.
Everything we do has a reason. I know shrinks figure they know
everything that goes on inside our heads, but you're so wrong.
We don't kill anyone who doesn't deserve it. There may be a

few who murder just for the love of killing. The thrill killers are a different beast. They want instant gratification and are usually ruled by lust, drugs, or are just plain crazy. Those of us who take their time and plan everything, are rarely caught. They could be the person working beside you, a local cop, or even your doctor. We don't fit into a type and usually the stranger-danger tag, or the dirty old man you warn your kids about, is a joke when it comes to most of us. People should me more afraid of the friendly person close by because, as sure as hell, that's where one of us is lurking. My mistake was confessing to my wife, and she went to the cops."

Claustrophobia gripped Jenna by the throat. She wanted to be as far away from this man as possible. Sucking in a breath, she met his gaze. "You say you're not violent anymore, so would you kill again if released? Or did you murder the prostitutes just to prevent them infecting your family?"

"I said I wasn't violent *in here*. Maybe this is because there seems to be a lack of prostitutes on death row." Vito gave Jenna a look that went straight through her in a jolt of terror, and his smile was pure evil. "A psychopath can't change how he thinks, honey, and those do-gooder eggheads who believe a psychopathic killer can be rehabilitated are the crazy ones." He chuckled and leaned forward, staring at her as if waiting for a reaction. "Would I kill if I was released? Now let me think. Yeah, in a heartbeat, but I'd figure out another way of making women suffer. I wouldn't hunt down prostitutes again—I'm over it. Maybe I'd target wives—you know, the newlyweds pushing shopping carts out to the parking lot at night. They're so vulnerable to people like me."

Jenna hadn't as much as blinked. "Wives? Do you have a reason or is it any woman under thirty?"

"I'm locked up because I trusted my wife, but now I know from talking to the guys in here they can be as treacherous as a black swamp. They need their tongues cut out and nailed to a tree. So, I suggest you never let me out because next time you won't be able to stop me."

"Okay, I'll keep that in mind." Jo stared at him expressionless. "If you claim to understand the psychopathic mind as well as you say, why not give me a profile on the man killing high-risk women and dumping them in Black Rock Falls—and a possible motive."

"Sure." Vito straightened in his chair. "You want my advice. Ha-ha, that's amusing. Okay, shoot."

After, Jo had given him the rundown on the current case, leaving nothing out, Jenna allowed him to view the crime scene photographs. They were taking a risk doing this, as any type of stimulation could trigger a psychotic episode. Surprisingly Vito looked at the images with a detached expression on his face. She waited for what seemed like fifteen minutes or so for him to absorb the images. "Well, do you have anything to offer us about the case?"

"The woman you believe to be involved isn't." Vito shook his head emphatically. "No way. Well not in the way you imagine. The domination and rape fantasies are personal, and he wouldn't share it with anyone and sure as hell not with someone he believes to be inferior to him. He might be ordering her to clean up his mess. I figure he'd enjoy seeing her do that, especially if she's trembling and afraid of him." He sighed as if tasting the idea and enjoying it. "You need to understand, this woman means nothing to him... She might as well be a mop or some inanimate object." He slid his gaze to Jo. "This guy has killed before, many times, and can never get enough." He wet his lips as if tasting the tension in the room and looked back at Jenna. "The thrill never goes away. We're always planning the next kill—I am right now. It's just as well I'm shackled. Being this close, I can smell you. Inside my head I'm seeing you squirming in agony."

Refusing to back down, Jenna met his gaze straight on and

lifted her chin. "I'm seeing you crying for your mama when they push that needle in your arm but that's beside the point. Can we get back to the case or is that all you have?"

"Feisty—I like a challenge." Vito smiled at her. "I have insights on psychopaths you can't read in books. I live with them. I know how their minds work and how they differ from each other. You'll get to understand as time goes by there are different types and all with their own demons. It's the demon who guides them that you need to understand—I know everything about how they think, but it will cost you." He shrugged. "I'll give you this one for free, like a 'come get me' offer. From what you've explained, your man is escalating fast and allowing Poppy to live might indicate he's losing control, which makes him unpredictable. Who do you have in your sights as suspects?" Vito pushed the iPad back across the table to Jenna.

After giving him a basic suspect profile, Jenna waited for him to process the information.

"This list of probable suspects is good. Any one of them could be the killer but look for someone with high intelligence. This man is smart." Vito nodded, looking pleased with himself. "If his women are, what did you call them, high risk, I figure you mean prostitutes, itinerants, women who hitchhike or hang out alone in bars, right? If he is killing them, he is selective and in control. Few are reported missing, which allows him to take his time with them. He is using skewers but that's a coincidence. I figure we're worlds apart. This isn't a copycat killer. I used skewers to represent a halo and salvation; this man is following a ritual that symbolizes important things to him." Vito sucked in a breath. "Bad memories from his childhood perhaps." He shrugged and drummed his fingers on the table thinking for a beat. "As no one is going missing from your county, then it's kind of obvious he kidnaps women from different counties or states. So, he travels around, which you've already figured out. Keeping the women alive is unusual. Most of us prefer to catch and kill." He smiled. "The chase is all part of the thrill, so this is unusual. He's keeping them for a specific reason. I would say as he beats and rapes them, his fantasy is domination. He's proving he can control and instill fear in women and needs to prove it over time. I doubt he gets bored with them. They must do something to trigger the final act of murder. He needs the women to validate their own deaths." He met Jenna's gaze with an ice-cold stare. "I would say he is like me in that way and is probably living a double life. It wouldn't be impossible for him to be someone who helps people during the day and kills at night." He turned his attention to Jo. "What did you call me? Ah yes—a classic case of double-life psychopathy. He could be the same."

"What about washing their bodies and displaying them in public? What's with the face mask and skewers? What do they symbolize?" Jo leaned forward slightly, her eyes bright with interest. "This killer seems to have so many facets it's hard to understand his motive."

"Oh really?" Vito chuckled. "You are this high and mighty expert on behavioral analysis and you don't understand the basic visuals we use as stimulation."

"Why don't you spell it out for me?" Jo lifted her chin. "This type of cooperation is very valuable to us. If you agree to continue to assist us, I'll make a request to have you removed from death row. Maybe if you continue to speak to us, I'll throw in a few luxuries as well."

"Okay." Vito pursed his lips. "The mask is pretty simple. It makes all the victims look alike, same as dressing them in negligees. This guy has a specific type of woman on his mind each time he kills. This trait is quite usual for many people like me because it's usually the face of the person who triggered the killing spree in the first place. That's what is on our minds when we feel the need to murder someone." He thought for a spell, staring at his hands and then lifting his gaze back to Jo. "He is like me to some degree. I would say the women he chooses do something that trigger the need to kill them, but killing them straight away is too easy. He needs to punish them for their sins, and once he is satisfied, he takes their lives. Bathing them and placing the mask over their faces gives them back their innocence."

"What about the skewers placed down the spine like a porcupine?" Jo paused her pen above her notebook. "What do you make of that?"

"It's obscure and only something that triggers a memory for him." Vito sighed. "If he moves around for work, then you could assume these women are hitchhikers. Maybe, he offers them a ride and place to stay. If so, they'd get willingly into his private vehicle. He'd take them to the place he's keeping them, which would be isolated, because he wouldn't want anyone disturbing him during his ritual. One thing is for sure, it wouldn't be close to where he lives or he'd risk being seen coming and going." He let out a long breath. "The displaying them is a myth and something shrinks believe is part of our tormented psyche. It means nothing and has no significance. The ritual was over the moment they died. The woman meant nothing to him anymore. He was just dumping the garbage." He stared at Jo. "I could fill your book for you with reasons psychopaths commit murder, but that's all I'm saying. Get me a deal and we'll talk again." He turned his head toward the door. "Guard."

Jenna waited for him to shuffle out of the door and turned to Jo. "That had to be one of the most terrifying interviews I have ever conducted."

"It was brilliant." Jo gave her a wide smile. "He really believed he'd taken control of the interview, didn't he? We milked valuable information out of him and I watched him go through every stage of his psychopathy. I hope we get the chance to speak to him again. That, my friend, was an interview behavioral analysts can only dream about."

THIRTY-FIVE

Head throbbing and eyelids heavy, Susie Hartwig dragged herself back to consciousness. Dim light surrounded her, and the cold from the hard surface beneath her seeped into her bones. Too afraid to move, she lay still and listened. Hearing nothing, she lifted her hands and ran her fingers over the back of her head and then peered at them, expecting to see blood. Her eyesight was out of focus, but she could make out the black granite walls surrounding a small room with a mattress on the floor, and a sink and toilet. Pushing down waves of panic she tried to control her fear. She'd read books about surviving situations like this. It had been advised by Mayor Petersham after the first six or so serial killers had come to town. Staying calm could be the difference between life or death. Swallowing her fear, she assessed her situation. Her first priority was her safety and the second was to escape.

Rolling onto one elbow, she scanned the small area. A metal box without a lid sat beside a sturdy door, and as her eyesight cleared, she made out bottled water and a pile of silver packages. Shivering, she touched the scanty negligee covering her nakedness and tried to pull it down to cover her. It didn't take a genius to understand that the man she'd helped last night had kidnapped her and locked her in this tiny room. The thought of him touching her made her sick to her stomach. As her eyes adjusted to the light, she noticed the bars covering a square toward the top of the door, but they were covered. She had seen similar doors in jails in movies set in the old West. Could he be holding her on a movie set? Or was this part of an old mine? She pushed to her knees and slowly stood. Her head swam and her stomach rolled as she ran her hands over the slimy damp walls. Her palms slid over the grooves the pioneer miners had left behind when they'd dug them out of the mountainside using pics and shovels. The hard black granite was familiar. It had been around her all her life. *I'm still in Black Rock Falls.*

The door had no handle, but she pushed her shoulder against it in the hope it might open, though it was shut tight. She heard a noise and, in fear of her life, froze on the spot. A whisper hardly more than an exhalation of air came through the crack in the wall.

"Are you okay? Be very quiet or he will hear us." The woman's voice paused for a beat. "My name is Poppy. I'm a deputy. Who are you?"

Heart thundering in her chest, Susie pressed her lips to the fissure. "Susie Hartwig. Where are we and why is he keeping us here? Is this anything to do with the bodies they found in town?"

"I think so. I figure we're his stock of murder victims. He's given us all a number and I'm twenty-five, so he's been doing this for a while. We're no longer human to him, and forget about reasoning with him. Pleading or crying is a big mistake, so try and keep it together." Poppy's voice was just above a sigh. "If you want to survive, don't make any noise. He likes you to be afraid of him, so look him straight in the eye and remain silent. There are more of us here, but the others are down another passageway. He moved me here yesterday, but I don't know why."

As terror lifted the hairs on her body, Suzie pressed her mouth to the gap. "What will he do if he hears us talking?"

"The moment anyone cries out or makes a noise, he drags them into the open space just outside, ties them up, and murders them." Poppy gave a muffled sob. "He seems to know everything we do. I figure he has CCTV cameras down here. I have a plan to escape. Keep your head down and don't question anything I do even if it seems as if I'm on his side—I'm not."

Trembling, Susie nodded, even though the woman couldn't see her. She had no idea if the person on the other side of the wall was the killer just trying to trick her. A rush of panic gripped her, and she pushed it aside and took a deep breath. Good people would be out searching for her. "I'll be missed. I know the sheriff and everyone in the department. She'll be out hunting for me right now. We'll just have to survive long enough for her to get here."

"I know her too and I hope she's as good as her reputation. I sent her a message on the last victim. Dr. Wolfe will find it for sure." Poppy let out a long sigh. "I guess we'll soon know if Sheriff Alton lives up to her reputation." Footsteps slow and deliberate came from outside. "Don't say a word. He's coming."

THIRTY-SIX

It was difficult to avoid attracting attention as Rio walked with Rowley to the front desk of the company where Lucas Davies worked. The sight of two deputies asking questions had everybody's ears pricked and he had serious doubts the suspect would cooperate with them. As he'd been released from prison only in the past three months, he would likely be working on a trial basis. Davies would no doubt consider any intrusion by the local law enforcement a threat to his job. He wondered why Jenna had considered him in the first instance. They were pursuing a killer, not an arsonist, and Lucas Davies had been convicted of setting fire to a neighbor's vehicle after he discovered his wife had had an affair with him.

The receptionist at the front counter showed them into the company's break room and then hightailed it off to find Davies. When a man in his thirties with neat blond hair and wearing smart casual dress came into the room, Rio stood and waved him to a seat. Lucas Davies? I'm Deputy Zac Rio and this is Deputy Jake Rowley. I know you've recently returned from a business trip, but were you in town at any time from last Thursday through Monday?"

"Do I need a lawyer?" Davies eyed them suspiciously. "Because you would only have to check with my employer to know where I was and when."

Flipping open his notebook, Rio shrugged. "Well, that's up to you. I know we could ask your employer, but we figured you'd prefer to answer a few questions rather than have him suspect you might be involved in an offence." He sighed. "We're asking anyone who was released from jail in the last six months or so the same questions. They're routine, is all. If we believe you're involved in a crime, we would read you your rights and take you in for questioning. You've been around the block a few times. You know the deal. So, what's it going to be? Answer my questions or do we take you down to the office?"

"Okay." Davies looked over his shoulder as if concerned someone might overhear him. "I left town on Thursday and spent the weekend in Helena. I visited a few of our stores on Saturday and Monday and then I drove home." He frowned. "We're required to keep a log of our visits, including mileage, which is checked before we leave and when we return." He sighed. "We aren't assigned a particular truck. They're all the same and we take the one with the merchandise packed ready for the stores. That's why the mileage is checked."

So, it's pointless checking for an oil leak. Rio made a few notes and nodded. "Did anyone see you in Helena over the weekend?"

"Yeah." Davies shuffled his feet. "I'm seeing someone, but I really don't want you calling them for an alibi. I'm not sure how she would react if she believes that you're checking up on me."

"If you show us your logbooks and they check out, you'll need to give us her name, should we need it to clear you." Rowley gave him a direct stare. "We don't have to inform her that we're looking at you for a crime. We have other ways we can use to protect your privacy."

"Okay, I'll go and get the logbooks." Davies gave them the

name of his girlfriend and her details and then hurried back to the office.

Rio stared after him. "His logbook should give details of the contacts he made during his workday. I'll use my phone to make copies of each page and make random calls to see if they are legit. If so, I think we can recommend the sheriff strikes this guy from her list of possible suspects."

"He sure isn't acting like a killer to me." Rowley tipped back his hat and rested one hand on the handle of his weapon. "He is cooperating. Well, I figure he's trying to make a new life for himself. When he set fire to his neighbor's vehicle, it was probably a crime of passion."

Rio checked out the logbooks when Davies presented them to him. Each page had been checked by the company and stamped as being correct. He copied each page using his phone and then handed the book back to him with a nod. "Thank you for your cooperation. I doubt we'll be bothering you again." He led the way out of the office and headed back to their cruiser.

As he slipped behind the wheel his phone chimed. It was Bobby Kalo and he answered using the Bluetooth device in his vehicle. "Don't tell me you've found a link between those trinkets and a murder?"

"How about three missing persons files? I've sent the details to the office. They go back seven years and are in three different states. The pieces of jewelry are distinctive and the missing people were wearing them in photographs, which made life easier. All three were single women who lived alone, known to frequent bars, and were in the high-risk category." Bobby tapped away on his keyboard. *"In each case, they were reported missing by people they worked with. There's no supporting evidence whatsoever. It was as if they vanished from the face of the earth."*

Exhilarated by the news, Rio smiled at Rowley. "It would be too much of a coincidence for someone to have all three of them in their house, wouldn't it? Did you cc Wolfe as well?

He'll send the victims' dental charts to all the dentists in Colorado. It will be a breakthrough if we can get a positive match on any or all of them. Thanks, Bobby. I figure we'll go and visit the Bright cousins again."

"My pleasure and, yeah, Wolfe has the files. Catch you later." Kalo disconnected.

"I'll call Jenna." Rowley pulled out his phone.

Shaking his head, Rio flicked on lights and sirens and headed toward the Brights' residence. "She won't have her phone with her during the interview, and if she's on the way home in the chopper, she won't be able to hear you. We'll just drag the cousins back to the office for questioning and I'll get the paperwork ready for an arrest warrant. We'll explain everything to Jenna when she gets back."

When they arrived at the Brights' house, the place was locked up tight. No vehicles were in the yard and the shutters had been closed. Needing to know if the two men had left town, Rio used his lock pick to open the front door. They moved inside, weapons raised and cleared the ground floor, and then moved slowly up the stairs. The bedrooms still held a few clothes in the closets but the personal items they'd spotted during the search of the property were missing. He holstered his weapon and turned to Rowley. "Dammit! It looks like we're too late. They're in the wind." He glanced at his watch. "The sheriff said she'd be back from the state pen before noon. I'll send out a BOLO on the Brights' vehicles, but they probably left town the moment they were released and have a twelve-hour start on us by now. Maybe something in the questioning spooked them or they knew the box of trinkets was a smoking gun?"

"We can't just sit by and do nothing." Rowley's mouth turned down in annoyance. "If they came into an inheritance, they'd have spare cash. I figure we contact the airport and see if they've taken a flight in the last twelve hours. If I were planning on making myself scarce, I'd take the first flight out of town."

With his mind running through different scenarios, Rio looked at him. "We can, but that's easy to trace and these guys are way too smart—and Sam Bright would send up a red flag the moment he purchased a ticket as he's a parolee. I figure they'd take the best option and go off the grid—they'll be holing up where they keep the women and biding their time to see if we connect the missing women to the trinkets. We'll send their pictures and descriptions of their vehicles to the local rangers and ask them to spread the word with the hunters and hikers. I figure it's our only chance of finding them."

"That sounds like a plan." Rowley smiled at him. "I'll make some calls."

THIRTY-SEVEN

Fear paralyzed Susie as the footsteps came closer. They were the slow deliberate footsteps of someone with confidence. Sweat coated the palms of her hands and she looked around wildly for a place to hide. Black damp walls stared back at her—there was no escape. Her previous bravado melted like last winter's snow. When the footsteps came to a stop outside her cell, trembling shook her and the need to run gripped her. Panic came in a rush, and she couldn't breathe. Terrified her jailer would see her fear, she clasped her hands and pressed her lips together. The hatch over the wire mesh peephole opened and the small light set high in the wall illuminated the dark eyes peering at her. The expression held no particular menace and reminded her of her pet Labrador's inquisitive brown eyes. Empowered by the comparison, she lifted her chin and, folding her arms across her chest, met his gaze. The only defense was attack and he'd expect her to be afraid of him. Dragging up every last bit of courage, Susie glared at him. "Is this the way you treat somebody who tried to help you?"

"One question." Obscured by the bars, his facial expression was difficult to make out. "Did I hit on you the other day in

Aunt Betty's Café? Or encourage you in any way whatsoever to make you believe I was interested in you, Twenty-Six?"

The fact he'd given her a number was all the proof she needed to know he intended to kill her. Trying to get her head on straight, Susie gaped at him. So many people came by the diner to eat or collect takeout, and she didn't recognize his voice, but she'd never make a pass at a customer. Trying hard to keep the quiver from her voice, she took a deep breath. "Do you figure I have the time to seduce customers? If you thought that, you'd be wrong. What do you imagine my reputation would be like if I started flirting at Aunt Betty's? Do you honestly believe townsfolk would eat in my diner if I made them feel uncomfortable?" She stared him down, hoping that her attitude wouldn't make him fly into a rage and murder her. "It's usually the other way around. Being a waitress in a diner, we're often the subject of unwanted attention. I try to make my customers feel at home and I've never had any previous complaints. If being friendly was a problem for you, then I apologize, but Aunt Betty's Café is known for its friendly atmosphere and that's never going to change."

As if she flipped a switch, her jailer's eyes transformed. The pupils seemed to get larger as if his eyes had suddenly turned black. The hatch slammed shut and Susie could hear a bolt slide just as the door swung inward toward her. The smell of cigarettes and male sweat rushed in the cell as the man filled the entire width of the door. He was not what she expected. In his late thirties, wearing coveralls, with a strong build and sour expression. Lines around his mouth turned down and deep frown lines gave him the appearance of being continually grumpy, but it was the eyes that terrified her. He tipped his head one way and then the other as if evaluating her. Chills ran down her spine, but she stood her ground. Where else could she possibly go? If Poppy was correct, cowering in front of him would only make her his next victim.

"You sure are arrogant. Didn't your daddy teach you to respect men?" He shook his head and observed her for a long minute. "You know I can't let you go, don't you?" A sadistic smile curled his lips. "Although, I don't figure I'd get much pleasure out of murdering you just yet. Maybe I'll make you watch what happens to the women in here. Or I'll beat some respect into you. I have all the time in the world to make you obedient. I figure everyone has their breaking point and I'll just have to be patient until you reach yours—then I'll enjoy killing you." He pulled the door shut and slid the bolt across.

Shaking with fear and teeth chattering, Susie dragged in deep breaths to steady her nerves and then pressed her ear to the crack in the door. The cell next to her opened with a whine of rusty hinges, and as he spoke to Poppy, the hairs on the back of her neck rose in terror.

"I'm guessing you know Susie Hartwig from Aunt Betty's Café?" He cleared his throat. "The manager? I know you were in the diner. I saw you talking to her when you arrived in town."

"Yeah, I know her. So what?" Poppy's voice drifted down the hallway toward her.

"I'd do her just to shut her smart mouth, and dump her outside the diner, but it's too hot in town right now to use a local with the sheriff and the FBI hanging around. The women from other states are rarely identified and the trail stops there." He was chatting to Poppy about murder as if he were discussing the menu at the diner. "I have a real screamer I'm anxious to get to. On second thoughts, I'll give Susie to you. I'd like to watch you play out your fantasy—I might even join in. We'll leave her in the formaldehyde bath for a few days and I'll dump her in Colorado on my next visit."

"When are you leaving?" Poppy sounded excited. "If you're planning on doing another one tonight, and dumping her locally, the cops are going to know you're in town."

"I'll need to check my schedule." His tone was conversational. "Phew! I can smell you from here and it isn't nice. I guess you've earned a shower. I haven't time or inclination right now to watch you, maybe later."

"Do you have to be here? I'm not going anywhere, am I?" Suzie's voice hardened. "Or don't you trust me alone in the passageway, even after I helped you."

Suzie pressed her eye to the crack in the door. Blood spatter matted Poppy's hair and was smeared over one ear. She stood naked not bothering to cover herself. Dear Lord, she'd helped him kill someone. Trying to stop her knees trembling with fear, she moved her attention to the man. He was rubbing the back of his neck, eyes staring into nothing, thinking.

"Hmm." He looked around and then shrugged. "I don't trust you. I never will, but I'm not stupid. I know after you helped me with the last one, you'll be useful to have around." He chuckled. "They're fun for a time, but once they stop breathing I lose interest. If I intend to continue my hobby, the cleaning is essential. I can't risk leaving my DNA on the trash." His mouth quirked up at the corner. "I wish I had a bigger garbage disposal. It would make life so much easier." He rubbed his chin. "Okay. This is a onetime offer. I'll allow you to take a shower and then go back to your cell. You'll have to prove I can trust you. Remember, I may not be here, but I'm always watching."

"I'll need something to wear." Poppy moved into the hall-way. "A clean dress maybe?"

"I guess so. There's a bag of clothes next to the desk." He looked at her for a long moment. "Don't make me angry, Twenty-Five. I'll so make you regret it." His fingers closed around Poppy's throat. "There's no way out of the caves. The gate at the end of the tunnel is locked. So, if you want to keep your freedom... *partner*... don't mess up, because you know the consequences for trying to escape. Don't you?" When she nodded, he dropped his hand.

Susie's teeth chattered as the horror of what was happening sunk in. She leaned against the wall, hugging herself as his slow footsteps moved away. A clang of a metal door and the grind of a key turning echoed up the tunnel accompanied by a low satanic chuckle.

THIRTY-EIGHT

After touching down at the ranch, Jenna wasted no time and climbed into the Beast. As Kane headed out of the driveway with Carter and Jo close behind in Jenna's cruiser, she called Aunt Betty's Café to place an order for takeout. It was a little after noon and she expected Susie Hartwig to pick up the phone. She gave the order to Wendy. "Do you have time to make up the order now, or can someone drop it by the office when it's ready?"

"I'll start on the order now, but delivery might be delayed. Susie hasn't shown for her shift." Wendy let out a long sigh. *"This will be the first time I think she's ever been late. She was planning to go to the beauty parlor this morning, so maybe she got held up. If she arrives by the time I've made up your order, I'll drop it by on my way home. If not, I'll call you. It's the lunchtime rush and we're snowed under."*

Not wanting to be disturbed when they arrived at the office, Jenna pulled on her bottom lip. "I'm just leaving the ranch now. We'll drop by on the way through town and wait until it's ready."

"Thanks, I'll see you soon." Wendy disconnected.

"Problem?" Kane gave her a sideways look.

Jenna shrugged. "I don't think so. Susie is late for work, is all, and you know how busy they are at this time of the day. We'll just stop by and pick up our order. We have a ton of things to discuss when we get back to the office. What Vito told us will help narrow down the suspects."

"You can't take everything he says as gospel." Kane shook his head. "I agree he made some good points, and you did get to see the inner workings of a psychopath's mind, but he's only talking to you because he gets a kick out of it. He's not doing it to help. For him, any violent stimulation, especially looking at crime scene photographs, is like giving him a box of candy."

Jenna's phone chimed. It was Wolfe and she put it on speaker. "Hi, Shane. I hope you have good news for me."

"It depends on how you interpret good news." Wolfe sounded exhausted. *"I've experimented with several different light filters to enhance the fingerprints. It took longer than I'd expected, but I've found a cryptic message scrawled in Poppy's sweat across the victim's stomach. It reads: Help! Underground cells."* He paused a beat. *"I checked every image of the victim and that's all she wrote. There's nothing to pinpoint her position, I'm afraid."*

Stunned into silence for a beat, Jenna held her breath as the images popped into her inbox. The case had blown out in another direction. She scrolled through the images he'd sent her. "This is incredible work. Thanks, Shane. You're a genius. Who would have thought Poppy was smart enough to think of doing that? When you said you'd found her DNA on a victim, I figured she was involved with the murders."

"Yeah, so did I. Before you go, I guess you haven't spoken to Rio yet? We've had a hit on missing women out of Colorado." Wolfe yawned explosively. *"Sorry, it's been nonstop for hours. Kalo sent me the information and I've forwarded the dental*

records to all the dentists in the state. I'll call you when I get a reply." He disconnected.

"It looks like Poppy's a victim after all." Hearing Kane's sharp inhalation of breath, Jenna stared at him. "What? This proves we have someone on the inside. Poppy has somehow made herself useful to the killer. She managed to get a message out. This is epic."

"I don't buy it. If she's a victim, how did she get access to the body?" Kane's mouth turned down. "Allowing a woman to get involved goes against the killer's previous behavior—so is dropping his guard and leaving DNA. Something's not right here. Even psychopaths have logic. It's just different to ours. There's no proof Poppy actually wrote the message, is there? Maybe he's giving us a surefire suspect so he can walk free, but it could also be a trap, Jenna. It wouldn't be the first time."

The interview with Bruno Vito was still playing through Jenna's mind. She'd gained insight into the current case but could understand Kane's concern. "You have to admit some of Vito's points made sense." She turned in her seat to look at him. "For instance, he believes that Poppy isn't involved in the murders and the killer works alone. If the message on the victim is legit, it also means all the time since Poppy went missing she's been in the hands of a psychopath."

"One who drives to Colorado on a regular basis and uses her credit cards to keep up the illusion she's safe and well." Kane took his hand off the steering wheel and rubbed his chin. "That will narrow the suspects down. I'll check over the case files again when we get back to the office."

Pulling her notebook from her pocket, Jenna thumbed through the pages. "Something else I figure is significant. Although Vito made a case for the killer to be working alone, the fact that he is keeping women prisoners would make me believe he had a partner. He'd need someone to watch the women in his absence. Yet, Vito believed the killer has a ritual, he likes to perform in private. This makes sense to me, although I know I shouldn't try and apply logic to anything a psychopath does."

"I agree. The entire interview was a valuable insight into the criminal mind." Kane pulled into the curb outside Aunt Betty's Café and waved at Carter, who was following them, to keep going. "I'll go and grab the takeout." He slid out of the door.

Anxious to start a search for Poppy, Jenna checked her messages and found nothing from Rio or Rowley. There were no missed calls either, which she found unusual as Rowley was a stickler for checking in with her. Five minutes later Kane emerged from the diner carrying a cardboard box and deposited it on the back seat next to Duke. "I wonder if Rowley and Rio have finished the interview with Lucas Davies. I haven't heard from them all morning."

"They probably didn't want to bother you." Kane headed along Main. "They know we're due back at noon, so they'll be waiting for us at the office. Rio is used to taking the lead in murder cases. I'm sure he'll have everything up to date when we arrive."

The vehicles parked outside the sheriff's department indicated that everyone was in the building. Jenna gave Maggie a wave as she walked past the front counter and went straight up to the conference room they were using for this case. The smell of fresh coffee brewing wafted down the hallway. She pushed open the door glad to see everyone at work around the long table. After dropping her things on the desk, she sat down and gave them Wolfe's news. Everyone inhaled at once when she showed the powerful images. "Our priority is finding Poppy. If she's with the killer, we need to be moving at warp speed to find her." She moved her gaze around the table. "This means in a covert way, no lights and sirens, no guns blazing. The killer is holding prisoners and by going off half-cocked we'll be giving him a reason to murder them." She swung her attention to Rio. "Okay, what have you got for me?"

She listened with interest as Rio brought her up to date. "Yeah, I know about the missing persons. Wolfe called. Nothing more on that as yet." She made more notes. "That's very interesting about the Bright cousins. Get out a press release saying they're persons of interest and set up a hotline. It's a shot in the dark because we have reason to believe the killer takes regular trips to Colorado and we know Sam Bright hasn't left the state." She took the cup of coffee Kane handed her with a smile. "Lucas Davies travels to Colorado. He needed special permission by the parole board to cross the state line, but they consider him such a low risk it was granted as it's part of his profession and, so far, he hasn't put a foot wrong." She looked at Carter. "Do you figure it's possible for him to somehow get back to Black Rock Falls with a body and then drive back to collect the truck?"

"Looking at the entries in his logbook, he travels the same route." Carter scanned the images on Rio's phone. "He frequently stays overnight, which gives him a window of opportunity. He could easily use the credit card in Colorado and have his final sleepover within driving distance of Black Rock Falls."

"We'd be looking for a place he stops overnight within a three-hour drive of town." Kane unpacked the box of takeout and placed it on the table. "So, he either uses a rental or he has a vehicle stashed somewhere along the way." He sighed. "The problem I have with Lucas Davies is that he has no priors other than arson. We know the killer in our case has murdered before and Lucas Davies doesn't fit the profile."

Jenna stared at Kane. "Sam Bright does, and I don't recall asking Derek Bright if he's been in Colorado recently because it wasn't relevant at the time." She scrolled through her files. "His occupation is listed as a road driver as well, so he could easily be the one using the credit cards in Colorado."

"Seems to me we should be including anyone with the opportunity of driving to Colorado over the last three months, that's how long Poppy has been missing." Carter stared at the whiteboard. "Did anyone follow up on Tom Parsons?"

"He's been out of town and isn't due back until today." Kane scanned his notes. "We spoke to his wife, but she didn't have too much information. He would be due to drop off his consignment at the warehouse. I'll give them a call and see if he has arrived yet. According to his wife, he isn't due to go out again until Friday." He reached for a sandwich. "His truck hasn't got an oil leak either. I checked out where he parks when he's at home."

Jenna sipped her coffee and sighed. "We'll keep him on the list until we can speak to him." She stared at the whiteboard. "With the Bright cousins in the wind, they have to be our prime suspects."

A knock on the door and the sight of Atohi Blackhawk brought a smile to her face. "Hi, Atohi. Did you find any caves?"

"It seems the old timers kept things underground." Blackhawk dropped into a spare chair and leaned on the table. "I know the historical sites but they're not plausible. Many years ago, way back in the 1800s, they mined for gold in the lowlands around these parts. You recall seeing the miners' cabins or what's left of them out past the industrial areas on the edge of the county? It seems that many of the miners carved out caves in the granite rock formation each side of the dry riverbed to store their machinery during the winter. Some sunk mineshafts all along the dry riverbed, but many of those mine shafts have been sealed as they are dangerous, but the storage tunnels into the rock meet the requirements you're looking for. They're deep and isolated. It's almost barren there, apart from the wheatgrass. No one lives for miles in any direction, so someone could come and go without being noticed. It wouldn't take too much to shore up the caves to make them safe."

Jenna pulled up a map of Black Rock Falls on her iPad and handed it to him. "Do you know where these caves are exactly? It's a massive area to hunt down one single cave."

"There are many, but with discussion they came up with the most likely caves. All agreed he must be holding the women here." Blackhawk moved the map and pointed to an area flanked by a granite wall of rock. "This is the old riverbed. It goes for miles and if someone is taking women there, they must have access. From what the elders remember from the stories, the caves here were extended by miners." He indicated to an area that widened from an old riverbed to an open plain. "The gold mines are all around here. Many holes in the ground. It makes sense if some of them stored equipment or used the caves for shelter, they'd be here."

The thrill of closing in on a killer gripped Jenna. She smiled at Blackhawk. "Thank you so much for tracking the caves down for us." She squeezed his arm. "Stay, we have fresh coffee and a ton of food."

"You're welcome." Blackhawk grinned at her. "And thanks, I'd appreciate a bite."

"I'll go with Jo and scout the area in the chopper." Carter pushed to his feet and looked at Jenna. "It will give us a better idea of where to start searching. If we see anything, we'll call you. If not, I'll drop the bird on the ME's roof when we get back, in case we need it in a hurry." He poured his coffee into a to-go cup and scooped up a cherry pie. "Come on, Jo, grab two forks, we'll eat on the way."

Jenna nodded. "Thanks." She turned to Rowley. "Go with Rio and hunt down Tom Parsons, see what he has to say for himself. If he can prove his whereabouts, we'll drop him from our list because it looks as if he was out of town when we discovered the last victim."

"I'm on it." Rowley led the way out the door with Rio on his heels.

"Okay." Kane stared at the whiteboard. "We should consider cutting down the suspects list while we're waiting. It will be an hour or so before Carter has done a sweep of the mining areas."

Before Jenna could open her mouth to reply, Maggie was at the door, her face distraught. "Is anything wrong?"

"Mrs. Jenkins out of Maple dropped by with this purse, said she found it and the phone in the grass alongside the road." Maggie held out an evidence bag. "They belong to Susie Hartwig. I called Aunt Betty's and she didn't show for work this morning. Wendy has searched everywhere. She went by her house and the beauty parlor, but no one has seen her."

Chills ran down Jenna's spine as she took the evidence bag. Now this is getting personal. She turned to Kane. "You took Susie through a self-defense course personally. She carries a weapon and knows how to use it. She wouldn't be easy to take down." Scared for Susie's safety, she swallowed hard, trying not to think of what might be happening to her this very minute. "He's taken her, hasn't he? This is a message aimed right at me. The others were strangers. Susie is our friend, and he darn well knows it." She slammed her fist on the table. "I want her found —today!"

THIRTY-NINE

Heart thundering in her chest, Poppy waited as the footsteps disappeared and then crumpled to the smelly mattress, too scared to move a muscle for at least an hour, before daring to stand. Disregarding her lack of clothing, she edged her way down the passageway. At the end, a metal gate barred her way. Closing her fingers around the cold iron, she pulled and pushed, but the gate was locked. Ahead, another passageway revealed a line of six cells, each with a metal door with the same peephole as the others. Not a sound came from within. No footsteps or heavy breathing—nothing. Convinced her jailor had left, she turned and hurried back and slid open the bolt on Susie's cell. "Help me to search for anything we can use as a weapon."

"What about the CCTV camera?" Susie was keeping her distance, her eyes wide with fear. "He'll be back and punish us if he catches us out of the cells."

Poppy had taken the opportunity to look for the camera when she'd cleaned up the mess from the previous murder. She hadn't spotted any cameras pointing toward their cells. A small lens set high in the roof of the cave pointed to the area where her jailer murdered his victims. She turned to Susie. "I figure he only films himself murdering his victims. I think everything else is just a threat to keep us in check. Don't worry, he's not coming back for a time. I know his routine. If he comes by early, he leaves around this time and doesn't come back for hours, sometimes days. It will be hours this time, because when he's going away for a few days, he always restocks our food supplies and this time he hasn't."

"I'm not sure I want to take that chance." Susie backed away from her.

Poppy wanted to shake Susie into action, but the woman just stared at her round-eyed. She glanced down at herself and guessed that taking orders from a blood splattered naked woman would be difficult. Turning away, she went to the desk and pulled out the bag of clothes. She sorted through them finding something suitable to wear and pulled on a T-shirt and a pair of jeans. She found some sweatpants and a T-shirt and thrust them at Susie. "Put these on. It will make you feel more comfortable and then we'd better start searching this place from top to bottom. Look for anything we can use."

"It's a cave. Where could anything possibly be hidden in here?" Susie pulled on the clothes and stepped tentatively out of the cell.

"Look anyway." Poppy headed back down the passageway. "I'm going to find the recording device. It has to be in here somewhere. We need to turn it off so we can move around."

Reaching up high, Poppy followed the cable leading from the CCTV camera and back toward the alcove near her cell. The dim light in the tunnels hid the small critters living in the cracks and crevices. Disturbed by her probing fingers, they scattered and ran over her hands and up her arms. Unable to control her shrieks of disgust, she brushed them away and shuddered. Determined to find the recording device, she ran her fingers over the cable. It led to high above the desk, and after searching all around, she noticed a small shelf set into the roof of the cave. She climbed onto the desk and, expecting to discover a recording device of some description, she gaped in astonishment at the laptop sitting on the shelf. She touched the keyboard and the screen lit up, showing the live feed of the killing area. Taking a deep breath, she pressed pause on the program and the live feed froze on the screen. "I've paused the video. It was pointing the other way anyway. He wouldn't be able to see us, but he might hear us."

"Is that a laptop?" Susie stood on tiptoes and stared at her. "See if it has an email service. It must have some type of wireless connection or it wouldn't be able to feed him a live stream."

It took Poppy a few seconds to find the email application. When she'd arrived at the sheriff's department, Maggie had informed her everyone in the office's email address was their last name, at Black Rock Falls Sheriff's Department. She sent an email to Kane.

I'm a prisoner in cells cut into underground caves with Suzie Hartwig and others. Can you get a fix on this laptop? Poppy.

She turned to look down at Suzie. "I've sent an email to Kane. It should go to his phone. The last one I sent him, he replied really fast."

"You should have sent it to the sheriff. You know she'll be out looking for me." Susie looked distraught. "I've looked everywhere. There's nothing here to use as a weapon, unless you count soap and a couple of towels. If Deputy Kane doesn't reply soon, you'd better delete that email or we'll be in big trouble. It will be better if this lunatic doesn't know we've been in contact with the sheriff's department."

Poppy waited, her legs trembling as she stood on the desk. A reply popped into the box.

Are you in danger right now? Kane

Typing, Poppy made the message to the point, giving as much information as possible.

No, killer left an hour or so ago. He is usually gone for a few hours. Average height, thick build, brown eyes and hair, smoker, smells of sweat. Poppy

---

Stand by. It will take time to trace. Thirty mins. Delete each email. Kane

---

Poppy turned up the volume on the laptop so she could hear the alert when the next message arrived, deleted the emails, and climbed down. She looked at Susie's hopeful expression. "Now we wait."

"How long?" Susie slumped against the wall.

Poppy shrugged. "Half an hour, maybe longer, before they can pinpoint the laptop's location. Don't worry. They'll find us now." She scanned the files on the laptop and bile seeped up the back of her throat. "Oh my God, he taped all the murders."

"The sick freak." Susie rubbed a trembling finger under her nose. "Why don't you go and wash off the blood? It's all through your hair. If this all goes to hell, he'll know something is up if you haven't taken a shower." She dashed a hand through her hair. "I'll listen for the email, and if I hear him coming back, I'll take the recorder off pause, and go back into my cell."

Nodding, Poppy stared down the tunnel. "You'll hear his vehicle's engine. It will give you time to do what you need to do. You have to be brave. Ready?"

"Okay. Go." Susie pushed off the wall and walked a little unsteadily down the tunnel.

FORTY

Rowley turned his cruiser into the Brights' driveway and followed Rio around the house, checking that the cousins hadn't returned home. The place was the same as when they'd left it and the cousins nowhere in sight. "I guess it was worth a try. I've known people to take off and then sneak back home. They figure we won't check twice."

"It was worth dropping by again." Rio climbed into the passenger seat and fastened his seatbelt. "I'll add Tom Parsons' coordinates to the GPS. With any luck he'll be back by now. I figure it's a waste of time talking to him, and we should be out looking for Susie Hartwig."

Rowley turned his truck around and headed back to the highway. Listening to the voice on the GPS, he easily found his way to Tom Parsons' ranch. "Kane mentioned this guy keeps his vehicle out back. I figure we should leave the cruiser here and go in on foot to see if his eighteen-wheeler is there. It will give us a chance to see if it has an oil leak." He pulled his cruiser off the driveway and behind a clump of bushes.

Keeping to the shadows from the pine trees lining the drive-way, they headed for a long tall garage out toward the back of the property. Rowley turned and smiled at Rio. "So, he's home then?"

Moving cautiously, they made their way into the garage and alongside the truck. They bent down and using their flashlights examined the cement floor. Water pooled alongside the truck and a hose looped over a tap still dripped. It was obvious Parsons had washed his truck recently. Rowley straightened shaking his head. "It looks clean to me. Let's see if he's willing to talk to us."

"We should go back and pick up the cruiser." Rio stood hands on hips looking at him. "He might figure we've been sneaking around without permission if we walk up to the door."

Rowley nodded. "Yeah, good idea." He led the way back to the cruiser and they drove to the end of the driveway, parking out front of the porch.

As they climbed the steps to the ranch house, the strong smell of dirty diapers oozed out of the screen door. Rowley wrinkled his nose and rapped on the doorframe.

A man walked toward the door carrying a newspaper and his eyes narrowed as he stared at them. As the door opened, Rowley introduced himself and Rio. "We're just following up on the chat Deputy Kane had with your wife."

"Sure, what do you want to know?" Parsons leaned against the screen door his hands pushed into the front pockets of his jeans.

Rowley went over the dates and times they'd discovered the bodies, watching him closely for any telltale signs of involvement.

"I don't recall seeing anyone on the side of the road on the way into town, but it's dark most times I'm on the move. Not on any of the days you mentioned." Parsons' head furrowed into a frown. "This is bad business. No woman is safe to walk around alone anymore." He looked steadily at Rowley. "I always avoid driving through town and take Maple. It saves me time with the traffic and all. So, I guess I missed seeing the body on the carousel and I haven't visited the landfill in at least a week."

"Think over those days and times again." Rio repeated them. "You must recall if you were here. It was only a few days ago."

"Yeah, it's possible, but I can't be sure about the times. Lately I've had a fast turnaround, so I'm literally dropping off one consignment at the warehouse and collecting another for delivery. I don't kind of check my watch every five minutes. It's load the truck and drive, unload the truck and drive. Most times I forget what day it is I'm so busy." Parsons shrugged. "I have a growing family, so I take the work when it's available. The last couple of weeks it's been nonstop."

"What about sleeping?" Rio looked at him closely. "There are rules about driving long hours without taking a rest."

"Oh, I get my sleep." Parsons smiled at him. "Most times it's at a truck stop or a motel. I usually grab a shower and I'm fresh to go." He sighed. "I'm home for a few days now, so I'll get the chance to see my kids and spend time with my wife before the next job."

A young boy walked up the hallway and wrapped his arms around his father's leg. Parsons picked him up and rested him on one hip. The child's thumb went in his mouth and his head dropped against Parsons' shoulder. Rowley exchanged a glance with Rio and nodded at Parsons. "I can see you've got your hands full." He smiled at the little boy. "Thanks for your cooperation."

"Anytime." Parsons turned away, allowing the screen door to slam shut.

As they climbed into the cruiser, Rowley turned to Rio. "What do you think?"

"He seems way too busy to fit killing into his schedule." Rio sighed. "Let's head back to the office so we can do some real police work."

FORTY-ONE

Chewing on her bottom lip, Jenna leaned over Kane's shoulder watching the laptop screen as he typed the emails to Poppy. She could just about cut the tension in the room with a knife. Kane had jumped into action at once, contacting Bobby Kalo and forwarding the messages as they came in in an attempt to locate the IP address of the laptop Poppy was using. Jenna contacted Carter to explain the situation. "How long before you take off?"

"I'll be leaving here soon but I need to stop by Wolfe's office to refuel. I'll be over the mines in thirty or forty minutes." Carter's boots crunched on the gravel as he headed toward the chopper. *"Jo will contact you by text as soon as we're over the mining area. I'll stay at altitude and make sure there's no vehicles in the area. If it's safe, I'll drop low and search the riverbed. Ask Poppy to listen for the chopper and then tell me when she hears it. I'll sweep the area until we get a fix on her position. I suggest you head out for the lowlands now."*

"Copy that." Jenna relayed the message to Kane. "Send the email to Poppy. Carter will need an accurate location, so message Jo the moment Poppy gets back to you. I'll get what we need from the gun locker. Contact Rio and Rowley and head them in the same direction."

"Maybe we should think this through some?" Kane sent the email and then rubbed the back of his neck. "If the killer shows while we're there, he'll hightail it out of town. That description Poppy gave us fits three of our suspects... both the Bright cousins and Parsons. If he gets back before we arrive, and we spook him, he might kill them."

Jenna considered the situation and nodded in agreement. "I agree. Susie and Poppy's safety comes first. We'll go in covertly, and if he's not there, we'll get the women out and lay a trap for him."

"That might not be so easy." Kane frowned at her. "Poppy seems to think he could be away for a few hours or days, and we sure as hell can't sit down there for days on end, hoping he'll show."

Allowing Kane's words to percolate through her mind, Jenna paced up and down, thinking through every angle. There was no way she'd leave anyone in danger. "Okay, you're the expert in covert operations. Do you think Carter can drop us somewhere close to the caves Blackhawk showed us? You'll be able to communicate with Poppy on your phone to find out if the killer has returned. If he hasn't, we'll go in and get them out and have them picked up by Carter. Once the victims are safe, we'll take shifts watching the entrance road to the mines for him to return. I know that area. If you recall, we found a body there. There's an access road for the maintenance of the electricity lines. Do you recall speaking to a linesman who'd spotted a body near a mine shaft?"

"Yeah, that's not something I'd forget in a hurry." Kane raised both eyebrows at her. "The area is open plains for many miles. It would be difficult to watch who comes and goes without being detected." He rubbed his chin. "Do you remember that old cabin along the mining road? We could hook up a camera in there to watch the road and be waiting out of sight a mile or so away—if we could get in and out before he spotted us. There's no telling when he will return."

Jenna considered the distance between the main highway and access road and took into account the time it would take to get back up to the area. "I figured we would be on our own if he is there or returns when we're rescuing the women. Carter isn't going to be able to do much when he's flying the chopper, and Rio and Rowley will be at least a mile away." She sighed. "We'll be on our own, but we've done it before. I'll go and get the gear. I assume we'll be repelling out of the chopper on the rockface beside the old riverbed?"

"Yeah. It's not going to be easy. Carter will have to drop us from altitude to avoid anyone seeing us. It will need to be a rapid decline." Kane gave her a long considering stare. "Are you sure you want to do this? Wolfe can fly the FBI chopper and Carter could go in with me. It's something we've done a million times before."

Jenna snorted. "You're not getting overprotective again are you, Dave?"

"No, it's not about being overprotective. It's about speed." Kane's lips flattened into a thin line. "Me and Carter can descend fast. We've had to because we've been under fire. You'll need to drop and trust the rope. It's not easy."

"I'll manage." She headed for the door. "I'm going with you. Call Rowley and see if he's got eyes on Parsons. If so, we can remove him from the suspect list. Poppy didn't mention two men, so we have to assume our killer is Sam Bright. He may or may not be alone." She turned to look at him. "The Bright cousins are already spooked. There's a good chance they're already heading back to the caves to kill the women. We can't wait for Kalo to pinpoint the laptop, Dave. We have to move now."

"I'll text Jo with the new plan." Kane pulled out his phone.

Running, Jenna rushed to the equipment lockers, pulled out liquid Kevlar vests, helmets, and harnesses. She grabbed rifles and their backpacks. Dressing, she'd strapped on her helmet when Kane came into the room. "Are we set?"

"Yeah, we'll head out to the rocks behind the riverbed. There's an old track leading out to it but most of it will be off road. Carter will pick us up, and once we get a location, we'll drop down. He'll take off to avoid attention, so we'll be on our own." Kane pulled on his liquid Kevlar vest. "Rowley had eyes on Parsons about half an hour ago. They were on their way back. I sent them out to the industrial area on the edge of the lowlands to await instructions."

Sighing with relief, Jenna nodded. "That's good, so we have one or both of the Bright cousins to deal with—if they show." She smiled at his worried expression. It wasn't like Kane to show any emotion before heading into a situation. "What's up with you today? We've handled worse killers than this one. At least he hasn't made personal threats against us. For once, I'm not his target."

"Jenna, you are. He hates women." Kane's gaze narrowed. "He especially hates women in law enforcement or he wouldn't have placed the cop's mask on his victims. He'll take great pleasure in taking you down and making you suffer. How Poppy has survived so long is a miracle."

Sobered by his revelations, Jenna nodded. "Okay, okay. It just seemed to me Sam Bright didn't pose too much of a problem. He was cooperative, almost passive." She swallowed hard at Kane's raised eyebrow. "A psychopath can fool anyone. Yeah, I know." She cleared her throat. "Talk to me."

"We have no idea what weapons they have, or what they'll do when cornered. An unpredictable psychopath could use the women as a shield, or just kill them in front of us." Kane turned a concerned expression to her. "You know, they'll do anything to escape."

Jenna squeezed his arm. "I remember when a killer had a knife at my throat and you killed him. They don't know what they're up against. We're a good team and I'm not planning on seeing Suzie or Poppy die today."

"Let's hope we get there before they do and can get the women out without a fight." Kane attached his earbud and turned on his com. "Discharging a weapon in granite caves is dangerous. Miss the target and the ricochet could kill one of us."

Jenna nodded and attached her com. "I know." His combat face was back, and the sight of it was like a wall of armor around her. He made her feel safe. She handed him a helmet. "It's just as well you never miss then, isn't it?" She went on tiptoes and kissed him. "Let's go."

FORTY-TWO

Susie Hartwig pressed against the bars, her ears straining to hear a chopper, but she heard nothing. Tentatively, she called out. "Hey, is anyone else in here? He can't hear you. We've turned off the recorder for now."

Voices, thin and hesitant, came back from the other passageway, none she could really make out but they'd understood her just fine. "Help is on the way. Stay quiet now. He might be back soon."

There'd been no more emails. She paced up and down, her nerves shattering with every minute that went by. She turned to look at Poppy standing on the desk, her attention fixed on the laptop. "Anything?"

"Not yet. I'm to let them know when we hear a chopper. It's been almost thirty minutes. They should be heading this way soon." Poppy waved her away. "Keep listening."

Taking her position at the gate, Susie said a silent prayer for the FBI agents to find them. She'd met Jo Wells and Ty Carter. They'd been very nice to her and given her a substantial tip each time they'd dined at Aunt Betty's. A rumble came in the distance and she pressed her ear to the bars. Not the *whoop,*

whoop of a helicopter but the roar of an engine. Fear had her by the throat as she turned and ran back to Poppy. "He's coming back. I can hear a vehicle."

"Get back into your cell." Poppy turned to the laptop. "Don't say a word. I'm sending a message for radio silence to Kane. I'll delete the messages and take the recorder off pause." A few moments later, she jumped down, looked all around, and went back into her cell. "Eat something. He'll expect us to act normally and it's way past lunchtime."

Sick to her stomach with fear, Susie searched through the box of supplies and pulled out an aluminum package at random. She selected a bottle of water and went to sit on a mattress pushed up against the damp wall. It took her more than a few tries to make her trembling fingers open the package containing crackers and cheese. She'd never experienced terror like this before, and her strength of will wilted like a cut flower in the sun. Is this what happened to the other poor souls kept prisoner in these caves for so long? Had the horror of being on a waiting list of victims make them complacent to their fate?

It seemed like forever before the familiar footsteps moved slowly through the tunnels. He checked on each of his prisoners and took his time, as if soaking up their fear. The threats he made to them made Susie's chin tremble. The cruelty of this man held no bounds. He tormented his victims with the slow death he'd planned for them. And then he'd laugh when describing how they'd be found. His intent to spread them out in an indecent pose so the world would recognize them for the scum they represented. He actually believed the local townsfolk would respect him for removing them from society. The clang as the gate to their section hit the wall sent shivers down Susie's back. The adrenaline flowing through her veins from the previous excitement was making it difficult to regain her composure as his footsteps came closer.

The bolt in her door slid across and the door swung open.

Her jailer stood there staring down at her with a cold soulless expression. In his hand he held a baseball bat and was casually slapping it against the palm of one hand as he observed her. Sipping her water in an effort to appear calm and in control, Susie lifted her chin and stared at him but said nothing.

"Did I give you permission to get dressed?" He looked over with narrowed eyes. "Just where did you get those clothes from? You don't deserve the dignity of clothes."

"I gave them to her." Poppy stepped out of her cell. "All the time you've been giving me the criteria of the women you believe need to be punished, and it's quite obvious that Susie isn't guilty of what you've accused her of doing."

"That wasn't your decision to make." He lifted his chin and looked down his nose at her. "Like most women, you try to over-step your mark." He swung the bat back and forth. A slow smile curled his lips. "You like Susie, do you?" He handed Poppy the bat. "Prove your loyalty to me and kill her."

FORTY-THREE

Heart racing with anticipation, Jenna ran to the front door, clinging to her backpack and rifle. Behind her, Kane was asking Maggie to care for Duke while they were away, and then his footsteps were thundering on the tile behind her. Throwing her gear into the back seat, she yanked open the front door of the Beast and jumped inside. Seconds later, Kane slid behind the wheel and the engine roared into life. With a squeal of burned rubber, the truck took off at high-speed, lights flashing and sirens wailing as Kane maneuvered the vehicle through the traffic. They reached the outskirts of town and the front of the Beast lifted as Kane pushed his foot to the floor. Fences and driveways flashed past as they headed for the onramp to the highway. The thrill of the chase had Jenna taking deep steadying breaths. She would never admit it to Kane, but the idea of dropping freefall from a chopper scared the hell out of her. As the lowlands came into view, she took in the vast vista. For miles, the long golden grass moved with each breath of wind as if it were an entity writhing across the open plains. She gripped the side of her seat as the speed increased. Kane's concentration was on driving, and he hadn't said a word since they'd left town. All Jenna could hear above the wail of the sirens was the roar of the engine and the *whoop, whoop, whoop* as the Beast flashed past other vehicles as if they were standing still. In the distance she made out the craggy rock formation that wound around the lowlands and once formed the sides of a river.

"Hold on tight. We'll be making a sharp left after that clump of trees ahead." Kane flicked her a glance. "Once we're on the dirt road, kill the lights and sirens. We don't want to give anyone a warning we're on our way."

Jenna held on tight as the Beast slid around the corner, sending up great clouds of dust and then bounced along an old dirt road filled with ruts and divots. Nature had reclaimed the old road a long time ago, but Kane pushed the Beast through the overgrown mass of branches and weeds. They bounced along, weaving past rocks and fallen branches. Up ahead, Jenna made out the chopper hovering high above the rock formation. "I see Carter." She pulled out her phone and sent a text to Jo. A reply came in a few seconds and Jenna punched the air. "We've found them. Kalo just sent the laptop's coordinates and Carter is setting down at the end of this road. It runs around the back of the ravine. The riverbed opens up on the other side."

"Yeah, I know where I am." Kane slowed to maneuver around a pile of fallen rocks. "I hope we get there before he murders anybody else."

Jenna's stomach clenched into knots. "The problem I see is, if it is the Bright cousins as we suspect, one of them will be acting as a lookout. He could pick us off before we even get to the mouth of the cave."

"I thought of that and we'll be repelling down to a position above the cave." Kane squeezed her hand. "Any last-minute orders?"

Jenna looked into the eyes of a warrior and understood his question. "Use necessary force as always. Our first priority is getting those women out alive."

"Copy that." Kane gave her a nod and turned his attention back to the road. "I see the chopper." He pulled up and leapt from the truck.

Grabbing their gear and leaving the Beast, Jenna climbed into the chopper with Kane close behind. Without warning, Carter took off and her stomach flip-flopped as the chopper rose high into the air. She could hear Kane over her com speaking to Carter about the location of the cave. Carter's reply chilled her to the bone.

"I made out a vehicle, heading for the cave. I'd have missed it, but it threw up a cloud of dust. He must be in a hurry. When I came around for a better look, the vehicle had vanished. I figure he's covered it with a camouflaged tarpaulin." Carter's eyes were fixed ahead. *"I didn't see who was in the vehicle or how many people. Don't take any chances. The late-afternoon shadows will hide you if you stick close to the ravine wall on approach."*

"Copy that." Kane was organizing the ropes and pullies for their descent.

"I'll supervise the drop." Jo climbed out of her seat and slid open the door.

Jenna fumbled for her phone and sent a text to Rowley, to start moving in silently with Rio as back up. She swallowed the rising fear and waited for Carter to reach the drop point. The wind from the open door buffeted the chopper as it hovered in midair, high above the ground.

The noise was deafening now, and keeping busy to avoid the rush of anxiety, Jenna attached her harness and allowed Kane to check the fastenings. He stared into her eyes and talked her through the drop, making sure she understood the technique required for a fast descent. She gave him a small smile and nodded. It wasn't the first time she'd jumped from a chopper, but he knew she hadn't attempted a fast drop before, and by his concerned expression, she obviously couldn't hide the fear in her eyes. She pressed her com. "I can do this."

"I know you can. Leave your com open so you can hear me. I'll tell you when to slow down, okay?" Kane touched her cheek. *"Ready?"*

With her goggles in position and chinstrap fastened, she gave him a thumbs-up. Seconds later she stood on the skids beside Kane, waiting for the command to jump out into the unknown. Forcing her eyes to remain open, she fell back on Jo's command. Freefalling high above the ravine, fear tumbled her stomach and she fought down a wave of uncertainty as the ground came up way too fast.

"Now, Jenna, now." Kane's voice came through her earpiece.

A rush of panic overwhelmed her as she flashed past him and the next second instinct kicked in and she went through the procedure to slow her descent. Breathless, she hit the ground and rolled. The next second Kane was beside her, hauling her to her feet and unclipping her harness. High above the chopper moved away. Kane's gaze moved over her, and she smiled at him. "I'm fine. How far to the cave?"

"When we reach the top of this hill, we should be directly above it. It looks like a sheer drop to the old riverbed." Kane scanned the area. "I hope we'll be able to find a way down from here. Carter mentioned seeing an overgrown track alongside the cave. We'll need to be very quiet and try to avoid loosening any rocks on the way down."

It was windy at the top of the ravine and loose pebbles made the way uncertain. Jenna moved cautiously toward the edge and leaned over. The ground seemed to be a very long way down, but she could make out a track carved into the rock face.

Long grass and weeds crisscrossed the black pathway, and in places the trail had crumbled away completely, leaving large patches of unstable ground. "Getting to the cave isn't going to be easy."

"Look over there." Kane pointed to a spot in the shadow of the ravine. "Carter was right, our suspect has covered his vehicle with a camouflage tarpaulin. He's smarter than I imagined. His vehicle is almost invisible from here. No one would notice it unless they drove right up to it. Carter could have flown over all day and not found him if he hadn't thrown up dust on the way here." He reached for her hand. "Don't look at me like that, Jenna. It's safer if I hold on to you. I'll go first. If you slip, sit down. It will stop you from falling."

Seeing the logic in his plan, she gave him a nod. "When we get to the bottom of the ravine we'll be without cover, so we head for the vehicle. We should be able to hear what's going on in the cave from there. I would assume it's like most mineshafts and has a series of tunnels. From what Blackhawk was telling us, the killer could have used storage areas carved out from the rock and turned them into cells."

"It wouldn't be unreasonable to believe that people who would have mined here used the caves to live in." Kane cut her a glance. "They're good protection from the elements and safe enough if you put a gate on the entrance. Especially if they've been mining for gold, they'd need somewhere safe to keep it. It's too heavy to be carrying around in your pocket all day."

After a nerve-wracking descent down the slippery pathway, Jenna pressed her back against the rock face searching in both directions for any sign of the Bright cousins. Kane had moved out ahead of her and had reached the camouflaged tarpaulin covering the vehicle. He disappeared beneath it for a few seconds before his head popped out and he waved her forward. She moved quietly across the sandy bottom to the old riverbed and joined him under the covering.

Jenna used her phone to run the plate on the town car. "That's not the Bright cousins' vehicle, they both have trucks." She waited a few seconds before the name popped up on her screen. "I knew it was him. My gut wasn't wrong after all. It's the man Rio and Rowley just interviewed and our other suspect —Tom Parsons. He fits the profile in so many ways, but then the Bright cousins up and vanished. Doing that and with the clothes and all, it made them look guilty." She shook her head. "He's so darn smart, making like he was a devoted family man to put doubts into my head, and he almost got away with it. I should trust my gut instinct more often."

"I sure do. He was more like the Michelangelo Killer than we imagined. He's well organized. Look at this." Kane indicated to a water tank hooked up to a rain collector with a pump attached to a series of pipes. A generator hummed beside it, cables feeding out along the ground and into the cave entrance. "See the antenna up there? It's probably linked to a satellite feed." He moved around, slowly scanning the rock face, and then turned back to her. "I don't see any surveillance cameras. I think we're good to go."

Heart racing with the adrenaline flowing through her veins, Jenna moved to the edge of the tarpaulin. "The gate is wide open. I'll go right and you go left. Wait and listen at the entrance. It's like an amplifier in there. We should be able to hear everything they're saying. Problem is they'll be able to hear us too." She turned to look at Kane. "I'll take the lead. Hang back. If he sees me, he'll assume I'm alone. I'll distract him away from the women. Looking at the equipment he has here, he could be packing for bear."

"Just remember." Kane's voice whispered through her earbud. "There could be any number of tunnels in there for him to hide."

Ignoring the sudden overwhelming desire to run in the opposite direction, Jenna straightened her spine. This killer was brutal and sadistic and she doubted she would ever get the images of his victims from her memory. Her mind filled with the faces of Susie Hartwig and Poppy Anderson. Determined to stop this maniac's reign of terror, she slid her weapon from the holster, inhaled a deep breath, and moved like a ghost into the dim light of the cave.

FORTY-FOUR

The door to Susie's cell slammed back and the next minute he was on her. Pain shot through her head as one large hand closed around her hair and dragged her across the floor. Before she had time to scream, she saw the flash of a knife, and cold steel slipped down her chest as he peeled the clothes from her. Tossed out into the tunnel, she fell hard and slid across a gritty granite ground to Poppy's feet. Knees torn and palms shredded, she tried to scramble to her feet, but in two strides he had her by the hair again. Terror shuddered through her as he dragged her through the gate that led to his killing area.

"Get down here, Twenty-Five." Her jailer turned to look at Poppy's pale face. "Time to prove your worth to me."

Shocked into action, Susie balled her fist and lunged forward, aiming a punch at her jailer's groin. It connected. With a howl like an injured wolf, he staggered away from her, clutching himself and falling to his knees. The next moment, Poppy emerged from the darkness with the baseball bat held at shoulder height. As she swung at the killer, he reached out a hand and grabbed her by the ankle pulling her feet from under her. Crying out in alarm, Poppy crashed to the floor and just lay still. Without a second thought, Susie grabbed the baseball bat as it slid from Poppy's hand. The man was cussing as he struggled to get to his feet and she swung the bat across his shins. When he took the blow as if it were nothing and calmly reached for the knife in the sheath at his waist, Susie tried to scramble away, but the cave wall was at her back.

"I'm going to kill you real slow." He moved toward Susie and kicked the baseball bat from her hands. "I've always wanted to skin somebody alive, and it looks like you're going to be my first."

"Nooo!" Poppy sat up, shaking her head. "She hasn't done anything to you. I'm the homewrecker, not her. I actually enjoy breaking up couples just to prove I can. I came here to lure Deputy Kane away from the sheriff. I had an inkling that they were a couple after speaking to him at the conference. The problem with Sheriff Alton is she thinks she's all that. I came here to prove otherwise." She climbed slowly to her feet and leaned against the wall. "The problem is the idea of killing me doesn't appeal to you, does it?"

"The idea is getting more appealing by the minute." He glared at her. "I've had others before who think they can take it, but they usually end up sobbing and crying and begging for their lives. I figure you'll be the same." He lunged toward her.

"Sheriff's Department." Jenna's voice echoed through the tunnel. "Tom Parsons, we have you surrounded. Drop your weapons. It's not too late to fix this. Think of your wife and kids."

Susie stared at Jenna in disbelief. "Shoot him for goodness sake, before he kills us."

A flash of movement darted in front of Susie as Poppy sprinted down the tunnel pushing Jenna out of the way in her haste. Susie gasped as the killer moved like lightning and tackled Jenna, around the knees. They rolled on the floor and Jenna's gun spun across the ground into the darkness and out of reach.

FORTY-FIVE

Concerned for Jenna's safety but following orders and keeping out of sight as she took control, Kane melted into the shadows. The next second footsteps came running toward him and he stepped out of hiding. His breath came out in a rush as Poppy threw herself into his arms, blocking his view of Jenna. He holstered his weapon to untangle her and pushed her away. "Move. Get outside. Rio and Rowley are on their way."

"Oh, Dave, I knew you'd come to save me." Poppy leaned against the wall panting. "He has a baseball bat and a knife. No guns."

Ignoring her, Kane started down the dim tunnel, and as he turned the corner, his heart skipped a beat at the sight of Parsons rolling around the ground with Jenna. The dim overhead lights caught the flash of a blade. Behind them, Susie Hartwig, stark naked and filthy, was trying to crawl away, not toward him and to safety but into a dark corner, searching the floor with her hands. He ran toward Jenna, but in that second, Parsons had rolled her over, dragged her to her feet, and pressed the knife to her throat. A slow smile crossed Parsons' face when he spotted him. Kane held out his hands. "There's no way out,

Tom. Cut her and I'll kill you. Let her go and you'll be able to have your day in court."

"How about you back the hell off, and I'll leave and take the sheriff with me?" Parsons' mouth twitched into a confidant grin. "I've always wanted a sheriff."

"What about your wife and kids?" Jenna's gaze shifted toward Kane. "Don't you think you owe them an explanation?" She sagged against Parsons, leaning to his left and keeping him off balance. Her intention to fight clear.

Inside warning bells screamed at Kane. One wrong move and the sharp knife would cut deep. That close to her carotid artery, he'd never be able to save her. What Jenna was attempting was dangerous but when she gave him the tiniest of nods, Kane exchanged a knowing glance with her. They'd trained for a situation like this, but the risk to Jenna would be fatal. One mistake and Parsons would kill her. Distracting him was his only option. "How do you think she'll feel when she discovers you've been raping women?"

"This has nothing to do with my wife and kids." Parsons wrapped his free arm around Jenna's waist, but she continued to sag, leaning away, knees bent to unbalance him. "Stand up straight." He swung his gaze back to Kane. "Move and I'll cut her throat. Even you can't draw that fast."

Really? Time slowed and Kane could see a trickle of sweat slide slowly down Parsons' temple. As the man tried to get his feet under him, the knife dropped away from Jenna's throat. In a split second, Kane drew his weapon and fired. The deafening shot shattered Parsons' right shoulder. The knife spilled from his unresponsive fingers, and he gaped at him, his mouth opening and shutting like a fish tossed onto a riverbank. In an instant, Jenna spun around, kicked his legs from under him, rolled him over, and heedless of his bleeding shoulder cuffed him. Kane dragged him up and sat him against the wall. "Don't move or my next shot will take out your kneecaps."

"You can't just leave me here bleeding to death." Parsons' face contorted with pain. "You have a duty of care."

Disgusted by his whimpering, Kane turned and stared at him. "You're breathing and, trust me, that wasn't my first choice. You're lucky the sheriff is a compassionate woman and I hate paperwork, or I'd have aimed a little higher and to the left."

"You have the right to remain silent—and as Deputy Kane isn't in a very good mood just now, I suggest you do." Jenna read Parsons' his rights and then looked up at Kane, blowing the tumble of raven hair from her eyes. "Nice shot." She stuck a finger in her ear and wiggled it. "My ears are ringing." She pointed into the darkness. "My weapon is over there somewhere. Can you find it for me?"

Kane pulled out his Maglite. "Sure. I can hear a vehicle—that will be our backup."

"Good. They can take Parsons into custody and we'll mop up here." Jenna looked around. "This place is a hellhole."

"He's not getting away with killing all those women." Susie, eyes wide in a sheet-white face, had found Jenna's gun and was waving it at Parsons. "Move out of the way, Jenna." Her hands trembled as she aimed the weapon at Parsons' head. "Did you see what he did to those women? It's on the laptop, all the torture, the rapes—everything." She let out a sob and then gathered herself. "He's a monster. He doesn't deserve to live."

"Susie." Jenna stepped away from Parsons. "I've known you since I first arrived in Black Rock Falls. Have I ever allowed a killer to get away with murder?"

"No." Susie hadn't taken her eyes off the prisoner. "But this is different. This one tried to kill me. Do you know there are other women locked up in one of the tunnels? He keeps us like animals and numbered us so he could murder us in sequence. He doesn't deserve a trial. He deserves to die. I want my revenge."

Kane cleared his throat. "I agree he deserves to die, Susie, though if you kill him, it makes you no better than him, does it? A killer is a killer. If you pull the trigger, you'll be just as guilty as him. It wouldn't be self-defense. It would be first-degree murder, and me and Jenna would have to testify against you, and we don't want to do that do we, Jenna?"

"No, of course we don't." Jenna moved closer to Susie and held out a hand. "You're not thinking straight right now. Give me the gun."

"Not yet and I'm thinking just fine." Holding the weapon out in front of her, Susie went to where Parsons was slumped against the wall moaning. She pressed the muzzle of the gun into his forehead. His eyes lifted to hers and then closed tight. Susie leaned in. "Are you scared? You should be. How does it feel knowing I could squeeze the trigger? I should release the women and let them deal out their own form of justice. You deserve that but I'm better than you. I have a conscience." She turned and gave the pistol butt-first to Jenna and, grabbing a blanket from a pile on the desk to cover her nakedness, walked, head held high, out of the cave.

FORTY-SIX

FRIDAY, WEEK TWO

The next few days had revealed the extent of Tom Parsons' evil mission. Spread across two states and involving over forty women, Jenna found it difficult to comprehend how he murdered so many women and yet his wife had never suspected a thing. She'd spoken to her at length and received a blank, shocked expression. In fact, Mrs. Parsons had been so traumatized by the revelations, she'd been hospitalized.

They'd discovered four other women in the cells and all of them wanted to tell their stories. The women had been held for as long as three years and all of them would require extensive psychiatric treatment. Their stories had been the same. They'd met Parsons at a truck stop or a bar and started talking to him with the intention of getting a ride to the next town. He told them about his wife and kids and how he enjoyed getting on the road to get a break from them. During the truck ride, he told them he enjoyed their company and offered them a place to stay if he could visit them from time to time. The women were all drifters. They moved from town to town looking for work just to survive. His offer sounded too good to be true, but they'd been desperate enough to accept.

They'd taken Poppy and Susie straight to the ER along with the other women, and although Susie was shaken, she'd given a concise statement detailing her kidnapping. After Jenna had peeled Poppy from Kane, she'd found her to be clearheaded and able to relay precise information. The revelation that Parsons had changed his MO with Susie and Poppy offered the team a new insight into the devious ways a psychopath would use to lure a woman into his trap.

The evidence they discovered in the caves sealed Parsons' fate. He'd documented every murder and saved them on numerous drives. The team had taken turns viewing the footage because of the graphic nature of the content, and even Wolfe had walked out of the communications room ashen and speechless for a time. They'd handed all the evidence over to the DA and everyone was anxious to interview the killer, but Parsons had remained silent, speaking only to his lawyer, Samuel J. Cross. The team had used the time to hunt down the missing Bright cousins. The assumption that they'd vanished because of their involvement had bothered Jenna, but to her surprise, the men had arrived home with a mess of fish after camping at one of the lakes.

She'd been sitting in her office bringing her files up to date when Sam Cross knocked on her office door. Not a slick dresser, Cross was the epitome of a cowboy, with his faded blue jeans, battered Stetson, and snakeskin boots—but he just happened to be the best defense lawyer she'd ever met. "What can I do for you, Sam?"

"My client is willing to be interviewed but he'll only speak to agent Jo Wells and you." Cross rolled his eyes. "I informed him he'd need to speak with the DA if he wanted a deal, but he's hedging his bets. I figure he wants to wring the last bit of horror from his story by telling you and watching your reaction."

Grimacing, Jenna dropped a pen into her chipped mug. "After watching those tapes, nothing will ever shock me again."

"We're coming to the end of the time you can legally hold him without charges. When will you be formally charging him?" Cross tipped back his Stetson and sighed. "I should inform you that due to the mounting evidence against my client, my advice to him to avoid the death penalty will be to plead guilty of all charges. I'll advise him to give you and the Colorado law enforcement as much detail as possible so they can pursue the identities of the women on the video files."

Jenna leaned back in her chair. "That would be good. We'd like to hear his side of the story. Once the interview is over, we'll be arresting him. I'll supply you with a copy of the warrant. Not knowing the identity of the victims made it difficult, but Wolfe has now identified the three victims by their dental records. As their murders occurred in Black Rock Falls, and we have proof Parsons killed them, the DA will be bringing three counts of murder against him. He'll also be charged with kidnapping, deprivation of liberty, rape, and assault of the women we discovered inside the caves. By the end of the day, we'll be shipping him off to County."

"That's what I expected. I assumed the paperwork would be finalized today." Cross sucked in a deep breath and glanced behind him as Jo walked past the door. "I see Agent Wells is still in town."

"Yes. When we discovered the murders covered at least two states and the number of women involved, we brought them in to assist." Jenna cleared her throat. "Do you wish to speak with Agents Wells and Carter?"

"Not at this time." Cross rubbed the bridge of his nose. "It's been a long few days. Now Mr. Parsons is willing to talk, when can you arrange an interview with my client?"

Jenna smiled at him. "I'll speak to Jo. She can't wait to hear his story and has a remarkable way with dealing with psychopaths. For some reason they seem to feel safe with her and give her information. It's as if they feel proud telling her what they've done." She noticed the usually calm and connected Sam Cross was a little jittery. She wasn't surprised if he'd been subjected to Parsons' harrowing story for the last two days. "Why don't you go into the office downstairs and grab a cup of coffee and something to eat? I'll set up the interview so that you can get back to your office. It will be when the DA can make it. He wants to be involved."

"Thanks. After this case, I'm going fishing... for a week." Cross pushed his hat back on his head and headed out the door.

"Absolutely not." Kane shook his head. "You can't possibly allow a prisoner to dictate terms."

"Kane's correct." Carter moved a toothpick across his lips. "We should be in the interview with you. I can't imagine why you'd even consider that SOB's demands." He moved his attention away from Jenna and stared at Jo. "I know you want to gather information for your book but in my opinion—if it's of any value to you—is that allowing him to take the upper hand is a big mistake."

Annoyed, Jenna moved her attention from one to the other. "It was part of the deal I made with Sam Cross. It wasn't my idea or Jo's." She looked at Kane's unyielding expression and shrugged. "Fine. We'll all go in together, but if he clams up, I'll be ordering both of you to wait outside—is that perfectly clear?"

"That works for me." Kane smiled at her. "For a time there, I figured we were having our first fight as a married couple."

Shaking her head in disbelief, Jenna looked at him and burst out laughing. "Trust me, if we were having a fight, you'd know about it, but this isn't about us, Dave, is it? It's not personal. This is about work. I welcome a lively discussion about a case, but I don't appreciate anyone questioning my orders." She turned her gaze to Carter. "Even though the two of you tried to pressure me, this time I see your point. You should know, Carter, once I've made up my mind it's pretty hard to change it."

"Oh, I know, but it won't stop me trying." Carter's mouth curled up at the corners. "Ma'am."

Jenna headed for the interview room. "Okay, the DA and Wolfe have requested to watch the interview, plus a few of the DA's staff. They're all waiting for us, so let's get this show on the road."

She led the way through the office and stopped when she arrived at Kane's desk to find Poppy perched on top, peering into a compact mirror. After caving in and giving Poppy back her job, the realization that she'd have to endure the woman's constant attention to Kane annoyed her. She'd figured after Poppy had proved she could cope in a crisis she owed her a chance on the team. Jenna shot a glance at Kane and caught his eyeroll and smiled. "You know, Dave. As deputy sheriff, I figure you deserve a desk in my office. As Poppy has an obvious attraction to your desk, she can have it. You can share mine for now and I'll have a new one delivered by Monday."

"I'd like that." Kane chuckled. "Thanks. Do I get a pay raise as well?"

Jenna laughed. "Don't push your luck."

Sobering as they entered the hallway outside the interview room, Jenna nodded to Wolfe and the DA and his associates. They would be able to hear and see everything once she set up the recording device. The video feed was also available to Rowley and Rio in the communications room. She stepped inside, Jo followed close behind, and they sat down. Kane and Carter came in behind them and stood each side of the door, like sentries. Parsons, chained securely by feet and hands, sat relaxed beside Sam Cross, as if waiting to be served coffee in

Aunt Betty's Café. With the video set up, the time, date, and who was present added, Jenna rested her hands on the desk each side of her iPad. She had notes but had questions set in her mind to ask Parsons. She wanted Jo to ease into the questioning in an effort to collect as much information as possible. Before she could open her mouth Parsons leaned forward, clanking his chains.

"My wife and kids." Parsons' expression changed and his eyes flashed with concern. "Are they okay? Did you tell her?"

Empathy wasn't what Jenna expected and met his gaze. This vicious murderer didn't deserve her compassion, but right now she'd do just about anything to make him talk. "Yes, your wife knows. Your wife is under care at the hospital and the children are staying with her relatives. I'm sure you'd imagine this has been quite a shock to her."

"Everything I did was to protect her and the children." Parsons dropped his head into his hands. "Everything I do is for them."

Astounded to see him showing any emotion, Jenna turned to look at Jo. This reaction was so out of character for a person with his lust for murder, she needed an expert to handle him. She gave her a slight wave of her hand to indicate she should take over from the get-go.

"Mr. Parsons my name is Agent Jo Wells. I'm a behavioral analyst with the FBI and currently writing a book to enable law enforcement to better understand why people murder. I'm here to listen to you and not condemn you for what you've done. Can you tell me in your own words what provoked you to murder the first victim?" She leaned back in the chair and the room fell silent for some moments. "Did something happen to your mom to make you want to prevent it happening to your wife?"

When Parsons just stared at his hands, Jenna exchanged a meaningful look with Sam Cross in the hope he'd be able to make his client talk, but he just shrugged. Beside her, Jo nudged her elbow and indicated for her to wait. Jenna nodded and leaned back in her chair. It was so quite in the room that she could have heard a pin drop.

"Okay, so how about we start with the skewers. They must be an easy part of the explanation." Jo leaned forward slightly. "What exactly do they mean to you?"

"Yeah, everything I do means something to me." Parsons lifted his head slowly and stared at Jo. "Why?"

"They were used in a similar crime, by the Michelangelo Killer." Jo held up an image of one of Bruno Vito's victims. "Did you copy him?"

"I've never heard of him, but he has an imagination that's for sure." Parsons shrugged. "I've been thinking how everything started, why I killed the first woman, and how I felt about it. Truth is, I didn't feel anything. I don't care about them—I fantasize about who is next and it becomes an obsession. I think about killing all the time—I figure I'm addicted." He chuckled and shook his head. "You've never heard anyone say that before, have you?"

"Okay, so let's go back to when you were a kid." Jo's expression was relaxed and open. It was obvious she didn't plan on allowing him to take over the interview. "Tell me about your parents."

"My pa was a major asshole. He had no respect for my ma. He was in sales and traveled all over. He probably had a woman in every town and came home stinking of perfume or not at all for weeks." He opened his hands wide. "I'm sure Ma knew he was seeing other women, but I guess she loved him and, when he said he'd be home, she'd cook a special roast dinner. It was always one of those rolled-up meat dishes with the skewers all down one side to hold it together. When he didn't come home, she'd throw it against the wall and we'd go hungry. I always had the job of cleaning up the mess."

"What happened when your pa came home?" Jo's face was

expressionless and she never once gave her feelings away to the people she interviewed. "Did they fight?"

"Oh yeah, he'd slap her around and then apologize. They always made up and then as soon as he went away it happened all over." Parsons leaned back in his chair. "If I asked him why he slapped my ma or if I got between them to stop him, he'd get mad, take off his belt, fold it over, and beat me with it so hard I couldn't walk the next day. He'd tell me to mind my business. He'd say that when I grew up, I'd understand that a man has his needs, and a wife's place is to respect them."

"So, you were helpless to do anything to help your mother?" Jo made a few notes and raised her gaze back to him.

"I tried and we spoke about it, but she'd get mad at me too. She'd tell me I'd be just like him when I grew, that all men were the same. She also told me, there are two kinds of women: those who married a man to be his wife and the homewreckers." Parsons shrugged almost nonchalantly. "It seemed my father was attracted to the latter."

Unable to help herself, Jenna stared at him uncomprehending. "What has all this to do with you kidnapping, raping, and murdering women?" She frowned. "And why the plastic masks?"

"You said they'd sit nice and just listen." Parsons turned to Sam Cross and then indicated to Jenna. "You need a good beating, woman, to put you in your place. Men rule the world. Don't you know? You only got your job to keep the women from nagging us to death. It was a compromise is all."

Unsettled by his comments, Jenna wanted to leave, but kept her gaze steady on him. "Do you beat your wife?"

"Never." Parsons glared at her, his eyes turning black. He clenched his fists and Jenna heard Kane and Carter shift position behind her. "I'm a good husband. I protect her."

"Can we keep this conversation on track?" Jo took a sip of water from a bottle she'd just cracked. "It's an easy question.

Why did you kill your first victim? You must have had a reason."

"The first one and all of them were the same." Parsons shrugged and his attention moved back to Jo. "I travel in my work and not a day goes by without some woman trying to hit on me. They want a ride or they want me. I've got a cabin in Colorado. I often stay there because it saves money on my trips. Every time I go to a bar or go out to buy something to eat there's some woman trying to get me to invite them to my place. You see how easy it was for me to become like my father? I couldn't allow that to happen. I had a wife and kids at home and I always made sure my wife knew exactly when I was going to be home. Yeah, I spent time with the women I'd collected in my trips, but I never went home smelling of perfume."

"You're saying that you considered the women you kidnapped a threat to your marriage and removed them?" Jo met his gaze head on. "So why rape them? Surely that was cheating on your wife?"

"Ah, see, you don't understand the way of things." Parsons smiled at her. "Those women broke the rules. They had a choice. I told them I was in love with my wife, but it made no difference. They didn't care if they hurt anyone, so I gave them a ride to hell." He clanked his chains and shifted his gaze slowly to Jenna. "They deserved to be punished. I set rules for them to give them a chance to change their ways. Watch the tapes and you will hear what they offered me. So, I gave them each a number and, because they were all the same, I took away their identity. I purchased the masks at a yard sale in Colorado. The fact it was a cop's mask isn't relevant. What was relevant is that they all looked the same, because homewreckers are all the same."

Jenna cleared her throat. "We found a bag of clothes in the caves. Where did you get them from?"

"They belonged to the women." Parsons met her gaze. "I

hadn't time to put them into storage. The negligees I purchased from Walmart. I gave them to my wife and then told her I like to see her in different ones all the time. I took away the old ones and gave them to the women."

"You said you put the clothes in storage?" Jo's eyebrows rose. "Where exactly would that be?"

"I've had a longtime arrangement with Mrs. Bright." Parsons frowned. "Would you believe she went and died on me and left the house to her grandsons? I couldn't tell them about the clothes now, could I? I tried to buy the house from them, but they refused. It didn't matter because when I went to see them they were hauling out everything and burning the clothes."

"How many women have you killed?" Jo leaned back in her chair, acting as if she were asking him how many cups of coffee he had a day.

"I'm not sure." He scratched his chin, making the chains clank against the metal loops on the desk. "I started giving them numbers a year ago, but I've been married seven years and that was around the time it started. I didn't plan on dumping the bodies in Black Rock Falls at all. It was just that we have a toddler and a young baby and I wanted to be home more often." He sighed. "It took so long for my wife to fall pregnant for our first one I was starting to believe I was cursed."

The skin on Jenna's arms pebbled as if someone had walked over her grave. "If you thought that to be true, why did you keep on killing?"

"Oh, surely you know that, Sheriff?" Parsons eyes moved up and down over her body and came to rest back on her face. "There's something about having a woman afraid of me that I enjoy. I have no, what you would call *feelings* for them. Keeping them for a spell, they become placid, but when I drag them out and beat them... well." He shot a look at Kane and then moved it to Carter. His mouth turned into a satisfied smile. "It feels so good to have a woman squirming and moaning—I like to control their pain and see just how much they can take." He moved his attention back to Jenna. "I didn't stop because I enjoyed it too much."

Horrified, Jenna fought hard to compose her expression. "So, the excuse about fearing you'd become just like your father was an excuse for murder?"

"You are so wrong." Parsons' expression changed to annoyance. "I never had an affair with any of them. I punished them for trying to break up my marriage." He shrugged. "None of them had the chance."

"Are your parents still alive?" Jo made more notes.

"My ma is alive, but my father unfortunately fell in front of a bus when I was eighteen." Parsons chuckled deep and sinister. "My ma remarried and moved to California a couple of years later. She's happy."

Jenna needed more information. "Why did you kidnap Poppy Anderson and, more importantly, why didn't you kill her? Seems to me, she had the run of the place when we arrived. Was she involved in the killings?"

"Involved? Nah. She washed the body of Twenty-Four, is all. I enjoyed watching her on her knees. She'd do anything I ordered her to do... She was my slave. It was what she deserved. You see, as smart and cunning as she might be, she's no different than the rest of the homewreckers." Parsons raised an eyebrow and smiled at her. "Surely you know that by now, don't you, Sheriff?" He flicked a look at Kane and winked. "He sure as hell knows what she's like. Encourage a woman like that and they never give up—do they, Deputy?"

Jenna just stared at him. "Go on. Just how do you have so much information on someone who's never lived in town?"

"I delivered a truck to Helena and took a flight back. She sat beside me." Parsons chuckled. "She told me why she'd come to Black Rock Falls. She was going to hook up with Deputy Kane. When I told her it was common knowledge that you had feelings for him, she brushed that away and made like that wasn't a problem." He leaned back in his seat. "By taking her out of the equation, I was doing you a favor, Sheriff. The funny thing was that Twenty-Five thought she could play me, but I'd planned to kill her next and I'd have enjoyed every second. She's just like the others." He leaned forward and stared into her eyes. "I'm over talking, but I'll give you a piece of advice, Sheriff. A leopard can't change their spots. Twenty-Five already has her claws in your man—and it's only a matter of time before she takes him from you."

EPILOGUE

SATURDAY, THE FOLLOWING WEEK

The smell of steak sizzling on the grill with onions had to be the best aroma in the world. Jenna leaned back in her seat and sipped a glass of aromatic red wine that Kane had selected from his extensive cellar. The rich taste spilled over her tastebuds in a sigh of delight. She'd needed to unwind after the harrowing case, and Kane's idea to invite their friends around for a cookout was just about as relaxing as it got. The videos Parsons had filmed of the murders would stay with her for a very long time. She'd had a few sleepless nights and needed some time away from the office. She had taken off this weekend after Maggie and old Deputy Walters had offered to take over to give everyone a well-earned rest. She rubbed her forehead as the memory of speaking to Mrs. Parsons again filtered into her mind. She understood the power of loving someone, but some things most people could not forgive. Yet Parsons' wife was standing by her husband, even though he'd pleaded guilty to all charges and would never see the light of day again.

Jenna had to admit that Parsons' warning about Poppy Anderson had played on her mind. She had no doubt that Poppy was a flirt and had designs on Kane. Both Emily and Jo had warned her about giving Poppy back her job, saying she would cause too much trouble. The decision hadn't been easy, but one she'd taken alone. Poppy had shown true grit in an untenable situation, and she figured she owed her a second chance. Although, partnering her with Rio hadn't gone down too well with Emily.

She glanced over to the group of men standing around the grill. As if he'd felt her gaze on him, Kane turned and smiled at her. The one thing that Emily and Jo hadn't taken into consideration was that Kane was an honorable man. When he gave a vow, he kept it. She trusted him with her life and her heart and figured it would take more than Poppy Anderson to come between them.

It was just Jenna, Emily, and Sandy at the table. Julie and Anna had taken themselves off to the stables with Zac Rio's siblings, Piper and Cade, to see the horses. Jo and Carter had left the previous week after taking over Parsons' murder cases in Colorado. Her friends were chatting, and it was nice to just sit back and listen for a change. She smiled at Emily. "So, Zac is here. Are you two an item now?"

"I'm interested." Emily's lips curled into a satisfied smile. "He is kinda special, don't you think?"

Unable to hide her grin, Jenna laughed. "He's a nice guy. I like him. How does your dad feel about you dating him?"

"Oh, we're not dating." Emily's gaze moved over to the men. "We're just friends right now but I'm working on it, and it's not up to Dad. It's up to me. I don't want anything to stand in my way of finishing my medical degree, and Zac is very supportive, so there's no plans to get serious just yet."

Jenna shook her head. "That's hard to predict, Em. Love kinda hits you like a tornado and sweeps you away."

"So, I've noticed." Emily chuckled. "Dave gets those puppy dog eyes every time he looks at you." She pointed at her. "You look like the cat that got the cream."

Sneaking another look at Kane, Jenna smiled. "Dave makes me so happy. Every morning I wake up hoping it's not a dream. I guess that feeling will wear off one day."

"It won't." Sandy, Jake Rowley's wife, sighed and smiled. "I feel like that too."

Jenna's attention moved to Sandy, bouncing her twins, Cooper and Vannah, one on each knee, and wondered how she managed to cope with the wriggling, giggling twins. They seemed such a handful, but it was obvious that Sandy was enjoying every moment. "Are you getting any sleep with the twins?"

"Not what you might call *sleep*." Sandy laughed. "It's fine unless they're teething, which at the moment seems to be all the time."

"Let me take Cooper over with the men." Rowley came to the table and swung his son into the air. "We have to start the male bonding at a young age, you know." He grinned at her and hoisted the little boy on one hip.

"I've always thought it was ingrained in them. You know, the way they all gather together around the grill. Although, my dad seems to be the cook all the time. What is that, the dominant male or something?" Emily wrinkled her nose. "They're weird."

Grinning, Jenna glanced over to the group of men around the grill. "I love it. We get the best end of the deal. We make a few salads, supply the condiments, and sit here waiting to be fed. I don't mind that tradition at all. It's nice to relax for a time and talk girl talk." She glanced at Kane as he came back to the table to refill their glasses. She smiled up at him. "How long for the steaks? I'm starving."

"Shane will have them ready soon." Kane looked around the table. "Is there anything else I can get you, while you're waiting?"

Jenna smiled at him. "Only you."

"You have me." Kane pulled her into his arms and smiled down at her. "Jake is going to drop by in the morning to tend the horses. I've booked the honeymoon suite at the Cattleman's Hotel for tonight." He bent and kissed her for a long time and then pulled back and smiled. "I figure we'll take the honeymoon we're owed one day at a time... maybe stretch it out over fifty years or so."

Happiness spread through Jenna in a warm glow and she wrapped her arms around his neck. "I'd like that just fine."

A LETTER FROM D.K. HOOD

Dear Reader,

Thank you so much for choosing my novel and coming with me on another thrilling adventure with Kane and Alton in *Kiss Her Goodnight*.

If you'd like to keep up to date with all my latest releases, just sign up at the website link below. You can unsubscribe at any time and your details will never be shared.

www.bookouture.com/dk-hood

Finally having Jenna and Dave together was a delight to write, but after reading this book, you'll know nothing is smooth sailing in my stories. Trouble is coming from all directions and Jenna's and Dave's lives will be turned upside down. A new type of serial killer has arrived in Black Rock Falls—and no one is safe. I hope you'll join me for my next thrilling ride as the team hunts down the Jack of Hearts killer.

If you enjoyed *Kiss Her Goodnight*, I would be very grateful if you could leave a review and recommend my book to your friends and family. I really enjoy hearing from readers, so feel free to ask me questions at any time. You can get in touch on my Facebook page or Twitter or through my blog. Thank you so much for your support.

D.K. Hood

KEEP IN TOUCH WITH D.K. HOOD

www.dkhood.com
dkhood-author.blogspot.com.au

facebook.com/dkhoodauthor
twitter.com/DKHood_Author

ACKNOWLEDGMENTS

I want to thank my husband, Gary, who endures my long author silences when I'm in Black Rock Falls, brings me coffee, and reminds me to eat when I'm in the zone. He laughs at my research history, rather than being worried. I mean who wouldn't be concerned to discover I'm researching poisons, chainsaws, and how to dissolve a corpse in acid? Instead, he listens patiently to a scene I've rewritten ten times over and encourages me to keep going. Every day I'm thankful for being able to spend my life with him. These past three months have been crazy, and without him, this book would never have been written.